Praise for the Accidental Alchemist Mysteries

The Masquerading Magician

"People who enjoy character driven stories with mystery, magic, supernatural creatures, and historical intrigue will greatly enjoy this inventive, well-written tale."

—*Portland Book Review*

"A fine, whimsical, paranormal book … this plot certainly holds your attention."

—*Suspense Magazine*

"[*The Masquerading Magician*] is enjoyable and holds together quite nicely."

—*Reviewing the Evidence* online

The Accidental Alchemist

A 2016 Lefty Award winner for Best LCC Regional Mystery

"Pandian … launches a supernatural cozy series that hits high marks for a modern twist on an ancient practice."

—*Library Journal*

"A whimsical and charming supernatural mystery. The rapport between Gallic gourmet Dorian and Zoe is delectable, and Zoe's chemistry with Detective Liu is sizzling."

—*Mystery Scene*

"What really makes this book stand out, however, is the originality … Pandian has managed to create an eccentric and charming cast of characters readers are going to want to spend more time with."

—*RT Book Reviews* online

D0843870

"*The Accidental Alchemist* is a recipe for a great read. Gigi Pandian's pen never disappoints."

—Juliet Blackwell, *New York Times* bestselling
author of the Witchcraft Mystery series

"Zoe and Dorian are my new favorite amateur-sleuth duo!"

—Victoria Laurie, *New York Times* bestselling author

"Mysterious, captivating, and infused with the rich history of the Northwest, along with scrumptious teases about tasty dishes, savory teas, and mouthwatering desserts! *The Accidental Alchemist* is fantastic and set so far apart from typical paranormal books that it creates an artful combination of several genres and reading categories."

—*Portland Book Review*

"A magical, whimsical cozy that will delight readers who enjoy Juliet Blackwell and Heather Weber mysteries!"

—Avery Aames, aka Daryl Wood Gerber,
author of the Cheese Shop Mysteries

"Readers won't want to put this book down."

—*Vegetarian Journal*

The
eLUSIVe
eLIXIR

Gigi Pandian

MIDNIGHT INK
WOODBURY, MINNESOTA

First Edition
First Printing, 2017

Book format by Bob Gaul
Cover design by Kevin R. Brown
Cover illustration by Hugh D'Andrade/Jennifer Vaughn Artist Agent
Editing by Nicole Nugent

Midnight Ink, an imprint of Llewellyn Worldwide Ltd.

Library of Congress Cataloging-in-Publication Data (Pending)
ISBN: 978-0-7387-4236-6

Midnight Ink
Llewellyn Worldwide Ltd.
2143 Wooddale Drive
Woodbury, MN 55125-2989
www.midnightinkbooks.com

Printed in the United States of America

WORKS BY GIGI PANDIAN

The Accidental Alchemist Mystery Series
The Accidental Alchemist
The Masquerading Magician
The Elusive Elixir

Jaya Jones Treasure Hunt Mystery Series
"Fools Gold" in *Other People's Baggage*
Artifact
Pirate Vishnu
Quicksand
Michelangelo's Ghost
"A Dark and Stormy Light" in
Malice Domestic 11: Murder Most Conventional

Short Stories
"The Shadow of the River" in *Fish Tales*
"The Hindi Houdini" in *Fish Nets*
"The Haunted Room" in *The Bouchercon 2014 Anthology*
"Tempest in a Teapot" in *Ladies Night*
"The Curse of Cloud Castle" in *Asian Pulp*

To you, my readers, for your
boundless enthusiasm for a gargoyle.

ONE

THE WOMAN WAS STILL behind me.

She was so close to me on the winding, irregular stone steps inside Notre Dame Cathedral that I could smell her breath. Sourdough bread and honey.

I could have sworn I'd seen her at the *boulangerie* near my apartment earlier that morning. Now her unwavering gaze bore into me. She must have been at least eighty and wasn't more than five feet tall. She didn't fit the profile of someone worth being afraid of. Most people would have dismissed it as a coincidence.

Unless you're someone like me, who always has to be careful.

We emerged from the cramped corridor onto the narrow Gallery of Gargoyles, high above Paris. I shielded my eyes from the sun. A warm wind swept my hair around my face as I looked out through the mesh fencing that covered the once-open balcony.

The gargoyle known as *Le Penseur*, "The Thinker," sat regally with his stone head turned toward the City of Lights, as he had for over 150 years. Unlike my friend Dorian, this gargoyle of Notre Dame wouldn't be stepping off his stone mount.

For a few brief seconds, the stunning details Eugène Viollet-le-Duc had added to his chimeras all those years ago made me forget about the woman. The grandeur even made me lose sight of the real reason I was at Notre Dame that day. My quest was never far from my thoughts, but for those fleeting moments, I allowed myself the space to appreciate the splendor of the craftsmanship of generations of artists and laborers.

A girl around eight years old squealed in delight as she noticed a set of smaller gargoyles perched overhead, grinning maniacally at us. Her younger brother began to cry. His father explained in a thick Welsh accent that gargoyles weren't to be feared. They weren't even real, for Heaven's sake! His father was right—in this particular case.

If I didn't get rid of my shadow and get what I needed here at Notre Dame, the Welshman's words would be true for all gargoyles, including my best friend. I followed the tight walkway for a few steps until I saw it. An unfinished slab of limestone where a gargoyle might have perched.

This was the spot.

I glanced behind me. The woman stood a few paces away. In stylish sunglasses with a perfectly knotted silk scarf around her spindly neck, she was simultaneously frail and glamorous. Unlike the crowd of tourists excitedly scurrying past each other on the balcony that was never meant for this volume of visitors, the woman stood stock still. She held no camera. Her gaze didn't linger on the dramatic cityscape or on the unique stone monsters that surrounded us.

She looked directly at me, not bothering to conceal her curiosity.

"May I help you?" I asked, speaking in French. Though the woman hadn't spoken, the style and care of her clothing, hair, and makeup suggested she was Parisian.

She pulled her sunglasses off and clenched them in boney hands. "*I knew it,*" she replied in English. "I knew it was you." Her voice was strong, with the hint of a rattle in her throat. The forcefulness of her words seemed to surprise her nearly as much as it surprised me.

My throat constricted, and I instinctively reached for my purse. Empty except for my phone, notebook, wallet, and homemade granola bars packed in parchment paper. I was thankful I'd had the sense to leave Dorian's alchemy book safely hidden far from me. I willed myself to relax. Things were different now. This wasn't a witch hunt. Being recognized wasn't necessarily a bad thing.

I'd flown from Portland to Paris earlier that week. Because of the urgency of the situation, while I was recovering from an illness and too sick to climb the steps of Notre Dame, I'd stayed busy with people I thought might be able to help me, several of whom blurred together in my mind. Librarians, academics, amateur historians, Notre Dame docents, rare book dealers. Still, I found it surprising that I'd completely forgotten this woman. No, that wasn't entirely true. Now that she'd removed her sunglasses, there was something vaguely familiar about her … And if she was one of the people who worked at the cathedral, that would explain how she was fit enough to keep pace with me on the hundreds of stairs.

"Please forgive me," I said, switching to English, as she had done. "I seem to have forgotten where we met."

She shook her head and laughed. "So polite! We have not met. You're Zoe Faust's granddaughter, aren't you?"

I let out the breath I'd been holding and smiled. "You knew *Grandmere?*"

The woman gave me a curious look, her eyes narrowing momentarily, but the action was so quickly replaced with a smile that I might have imagined it.

"During the Occupation in 1942," she said. "My name is Blanche Leblanc."

"Zoe Faust," I said automatically.

The quizzical look on her face returned.

"Named after my grandmother," I added hastily, stumbling over the words. I'm a terrible liar. Personally, I think it's one of my more endearing qualities—who wants to be friends with someone if you never know if they're being honest?—but in my life it's also a most inconvenient trait. "It's lovely to meet you, Madame Leblanc." That was a lie too. I'm sure she was a nice person, but I didn't need this complication.

Three out-of-breath tourists, the stragglers of our group, burst through the top of the winding stairway. While they caught their breath, I led Madame Leblanc away from the crowded section of walkway next to the gargoyles. There wasn't much space on the gallery, but by stepping back a few feet, at least we wouldn't be jostled.

"You look so much like her," Madame Leblanc said, speaking more softly now. "When I was a young girl, my mother once brought me to her shop. What was the name?"

"Elixir."

"Yes. Elixir. Many foreigners left Paris, but your grandmother stayed and helped people during the war. Her healing remedies saved many lives. But then she left. After the fire ... "

I returned her sad smile. These days, people think of me as an herbalist. In the past, people thought of me as an apothecary. Not many people have ever known the truth, that I'm an alchemist.

I've never gotten the hang of turning lead into gold, but ever since I was a small child I've been able to extract the healing properties of plants. My ability to heal people was one of the things that made me think my accidental discovery of the Elixir of Life wasn't entirely a curse. But the dangers of living a secret life created a heavy burden. My "grandmother" Zoe Faust is me.

Since I've always been good with herbal remedies, I've been able to help both sick and injured people.

And war leads to far too many of both.

"Yes," I said, "*Grandmere* finally left Paris to help a family that was fleeing with a child too sick to travel."

Madame Leblanc's painted lips quivered. "My first thought was the right one, *n'est pas*?" Her silk scarf swirled in the wind.

"Are you all right?" I asked.

"Don't touch me," she hissed, twisting away from me. "My mother was right. *You are a witch.*"

The Gallery of Gargoyles was loud with the excited voices of tourists of all ages, but suddenly I couldn't hear anything except the beating of my heart. The multilingual voices of the tourists around us dissipated as if sucked into a vortex. It felt like the only two people left on the Gallery of Gargoyles were me and Madame Leblanc. My stomach clenched. I wished I hadn't eaten a hearty breakfast from that *boulangerie*. "You're confused, madame."

"You were in your late twenties then. *You have not aged a day.* There is no anti-aging cream that good. I know. I have tried them all. You stand before me through witchcraft or some other deal with the devil."

I choked. "I'm told my grandmother and I look very much alike," I said, trying to keep my breathing even. "These things happen—"

"I am eighty-two years old," Madame Leblanc cut in. "My eyesight is not what it once was, but my hearing is perfect. Even with the cacophony around us, I would know your voice anywhere."

"I'm told that I sound like her, too—"

"I remember the voice of the soldier who told me that my father was dead." Her words were slow. Crisp. "I remember the voice of the nurse who handed me my healthy baby girl. And I remember the voice of the apothecary named Zoe who saved many lives in Paris—but not that of my mother."

Momentarily stunned by the heartfelt speech, I was at a loss for words. I looked from the woman to the gargoyles surrounding us then out at the Eiffel Tower stretching into the blue sky, Sacre Cour's man-made grandeur, the flowing river Seine, and wisps of smoke from chimneys. Air, earth, water, fire. Elements I worked with and craved.

"I don't know what sort of bargain you made with evil forces to be here today," Madame Leblanc said, her voice nearly a whisper, "but that woman was not your grandmother. She was *you*. I know it is you, Zoe Faust. And I will find out what you are. You cannot hide any longer."

TWO

My heart galloped loudly in my ears. I feared I might be overcome with vertigo high atop the cathedral. This was a complication I didn't need.

"My grandmother always said she felt bad about the people she wasn't able to help," I said, forcing myself to speak calmly. "What was your mother's name? Perhaps she mentioned her to me."

"Oh, you tried to help her," Madame Leblanc said, a snarl hovering on her wrinkled lips. "You gave her a tincture that day she brought me to the shop. But at home, she refused to take it. She said it was witchcraft. She said that nobody's herbal remedies could be as good as yours without the work of the devil."

"I'm sorry," I said. "My grandmother wasn't—"

"Stop lying!"

The breathless tourists glanced our way before edging their way past, giving us as wide a berth as possible on the narrow parapet. Maybe my hope of salvaging the situation was misguided. I looked longingly at the exit, wondering if Madame Leblanc would be as quick on the stairs down as she was on the way up.

"The strong family resemblance has confused you," I said.

"I'm not crazy," Madame Leblanc said.

The ferocity in her eyes shocked me. Had she harbored this grudge against me since she was a child? I felt bad for her, but I couldn't say more. The world wasn't ready to know about alchemy.

"I'm going to find out what you are," she said. "You made a grave mistake returning to Paris."

"Madame—"

I broke off as a security guard approached us. He asked if everything was all right, but his bored eyes told me he was more concerned about moving us through the narrow stone gallery than with finding out what our disagreement was about.

With the distraction from the guard, I wondered if I could make a run for it.

Six months ago, my life had turned upside down. Perhaps not quite as upside down as it had in 1704 when I accidentally discovered the Elixir of Life, but it was the second-biggest shakeup in the intervening 300 years. Half a year ago, I learned that dangerous backward alchemy was real.

Alchemy is a personal transformation. Its core principle is transforming the impure into the pure, be it lead into gold or a dying body into a thriving one. Backward alchemy's Death Rotation skips the natural order and sacrifices one element for another. Backward alchemy takes more than it transforms. Backward alchemy and the Death Rotation are based in death, not life.

I've been running from alchemy for a long time, so I didn't make this discovery on my own. I'd been sought out by Dorian Robert-Houdin to help understand a book of backward alchemy, *Non Degenera Alchemia*, which roughly translated to *Not Untrue Alchemy*. Dorian's fate was linked to that of the mysterious book filled with disturbing woodcut illustrations and strange Latin text. The book was changing, and so was Dorian. He was dying an unnatural death. He would soon be alive but trapped in stone—a fate that struck me as far worse than death. I couldn't let that happen to the quirky fellow who had quickly become my best friend.

Did I mention that Dorian is a gargoyle?

Dorian Robert-Houdin was originally carved in limestone for Notre Dame's Gallery of Gargoyles. He'd been a prototype carving by Notre Dame renovator Viollet-le-Duc, created for the brand-new Gallery of Gargoyles built in the 1850s and 1860s. The statue turned out to be too small for the balcony, so Viollet-le-Duc gifted the creation to his friend Jean Eugène Robert-Houdin, the French stage magician credited with being the father of modern magic. Neither man was an alchemist, but a stage show magic trick went very wrong one day when the retired magician picked up a beautiful alchemy book. The gargoyle statue came to life as the magician read from the alchemy book he believed to be merely a stage prop. On that day in 1860, Dorian the living gargoyle was born in Robert-Houdin's home workshop.

Madame Leblanc and I were now nearly alone with the gargoyles and the security guard. Tourists were divided into groups that the staff sent up the stairs of the cathedral in waves, to prevent an unsafe level of crowding on the gallery. While Madame Leblanc assured the guard we'd be moving on shortly, I tried to ground myself in reality.

In addition to the stragglers who'd only recently reached the gallery, the only other person nearby was a man in a priest's collar who was staring intently at one of the gargoyles. Now there was a respectable fellow. If a living gargoyle came to him for help, I bet it would be a calm, well-mannered creature—not like the opinionated Dorian, who thought of himself as a French Poirot and was constantly getting into trouble. Though my fellow misfit Dorian was dear to me, he didn't listen. Ever.

I clung to the small amount of relief that I hadn't followed Dorian's advice for me to take him with me to Paris. He could shift between life and stone within seconds, so he'd suggested I carry him around Paris in a backpack in stone form. I had no doubt that he would have peeked out of the bag regularly and ruined any hope I had of convincing Madam Leblanc she didn't need to tell the world I was an immortal witch.

The guard left us to scowl at two teenage backpackers who were attempting to reach through the mesh barrier to touch a gargoyle. When I turned back to Madame Leblanc, she was blushing.

"I'm sorry," she said. Her lips were pinched. It was a difficult phrase for her to utter. "I have been foolish, no? I don't know what came over me. I hope you will forgive an old woman. It is only that you look so much like her."

"*De rien*," I said. "Think nothing of it. Good day, madame." I turned away, giving my attention back to the perch I wanted to verify with my own eyes. There was no doubt in my mind that this section of molding had been constructed to support a gargoyle. *It was true.*

Another gargoyle *had* once perched here. Local history held that a group of drunken Parisians had stolen the stone creature 150 years ago. But I knew the truth. A gargoyle much like Dorian had once stood here. *A gargoyle that had come to life and vanished.*

A hand touched my elbow.

"I would very much like to hear your memories of your grand-mother," Madame Leblanc said. She stood uncomfortably close to me in the confined space. "Your fond memories of her will help me push my mother's angry memories from my mind. I do not wish to die with such bitterness. It will also allow me to apologize for my foolishness that must have disturbed you. May I treat you to lunch?"

"It's truly not necessary to apologize," I said. "And I, uh, have a phone call I need to make."

10

"I insist. I will wait for you to complete your call. You only bought enough bread for breakfast at the *boulangerie* this morning, so I know you haven't already prepared lunch."

I'd been right about seeing her at the bakery next to the apartment I was renting. She must have known where I was staying. It wouldn't be easy to back out of the invitation. And in spite of my discomfort, I didn't want to leave this woman with so much anger over an old misunderstanding.

Taking advantage of my hesitation, Madame Leblanc wrapped her bony hand around the crook of my elbow and led me toward the exit. Her cold fingers tightened around my arm like the brittle fingers of a skeleton, making it impossible for me to break away discreetly.

I didn't trust that her change of heart was genuine. But if it wasn't, I could use this opening to convince her I *wasn't* over 300 years old. I just had to lie convincingly.

No question, I was in trouble.

THREE

WE EXITED THE CATHEDRAL through a twisting metal gate, a modern affront to the majesty on the façade above. I stole a glance up at the limestone carvings that adorned the front of the iconic cathedral underneath the Rosetta stained glass window. Hidden in the Christian imagery were a few alchemical symbols that had been added over the centuries. As an accidental alchemist, I had taken months to brush up on the more obscure alchemical codes in Dorian's book, but the symbols on Notre Dame were straightforward—if you knew what you were looking for.

In a row of saints, a saint was shown defeating a dragon that looked suspiciously like an ouroboros, the serpent who swallows its own tail, thus representing the cyclical nature of alchemy. In a different panel, a salamander was engulfed in flames but not burning, symbolizing how the animal can protect itself from fire, just as Dorian's alchemy book had done when caught in a fire. As we hurried along to reach the quieter side of the cathedral my eyes flicked to an unassuming carving of a simple man holding a book. If you looked closely, you could make out the chiseled letters NON DE-GENERA AL. *Non Degenera Alchemia.* The alchemy book that had brought me here.

In the walled park behind Notre Dame, filled with Parisians walking their dogs, Madame Leblanc deposited me on a wooden bench. She strolled along the path, giving me privacy to make my phone call.

I'd been bluffing that I had a call to make. Yet after being shaken, I had an impulse to call Dorian or Max. I wanted to hear a friendly voice. I scrolled through the photos on my phone of my life in Portland. A hurricane-strength wave of homesickness nearly knocked me from the bench. I hadn't felt the emotion in so long that it took me a few moments to identify it. Homesick? The bittersweet emotion meant that after all these years, I truly had a home.

From my small phone screen, the image of my sort-of-boyfriend Max Liu looked up at me from behind a jasmine bush in his backyard garden. Max didn't yet know everything about me, but we'd come to care deeply for each other since I moved to Portland.

The photo of my misfit best friend was far less personal, because I didn't want to risk anyone else seeing the image of a supposed statue cooking up a storm in the kitchen. Therefore my photo of Dorian was of him standing next to the fireplace in the posed form he took when he returned to stone. I liked this particular snapshot for the mischievous gleam in his eye.

The sun hadn't yet risen in Portland. Max would be sleeping, but I wouldn't be stirring Dorian from slumber. The gargoyle didn't need to sleep, and the predawn hours were his favorites because he could move around most freely. I slipped earbuds into my ears, made sure there was nobody behind me, then hit the button to call him for a video chat.

"I am so pleased you called," Dorian said in his thick French accent. The formal voice didn't match the excited grin on his face. "I have made the most amazing discovery."

"You have?" In spite of the shock I'd received from Madame Leblanc, Dorian's enthusiasm was contagious. "What have you discovered?"

"Avocado!"

"You discovered … avocados?"

"Yes. They are *magnifiques*! Once you are home, we must share this with the world."

I let out a breath and lamented the fact that my dying friend was far more skilled at culinary creations than alchemy. "I'm pretty sure people already know about avocados."

A blur of claws flashed across the screen as he waved away my concern. "*Oui.* But do they know they can use avocado *in place of cream* to make a perfect chocolate mousse, pudding, or even frosting?" He was sitting so close to the screen that his horns bumped into the monitor.

"Is something wrong with the video camera?" I asked. It was mildly disconcerting to have such a close-up view of stone pores.

"*Pardon?* No, I am simply busy baking. I was skeptical of the skinny women on the Internet at first, but the flavors of cocoa and salt are stronger than the flavor of the avocado. It works perfectly! But I am speaking over you. You have something to tell me as well? Have you seen my brother yet? Yes, this must be why you are calling!"

"No, I'm sorry, Dorian. I haven't been granted access to see the stone gargoyle yet."

"Oh. *C'est regrettable.*"

"But Dorian, I found his empty perch at Notre Dame."

"*Vraiment?* This supports our suspicions that he is a creature like me."

"It does. I'll find a way to see him."

He narrowed his liquidy black eyes. "The professors continue to hold him captive?"

I wouldn't have described the study of an unmoving statue quite so dramatically, but he wasn't wrong.

Shortly after the Gallery of Gargoyles opened in the 1850s, one of the stone gargoyles was stolen. It was thought to be a prank, perhaps perpetrated by drunken artists or writers inspired by Victor Hugo's *Notre Dame de Paris* who found a stone chimera not properly secured and therefore made off with it. The great cathedral had been defaced many times before in its long history, so Parisians gave a Gallic shrug and moved on. The gargoyle wasn't seen again for over 150 years—until last month.

A gargoyle that looked suspiciously like the missing stone gargoyle was found on the Charles Bridge in Prague and repatriated to France from the Czech Republic. My friend and I suspected he was another creature like Dorian, who'd been brought to life but was reverting to stone. The Charles Bridge gargoyle had turned completely back to stone more quickly than Dorian. Was he alone in the world without an alchemist like me to help him?

"He's still under lock and key at the university," I said. Since the statue's pose was anomalous, architecture scholars at a local university were studying the gargoyle.

"You will find a way. But ... you have other news, no?"

"Why do you say that?"

"Your face. It reads like an open book."

Now that I had him on the line, what was I going to tell Dorian? There was nothing he could do to help, so did I really want to worry him by telling him that I'd been recognized by someone who could expose me?

Furthermore, he would probably *try* to help, which would only make things worse. I could imagine him suggesting I find an underworld contact in Paris who could "convince" Madame Leblanc to leave well enough alone. In addition to being a food snob and a talented chef, Dorian was an avid reader with a vivid imagination. Since he lived a relatively solitary life out of necessity, Dorian had more interactions with fictional characters than real people, and his ideas about real life needed reining in. Frequently.

"I was worried about you," I said. "I wanted to see how you were doing." It was the truth. His backward transformation had been speeding up. Every day his progression back to stone was happening more quickly.

"My arm is not troubling me."

"Your arm? There's something wrong with your *arm* now?"

"I think we have a bad connection," he shouted. "*Allo?* I cannot hear you, *mon amie*. I will sign off and return to my new recipe. I seem to have misplaced my cardamom. *À bientôt.*"

His face disappeared from the screen and I was left alone.

I'd left my Portland home a week ago in order to save Dorian's life. When I moved to Oregon earlier this year I'd been hoping to have a semblance of a normal life for a few years. With its quirky people, respect for nature, and health food culture, the city of Portland spoke to me from the moment I'd rolled into town with my Airstream trailer, thinking I'd stay for a brief time. I'd gotten far more than I'd dreamed. Friends as dear to me as any I'd ever had, a guy I was falling for, and a house that truly felt like a home. I'd put all that on hold to come here. Madame Leblanc had thrown my carefully constructed plan into disarray.

I looked across the park toward the Seine. Parisians strolled with their heads held high, walking dogs, puffing on cigarettes, meeting lovers. An artist with a hat to collect donations was sketching on the pavement in colorful chalk. Next to the surrealist image of pigeons with musical notes in place of eyes, he'd lettered in bright yellow chalk, *Life without art is stupid.*

I wasn't feeling the pull of the romantic City of Lights. Alone in a city that wasn't home, across the world from everyone I cared about, the only person in Paris who cared at all about me was a tenacious woman who could very well expose my secret and prevent me from saving Dorian's life.

FOUR

TEN MINUTES LATER, I found myself seated at an impossibly tiny table squeezed into the darkest corner of a café in the Marais neighborhood, walking distance from Notre Dame. The scent of cigarette smoke lingered in the air, seemingly from ghosts but more likely from centuries of smoke-filled conversations the walls had absorbed.

"There was hunger, fear, and death during the war," Madame Leblanc said, "but it elevated our senses. That's why I remember your grandmother so clearly. She was a flame that burned brightly. Too brightly, some said. That's why they said she was a witch."

I shivered. "She never told me that." I'd been called a witch many times, but until now I hadn't realized people in Paris had thought the same of me. I'd been careful here. Though I owned my shop for decades, I'd only stayed for a few years at a time, leaving the shop in the capable hands of an alchemy student while my beloved Ambrose and I were living in England or traveling elsewhere.

Madame Leblanc kept her eyes locked on mine as she raised a glass of wine to her lips. Her makeup was perfect. I didn't even want to think about what I looked like. I'd been sick in the weeks leading up to my trip to Paris, due to an alchemy experiment gone wrong. I've always been good at taking care of myself with healing foods, tinctures, and teas that I make myself, but understanding backward alchemy was taking a huge toll on me. I never would have left my cozy midcentury kitchen and gotten on an airplane had time not been running out for Dorian.

"Being so young, you would not understand how different things were," Madame Leblanc said. "The war ... It's not like in the movies. We weren't living in black and white, or even sepia. It was a more vibrant, heightened state of existence."

I knew what she meant. Being an alchemist is both a blessing and a curse. I've helped thousands of people, but I've also seen many of them die. I've seen more of this wondrous world than most, eating and drinking and laughing and crying with people from cultures simultaneously identical and poles apart. In those travels, I've seen the best and worst of humanity. This was especially so during traumatic times like plague, famine, and war.

But I couldn't say that out loud. I had to check myself before I spoke—it would have been all too easy to reminisce with her. Digging my fingernails into the palm of my hand, I reminded myself that I was twenty-eight-year-old Zoe Faust of Portland, Oregon, who'd been living out of her silver Airstream trailer for the last few years, bumming around the United States after a bad breakup, not my namesake who'd owned a shop in Paris.

I had closed my shop and returned home to America in 1942. Ambrose had died a few years before, followed a short time later by a fire at Elixir. My collection of herbs, tonics, and elixirs was destroyed, along with the *potager* back garden where I grew herbs and vegetables. The alchemy student who'd helped me at the store off-and-on, Jasper Dubois, had already left Paris, so there was nothing keeping me there. The side of the shop with alchemical equipment was spared, which allowed me to stay afloat selling paraphernalia at flea markets across the US. I had put the larger items that survived the fire into storage, wondering if they'd survive the war and whether I'd ever return to Paris.

Instead of answering Madame Leblanc, I took a bite of my arugula salad with roasted chickpeas and potatoes, which I dressed with olive oil and vinegar. Madame Leblanc ate a crème frache and steak tartar tartine. I'd declined sharing a carafe of wine and opted instead for tea. I needed to keep a clear head.

"You appear to be more lost in your memories than I am, mademoiselle," Madame Leblanc said.

"I was thinking of how little I knew of my grandmother's life here. What were your impressions of her and her shop?"

She sat back and inhaled deeply. The lines around her mouth grew deeper as she pressed her lips together. Her hands tugged at the starchy cloth napkin in her lap. I wondered if she was nervous that her recollections might upset me. No, she didn't seem like one to shy away from controversy. I thought it more likely she was craving a cigarette.

"At first," she said, "I didn't know it was your grandmother's shop, because an elderly man was there when my mother first took me. But a few months later, your grandmother appeared. She was much more pleasant, no?"

I smiled. Jasper had been a young man when he began minding the shop for me. He was a student of alchemy. Not *my* student, because that would never do for Jasper. He was a product of the times. Born into a title but no money, he was convinced of the superiority of the French, the bourgeoisie class, and the male sex. I doubt it had ever occurred to Jasper that I could have taught him anything. I discovered alchemy's secrets accidentally and therefore wasn't prepared to take on apprentices, but Jasper had never asked how I found alchemy so he didn't know my transformation had been accidental. He simply appreciated the availability of an alchemical laboratory behind the shop, making it a mutually beneficial relationship. Every decade we would switch places as the proprietor, and Jasper continued to age while he sought out a worthy alchemy teacher. The last time I'd arrived in Paris, I found the shop closed and Jasper gone. I was never sure if he'd found the alchemy teacher he was looking for, or if the war had scared him off.

Madame Leblanc returned my smile. "In spite of what my mother told me that soured my memories, I remember that your grandmother was beautiful, like you. She had gone prematurely gray too. No no, don't be self-conscious. I can tell you haven't dyed your hair white to be *avant-garde*, but the color suits you."

"Thank you," I said simply. It wouldn't do to elaborate. My hair turning white was what had alerted me to the fact that I had indeed discovered the Elixir of Life. It was the one part of me that aged.

"My mother told me your grandmother gave remedies even to those who could not pay, and her *potager* was the envy of the neighborhood. That garden flourished even in winter. It was unnatural. That is what convinced my mother it was witchcraft."

I was about to speak when a police officer appeared in the doorway, his eyes methodically scanning the cafe. His stiff stance and uniform suggested he was with the military branch of the police, the *National Gendarmerie*. Tall, dark-haired, young. Most people look young to me these days, but he was truly a boy, only a year or so out of university, I guessed. His gaze came to rest on my table.

Madam Leblanc waved him over. "My grand-nephew," she said to me, beaming. As she turned to the young man, her smile tightened, shifting from pride to a different emotion. *Scheming*.

"Gilbert," she said, "this is Zoe Faust. I trust you had time to look into what I told you?"

I gripped the table. I was being ambushed.

While Madam Leblanc had considerately given me "privacy" at the park outside Notre Dame, she'd made her own phone call. She called her *gendarme* grand-nephew. But surely he couldn't believe a fanciful tale that his grand-aunt was lunching with a 300-year-old woman, could he? Why was he here? Humoring his auntie?

"*Bonjour, mademoiselle*," he said, bowing his head in friendly greeting as he sat down at the table.

"Is there a problem?" I replied in English. Better to play American tourist Zoe Faust.

"Could I see your identification *sil vous plait*?"

"What's this about?" *Breathe, Zoe.*

He shrugged as if he had not a care in the world. Turning away from his aunt, he gave me a conspiratorial smile. "I expect it is nothing. Your passport please?"

I handed him my US passport. I wasn't too worried. It was a real passport. Every decade I received a new birth certificate from a man who'd been a prop-maker in Hollywood in the 1950s before his career was destroyed by the McCarthy hearings. I'd helped him through an illness when he was destitute, and even though he didn't understand the reason why I needed those birth certificates in my name, he'd always happily supplied them until his recent death.

The smile evaporated from the police officer's face as he looked at my passport. "Zoe Faust? You? *C'est vrais?* This cannot be. *Tante* Blanche?" He looked to his aunt.

"I was named after my grandmother," I explained.

"Ah." A chagrined smile appeared on the *gendarme*'s innocent face. "But of course. Is your grandmother still alive, mademoiselle?"

Madame Leblanc scowled at the young man as he accepted my statement.

"Why are you asking about my grandmother?" I asked.

"It is believed that she has information about a fire in 1942. It killed one … " He paused and consulted his notes. "Jasper Dubois."

I stared at him. "Jasper?" I whispered. "Jasper died in the fire?" My God. Poor Jasper. I always believed he'd been a coward and had run off when the war began. It wasn't as simple to find people in those days.

"Aha!" Madame Leblanc exclaimed. "You admit you were alive in 1942."

My shoulders shook. "My grandmother mentioned him often. He helped her with the store."

"Yes," Gilbert said. "The shop called …" He consulted his notes again. "Elixir."

"Yes, that was my grandmother's shop. But I didn't realize anyone was killed, or that the police would investigate such an old fire."

"There's no statute of limitation on murder, mademoiselle."

"Murder?"

"The fire was arson. The person who owned that shop is quite possibly a murderer."

FIVE

A MURDERER? A MURDERER. A. Murderer.

My brain was having trouble processing the information. Slipping up and being found out to be over 300 years old, I could understand. But a murderer?

"There must be some mistake," I said. "I—my grandmother, she wouldn't have killed anyone."

"We all think we know people," the policeman said in his heavily accented English, "but we do not truly know the depths of their souls."

What an utterly French thing to say. Under other circumstances, I would have been amused, and perhaps had a conversation with him about Sartre or Foucault.

"You say she is dead?" he continued.

"Yes. Many years ago."

"Where is she buried?"

"What? Buried? No, she was cremated."

"At what crematorium?"

"I have no idea. My mother was the one who handled it."

"Where can we find your mother?"

"She died many years ago too." My head throbbed. "Why do you need that information?"

"We need to confirm your grandmother is truly deceased. You must understand, she has been on the run since 1942. What is it you Americans say? On the lam?"

My mind raced as I willed hazy memories to come into focus. The fire had been an accident, started by someone trying to stay warm, and nobody had died. But what if that wasn't true? What if the fire that drove me from Paris had been deliberately set, and had killed Jasper?

Who would have done that? And why hadn't I known?

It was the fire that had prompted my immediate departure from France in 1942, but I'd been ready to move on. Ambrose, the man I loved, had killed himself several years before, after the death of his son Percy had driven him insane, so there was nothing keeping me in Paris.

I still felt this policeman must be mistaken, but I thought back on that place and time, so different than today. In Paris during the Occupation, the rules of life were different. People looked out for each other on an individual level more than in times of peace, but at the same time, authorities had more pressing problems than sorting out the aftermath of a fire that seemed to be accidental.

After Paris was taken, an underground network sprang up that made it possible to travel to neutral European countries and leave for the United States from there. I'd left with a family that was fleeing Paris with a sick child. One of their daughters, Cecily, was stricken with influenza and shouldn't have been traveling at all, but the family insisted it was more dangerous to stay in the city. Ambrose and Percy were dead and my shop was destroyed, so I took the opportunity to help Cecily and start anew. I'd been so focused on administering to the child and hurriedly packing the intact half of my shop that I hadn't sought out the authorities to make an official report. It wasn't the kind of thing that mattered at the time.

"I'm truly sorry to have distressed you, mademoiselle." Gendarme Gilbert's demeanor shifted. He appeared genuinely distressed to have upset me.

"I know you're only doing your duty." I looked at his young face, which might not have been as young as I originally suspected. As he leaned across the small table, I saw that his skin was drawn and sallow, especially around his eyes. He wasn't sleeping well. I found myself thinking of tinctures that might help him.

I shook off my natural inclinations and got back to the matter at hand. "I can look into the information you requested, but it will take time. I simply can't imagine … Can you tell me more about the fire?"

A shrug. "I do not have all of the details. It was only my aunt's call that alerted me and caused me to make inquiries. I'm not sure how much you know about the French police, but this is not my jurisdiction. I am not with the *Police Nationale*." Another shrug. "But my aunt is a persistent woman."

"I understand," I said, wondering what a Leblanc family Christmas was like.

"The crime did not come to light at the time but was noted after the war. Perhaps it was disguised as a casualty of war by the person who owned this shop." He paused and consulted a palm-sized notebook. "Yes, the murderer had intimate knowledge of the shop. A note was made in *l'ordinateur—comment dites-vous?*"

"She understands French," Madame Leblanc said. "She knows you said *computer*."

"*Bon*," he continued. "A note was made on the computer decades ago when the records were entered in, but no suspects had been found. *Alors*, it was forgotten. Until my aunt called me today."

"I see."

"In this modern age, forensics can find many things that were once not possible. Again, I am sorry to have distressed you! You look like an honest woman, mademoiselle. You are too young and innocent to have this burden." He shook his head. "If you give me your word that you will send me evidence of your grandmother's cremation, I see no reason to confiscate your passport. But if you do not—"

"Gilbert!" Madame Leblanc cut in abruptly. Her face flushed. "You're letting her *go*? I remembered the dead man found in the shop after she left and called you to exact justice, yet you betray me?"

"*Tante*, what can I do? This woman was not even alive in 1942. She is not responsible for anything that happened seventy-five years ago."

What *had* happened all those years ago? Killing is the antithesis of what true alchemy stands for. It chilled my 300-year-old blood to think I could have been so close to a murder and not prevented it.

Alchemy is about life, not death. Alchemical transformations strengthen and purify the basic nature of both inanimate objects and people. Corrupted metals being transmuted into pure gold and mortal people stopping the deterioration of their bodies. The Philosopher's Stone and the resulting Elixir of Life are found through rigorous scientific study and focused pure intent.

We alchemists aren't immortal. It's an oversimplification to say the Elixir of Life is a path to living forever. We *can* be killed; we simply don't age in the same way as normal people. It's a science that the world hasn't proven ready to embrace. Those of us who've gone public have rarely met with a good end. That's why there was no way I was speaking up now.

I felt the gold locket I wore around my neck, with a miniature painting of my brother and a photograph of Ambrose. I'd always felt responsible for the deaths of my little brother and the man I'd loved with all my heart. Was I responsible for Jasper's death, too?

"This is very serious, you understand. I realize she is your grandmother, but if we find you are shielding her because she is elderly—"

"I'm not."

"I'm trusting you, mademoiselle."

I nodded in what I hoped was a show of meek acquiescence. One of the advantages of looking young is that people underestimate you. Even when I truly was only twenty-eight, most people had no idea what I was capable of. I was an accomplished simpler—a person especially good with plants—by the time I was a teenager, and I unlocked alchemy's deepest secrets a decade later.

"I am truly sorry about your grandmother," Gendarme Gilbert said. "I hate to see it trouble you so. Remember her for the woman you knew. You are not the same woman as she, not responsible for her deeds."

I stole a glance at Blanche Leblanc. She wasn't convinced.

The world is a constantly changing place. Technological advances made it both easier and harder to hide. Yet I've always found that the best way to stay safe is to hide in plain sight. I was so certain I would no longer know anyone in Paris. It never occurred to me that a *child* would remember me.

I tossed a handful of Euros on the table and fled from the ambush. It took every ounce of my willpower not to break into a sprint as soon as I stepped out of the café. When I turned the corner, I ran.

My chest burned. I was still weak. Too weak to be running across Paris from a threat out of the past.

I was out of breath and wheezing when I unlocked the heavy blue door to my building, pushed on the thick brass knocker in the middle of the door, and used the worn wooden railing to pull myself up the three flights of stairs. My lungs were on fire by the time I reached my apartment. I caught my breath and bolted the door behind me.

In addition to my pounding heart and burning lungs, my ears buzzed. At first I thought it was the stress of the situation taking over my whole body, but then I saw the source of the sound—half a dozen bees circled outside the kitchen window. Though I'd wrapped *Non Degenera Alchemia* well, it wasn't good enough. Its scent was still attracting bees. Not the musty scent of a decaying antique book, but the smell of sweet honey and spicy cloves. It was as if the book was aging *backwards*.

I walked across the main room to the kitchenette. A wood-framed window of thick glass separated me from the bees. I wasn't normally frightened of the small insects. They lived in harmony with nature and were essential to the plant cycle of life. But these bees... I looked more closely. One of the swarm flew away. I hoped his comrades would follow suit. And then I saw my mistake. The bee that had flown away hadn't given up. He was giving himself space to achieve more speed. He flew straight at the window. I jumped back as he smashed the glass with a splat. His fuzzy body fell to the window sill below.

I looked away and shivered. I didn't want to end up like the kamikaze bee. I hadn't yet found what I needed to in Paris, but how could I risk what would happen if I stayed?

There was no way to prove Zoe Faust from 1942 was dead, because she wasn't. I'd have to fake a death certificate, which was possible but inadvisable. I keep my secret by being careful, and the one man I knew who could forge documents was dead. Plus it would take time I didn't have. If I remained in Paris, I risked bringing my secret into the open. My life would be under a dangerous level of scrutiny, especially with Madame Leblanc and forensic evidence to fuel the accusations.

I lit a burner and set a kettle of water on the stove. Tea would replenish my body, calm my nerves, and allow me to think. As I contemplated my options, a knock sounded on the door.

"I know you are inside, Zoe Faust," Madame Leblanc's voice echoed through the door. "I have the information about your past that you crave. I can tell you what my nephew cannot."

SIX

I FLUNG OPEN THE door and immediately regretted it. Though I was careful about leaving any evidence of alchemy in the open, I hadn't been expecting guests and hadn't taken stock of what was visible at the moment.

"What do you want?" I stood blocking the doorway.

"I want the truth," Madame Leblanc said. "In return, I will tell you what you wish to know."

I gripped the side of the door, hesitating with the door open barely wide enough to see all of Madame Leblanc's face.

"The reason I remember you so clearly," she continued, "enough to know the truth that you and your 'grandmother' are one in the same, is because the image of that man, Jasper Dubois, is seared into my mind. I will never forget it."

"What did you see?" My heart beat in my throat.

"When the ashes from the fire were cleared, my friend Suzette and I played in the ruins. We were five years old. We were the ones who found him."

"I'm so sorry," I said. I meant it. What an awful discovery for a child to make.

She tilted her head in acknowledgment of the sympathy.

"My grandmother didn't tell me that Jasper was still in Paris when the fire broke out," I said. Had he been hiding from me?

"You are either wrong or lying. This is why I called my nephew. Jasper Dubois did not perish in the fire. He was *stabbed to death*."

I didn't have time to react because a precocious bee had squeezed its way through a joint in the thick window frame. It flew straight toward Madame Leblanc. It landed on her wrist. She swore creatively and slapped her hand. The dead bee fell to the floor, but not before it left its stinger in her tender flesh. She pulled up her sleeve and I caught a brief glimpse of a black tattoo on her forearm. Had she been branded by a concentration camp? Was the discovery of a body one of her last memories of childhood freedom?

"Come inside," I said, my mood involuntarily softening. I could never resist helping people when I had the resources to do so. Refusing assistance wasn't in my nature. "I have a calendula salve that should help the sting."

Madame Leblanc gave me a curious look. She hesitated for only a moment, then followed me inside and accepted the salve.

"You should—" I began.

"I know how to apply a salve. I'm familiar with most forms of medicines. Getting old has as many frustrations as it does pleasures. I do envy you."

"My grandmother taught me—"

She snorted. "*Grandmother.*"

"You truly believe in witchcraft, madame? I'm sorry it's disturbing that I look so much like my grandmother."

Madame Leblanc walked to the narrow kitchen window overlooking the courtyard.

"Those must be fragrant flowers in the window sill. I have never seen so many bees." She closed her eyes and swayed.

"Can I offer you a seat?"

"You are still as kind as you always were," she said, refusing the seat and standing as tall as her frail frame allowed. "But this is not over. You may be able to fool the rest of the world, but I know you are the same woman who disguised a murder as an accident. I will be sure Gilbert uncovers the truth about what you did to poor Jasper Dubois. My nephew will figure out what you did—and I will figure out what you *are.*"

With that she tossed her silk scarf across her shoulder and turned on her designer heel. "*Au revoir*, Zoe Faust," she called out from down the hallway. "For now."

Standing stunned in my doorway, I wondered where I'd gone wrong. My plan had seemed so simple a week ago. The book that had brought Dorian to life had pointed the way to Notre Dame. It was here I would find the last piece of the puzzle to save Dorian's life.

Only it hadn't proven that simple.

I'd been naïve in thinking Paris would hold obvious answers. I'd been hopeful because I hadn't known about Notre Dame's history with backward alchemists until Dorian's book caught on fire that spring. Instead of reducing the book to ash, the fire had brought forth hidden ink and revealed its connection to the cathedral. The unexpected transformation was significant, I knew, yet I couldn't see what exactly it told me about Notre Dame. I was missing something.

I thought the second living gargoyle might shed light on the solution. Unfortunately because I wasn't an academic, an architect, or a stone carver, I'd been refused access to the gargoyle who was trapped in stone. The university's staff studying the bizarrely posed statue didn't realize a living being was trapped inside, and I couldn't very well tell them. I had to find another way to see the creature. And until now, I thought I'd have time to do so.

I also wondered if there might be other backward alchemists out there. If there were, they might be able to help me. I hadn't been able to decipher parts of Dorian's backward alchemy book, which wasn't surprising since alchemy is filled with secrets, obfuscation, and codes. Most alchemists learn through a combination of personal experimentation in a laboratory and an apprenticeship with a mentor. I hadn't worked with a mentor since studying with Nicolas Flamel nearly three centuries ago, and I'd fled from my training before it was complete. I was only in touch with one alchemist—a former slave, Tobias Freeman, who hadn't studied alchemy formally either, and who didn't know any alchemists besides me. Even among properly educated alchemists, most don't know each other because secrecy and suspicion are so ingrained in our training that we hide the truth from everyone. There was no one to help me.

In other words, my trip had been a bust. And now, on top of everything, there was the murder of Jasper Dubois. What had I gotten myself into by returning to Paris after all these years?

I locked the apartment door and breathed deeply. I closed my eyes, but the buzzing of the bees prevented me from relaxing. Rooting through drawers, I found a roll of tape and sealed the joints of the war-time building's window frame to foil the bees.

I wished I could call Tobias to think through my dilemma. But there was nothing more my one true alchemist friend could tell me about backward alchemy or alchemy's connection to Notre Dame, since he'd had even less formal training than I'd had. It was his nonjudgmental friendship I craved.

But I couldn't bring myself to burden him. Not now. Though I knew he'd want to help me, he had his own life-and-death situation to deal with. He was caring for his wife of sixty years, Rosa, who was dying of old age in their home in Detroit. Rosa wasn't an alchemist and had continued to age. Still, Tobias and Rosa had loved each other for more joyous years than most of us get.

Instead I sat down, pulled out my phone, and searched for references to Jasper Dubois online. Millions of hits, but none of them my Jasper. Narrowing the search, I found reference to the 1942 fire in a French library's online newspaper archives. It was only a small article, providing no insights. Much more space was devoted to the war. I wouldn't find answers with the tools of the modern world.

My fingers hovered over the screen for a moment, then typed a search I hoped I wouldn't use until I had an answer about how to save Dorian's life. Flights home to Portland.

The more affordable flights connecting to Portland left in the morning, but Madame Leblanc's nephew would probably look for me the next day. I bought a ticket for the last flight that left that night. I would arrive home in the wee hours after a nineteen-hour journey, but I had little choice.

I opened the floorboard under which I was hiding *Non Degenera Alchemia*. I'd chosen this apartment rental because the building had been around for centuries. I knew it would have little nooks where I could hide things I didn't want anyone to find. Not that I was expecting trouble, but old habits die hard. Now I was glad I'd taken the precaution.

The book was safely ensconced in its hole. In spite of my overzealous wrapping, two now-dead bees had made their way underneath the top layer of plastic. They had squished themselves to death in their quest to reach the book. Bees are a minor symbol in alchemy and they are used even more in backward alchemy. Many of the disturbing woodcut illustrations in Dorian's book showed bees circling counterclockwise above a menagerie of dead animals. Beyond the scent of honey that permeated the pages as it aged, was there something more drawing the insects to it?

I didn't have to open the pages to see the woodcut illustrations. The twisted imagery was unforgettable. My mind saw bees filling the skies in a counterclockwise formation, stinging the eyes of the people and animals that writhed on the ground.

From those unsettling coded images in the book, I'd taught myself how to create an alchemical Tea of Ashes that temporarily stopped Dorian from returning to stone. Superficially, the process looked easy—mixing ingredients in fire that quickly transformed into salt. Much easier than true alchemy, which in addition to basic ingredients involves pure intent, time, and energy. Backward alchemy is a shortcut, a straight line through what should be a labyrinthine maze of discovery leading to true knowledge. Because the shortcuts here were backward alchemy, it was a delicate balance between adding life to Dorian and taking it from me.

Before leaving Portland I thought I'd found the right balance to make Dorian a large enough batch of Tea of Ashes for him to stay healthy while I was gone in Paris. I was wrong. The transformation had failed, and even worse, it left me sick for three full days—too sick to travel and too sick to do anything much beyond lie in bed. I'd lost so much time, and now I was being forced from Paris after less than a week.

But I wasn't giving up. I had five hours until I was due at the airport.

The question was, with five hours left in Paris, could I do what I hadn't been able to do in five days?

SEVEN

SITTING AT THE EDGE of the sagging bed in the small apartment, I rubbed a bee sting on my arm that was still noticeable and looked through the small set of tinctures and salves I'd brought from home. Traveling with the preparations was a force of habit, but in this case it was also necessary after I'd been sickened by the Tea of Ashes and stung by bees interested in Dorian's book.

After arriving in Paris I'd taken *Non Degenera Alchemia* to Notre Dame to compare its illustrations to the carvings on the façade of the cathedral. For the record, bringing a book of unknown power to an ancient cathedral to which it's tied is a very bad idea. That experiment led to many stings as I shooed bees away from the book; I used my photocopies for reference after that. I'd also visited many libraries and bookshops in hopes of discovering obscure references to Notre Dame's connections to alchemy that I hadn't been able to find in my own alchemy books or in mainstream publications.

One of the places I'd visited was a narrow bookshop within view of Notre Dame. Appropriately, it was called *Bossu Livres*—Hunchback

Books. It was presumably named for the famous character Victor Hugo's *The Hunchback of Notre Dame*. The bookshop's specialty was the history of Paris, with a large section on Notre Dame Cathedral. The bookseller thought I was a graduate student conducting research for my dissertation, so he didn't bat an eye when I asked about information on any secret societies that used to meet at Notre Dame. I bet it wasn't even the strangest research question he'd received. He was the only bookseller who'd taken my request seriously and spent more than a few minutes looking through his files. Though he hadn't been able to help at the time, he'd told me to check back in a few days.

Hoping to continue the research Madame Leblanc had interrupted that morning, I hurried across Pont Notre-Dame to the small Île de la Cité island where the cathedral stood. Normally I took time to appreciate my surroundings, especially when I was in a city as storied as Paris. But not today. If I let myself slow down, I knew I'd imagine Madame Leblanc and her nephew over my shoulder and the ghost of Jasper Dubois in front of me.

It was a warm day, close to the start of summer, and the scents of Paris swirled around me. Strong coffee, smooth wine, freshly baked bread, and … something smoky that stirred a memory I couldn't quite place. I glanced upward. The Gallery of Gargoyles was visible from the ground, though the personalities of the stone creatures were left to the imagination at this distance. "What are your secrets?" I whispered.

I pulled my eyes from the limestone façade, once painted brightly but now a natural golden tan, and continued to the narrow street that housed the bookshop. The shop was barely wider than I was tall, probably the same square footage as the interior of the Airstream trailer that was parked in my driveway in Portland. The small space was filled with treasures, stacked from floor to ceiling.

I pushed on the solid door, painted a bright blue. It resisted. The brass handle didn't budge either. I peeked into the window. A ray of sunlight shone over a display in the window of Paris-based poets from the nineteenth century. Aside from that illuminated corner, the interior of the shop was dark. A sign in the window read FERMÉ. The shop was closed.

I leaned against the stone wall and tried to keep my spirits from being completely crushed. At every turn, I faced another obstacle.

I gave a start as the bell jangled and the door of the bookshop swung open.

"I didn't mean to frighten you, mademoiselle," said the man who opened the door.

"It's quite all right. I'm pleased to find you're open after all."

He waved me inside. Only then did I realize it was the same bookseller I'd previously spoken with. A plain man in his forties, he had a forgettable face. The impression was rounded out by thinning brown hair, leathery skin, and the hint of a stoop. If he were to lean against a shelf of his leather-bound books, I had the feeling that he'd blend in and be invisible to customers. He'd told me his name just yesterday, but I struggled to recall it. "It's good to see you, Monsieur Augustin."

"Please, call me Lucien." He turned the sign from FERMÉ to OUVERT.

My eyes swept over the shelves as I breathed in the scent of books made over the centuries from various wood pulps and animal skins. These books were decaying as normal books did, with a faint hint of mildew detectable in the older ones and nary a bee in sight. Normally I loved spaces crammed full of books, but the haphazard nature of this room kept me off balance. If they had a filing system, it was unlike anything I'd ever encountered.

"I was wondering if you'd had a chance to look for the book on Notre Dame secret societies you mentioned," I said. "I know I told you I'd check back with you in a few days if I didn't receive a call from you, but I'm leaving Paris sooner than expected."

"Finished the research for your thesis already?" Though he spoke with a French accent, the inflection in the question suggested he'd lived elsewhere for a time. Under other circumstances I would have asked him about it, because linguistic nuances tell you so much about a person, but that conversation wasn't meant to happen today.

"Unfortunately a family emergency came up. I have to leave Paris immediately." I feigned interest in a photographic history of the cafés of Paris to avoid meeting his gaze as I lied.

He frowned. "I'm so sorry to hear that. Because I found something of interest."

My eyes snapped up. "What is it you've found?"

"A slim volume, probably produced in the fourteenth century." He hesitated. "Probably not what you're after. Never mind."

"No, please tell me what you found."

"It's called *The Backward Alchemists of Notre Dame.*"

My breath caught.

"Bizarre, no?" Lucien said. "I didn't think it was what you were looking for," he added with a shake of his head, misinterpreting my expression. "*Dommage.* I thought it was worth a try. It sounded like a secret society. The type of thing you mentioned as a possible interest for your thesis."

"I'd love to see it." Hope welled in me again. It was exactly what I needed. *This could lead me to a backward alchemist.*

"*Bon.* I am glad I requested it. The book is being sent here to the shop from a storage facility. Perhaps if you came back tomorrow morning—"

"I'm leaving Paris tonight." I didn't want to think about what awaited me with Madame Leblanc pressuring her nephew to flag my passport.

"Let me check on the status of the shipment. Maybe we'll get lucky." He disappeared through a door shaped like an embrasure of a castle and nearly as narrow as an arrow-slit. I let my eyes wander across the high shelves crammed full of books in a dozen languages, all related to the history of Paris, but none of them organized with any system I could discern. I picked up a book on unique Parisian architecture from the nineteenth century with a focus on abandoned buildings. I turned the pages, stopping at a photograph of *le Cabaret de L'Enfer*. As was typical of the French, the old nightclub was a complete embodiment of its theme: The Nightclub of Hell. It typified the quirky French ethos.

I knew the famous nightclub. *Le Cabaret de L'Enfer* had been one of Ambrose's favorite late-night clubs in the early 1900s. He was a country lad at heart and always felt most comfortable when we lived in the countryside. But because I could help more people when we lived in more populated areas, we always returned to Paris. After a time, he came to love it as I did. *Le Cabaret de L'Enfer* was one of the places that captured his imagination. He wasn't alone. His son Percy had once thought of opening a similar club in London, but he was a lazy, lazy man, so his talk never turned into action. But more ambitious entrepreneurs had opened a parallel nightclub next door to the Paris cafe: *Le Ciel*. Heaven.

I was stirred from the memory of a bygone Paris by a movement at the corner of my eye. Lucien had returned, shaking his head. "*Je suis desolé, mademoiselle.* No luck."

"Could you mail it to me in Oregon? I'll pay in advance for expedited shipping. Plus extra for your trouble."

"Extra is not necessary, mademoiselle. But you are kind." His eyes turned to the book in my hands. "*Le Cafe de L'Enfer.* You know of this landmark? It has quite a history."

"I've read about it. It's too bad it wasn't preserved."

"I have something you might like. I believe I have an old postcard of the Hell-mouth doorway."

He flipped through a stack of postcards on a stand near the cash register, then drew his hand back abruptly. "*Merde*. Damn these frail fingernails."

I winced as he held his finger, clearly in pain. "I might have something that can help, monsieur."

I wound a finger around my white hair as I reached into my purse with my other hand. I carried a tincture with me that would be good for frail fingernails. It was an herbal remedy that helped me with my hair, which would have been thin and brittle without extra care. Through healthy eating and topical treatments, I was able to keep it looking and feeling similar to how it did when I was young. Though I'd never again have thick, long hair, my hair was healthy enough to fool people into thinking I dyed it white as a trendy fashion statement and that I followed a vegan diet because it was the latest fad.

Lucien gratefully, if skeptically, accepted the tincture. I wrote out instructions for how to use it while he completed my order. I'd just have to hope that the book would provide useful insight whenever it did arrive to me in Portland.

The bell above the door sounded. Lucien's friendly eyes turned dark as the young woman with an overzealous application of eyeliner asked if he had any books containing maps of the catacombs of Paris, the tangled tunnels lined with human bones.

"*Je suis desolé, mademoiselle*," he said, and the customer departed.

"I think I saw a book on the subject in a pile over there." I pointed to a jam-packed bookshelf. "I bet I can catch her."

Lucien shook his head firmly. "*Moutards*. Maps of the catacombs are not for them. They sneak into the catacombs with complete disregard for their history. They use it as a *bôit de nuit*, their own personal nightclub. As if it were *le Cafe de L'Enfer*. This desecration of the catacombs has become acceptable!"

"Urban explorers," I said.

He narrowed his eyes at me.

"I'm not one," I added hastily. "But I've heard about it. Adventurers, kids staging raves, artists." They seemed harmless enough to me. Kids enjoying their youth in Paris. I was too old to understand the appeal myself. Or perhaps the underground crypts disturbed my alchemical sensibilities. Relics like human bones were to be revered, not made into entertainment. I'd visited the ossuary once, shortly after the underground graves had been opened to the public in the late 1800s, when an appreciation for macabre curiosities turned the rows of skulls and bones into a tourist attraction. I'd never had a desire to return.

The bookseller looked from his dim sanctuary to the vibrant street outside. "I do not know what this old city is coming to."

The wind was picking up as I stepped out of the shop. I turned up the collar of my silver raincoat, touched a hand to my locket, and glanced at my watch. I had time for one more errand. It was time to see a possible member of the family: Dorian's brother.

EIGHT

THE PREVIOUS MONTH, A gargoyle resembling the chimeras of Notre Dame had been found on the Charles Bridge in Prague. There were no witnesses aside from a drunk who slept outside near the bridge. The man swore the five-foot statue had limped onto the bridge by itself as dawn was breaking. Needless to say, his testimony was dismissed as the ravings of a drunken fool.

Authorities thought there must have been at least one other witness, because a half-empty bottle of absinthe was cradled in the statue's stone arms. The liquor had been bottled this year. Yet no witnesses could be found. It must have been a prank, the police surmised. Someone who shared a similar sense of humor with the thieves who were leaving gold dust in place of gold figurines in museums across Europe, offering no trace of how they got in or out.

I knew the true explanation for both of these occurrences. There were no thieves, and there was no prankster. Gold created through backward alchemy was reverting to dust. And this was a gargoyle like Dorian, who was brought to life but was now reverting to stone.

Architectural scholars recognized the statue as being one of Viollet-le-Duc's creations for Notre Dame, and it was quickly asserted that this was the stolen carving that hadn't been seen in over a century.

Only sketches of the gargoyle existed, and without any photographs it was all scholarly speculation. It was determined that more study was needed, and that architects and stonemasons would be the most appropriate people to study the beast.

The Czech authorities readily handed it over to France. Now the gargoyle frozen in stone was under study at a Paris university's architecture department.

In spite of my deferential tone and fluent French, I'd been denied admittance to study the statue by the scholar in charge, Professor Chevalier. I'd been confident I'd win him over with enough time, but time was no longer an option. An idea began to take shape in my mind. One that my young friend Brixton would undoubtedly call "wicked."

As I walked back to my apartment to pick up *Not Untrue Alchemy*, I made a phone call to check with Professor Chevalier's secretary, making sure he wasn't allergic to bees. I claimed to be a nurse who wanted to check how an allergic patient was doing, and the secretary assured me I had the wrong number, because she was certain the professor wasn't allergic to bees. If I wished to hear it from his own ears, I could call back when she expected him to return to his office within half an hour.

Perfect.

I freed *Not Untrue Alchemy* from its hiding place, made sure the book was carefully bundled, and pressed the few possessions I'd brought to Paris into my rucksack. Hurrying down the stairs and into the courtyard, I cast what might be my last glance at the centuries-old building. Would this be the last time I was ever in Paris? Instead of walking toward the university, I made a two-block detour to a spot I'd been working my way up to visiting.

Two minutes later, I stood outside the Auberge Nicolas Flamel, the Michelin star restaurant and oldest house in Paris. It had also once been the home of my mentor.

The plaque that adorned the building began with the words *Maison de Nicolas Flamel et de Pernelle sa femme. Pour conserver le souvenir de leur foundation charitable.* The home of Nicolas Flamel his wife Pernelle, honoring their charitable work.

I ran my fingertips across the rough stone that had stood since they built their home in 1407, and that had served as a restaurant for over a hundred years. His building had stood the test of time much better than the building that had housed Elixir. Because of the fire ... I pushed thoughts of poor Jasper Dubois from my mind.

Alchemical symbols were carved into many of the stones on the Auberge Nicolas Flamel, though I knew for a fact they hadn't been made by Nicolas or Pernelle. The carvings came later, long after they had faked their deaths and abandoned their city home for the French countryside. These symbols hadn't been made by true alchemists, but were instead laymen's ideas of what alchemical symbols would look like, added once Nicolas had become infamous. The decorative letters and animals of the faux alchemists had worn smooth over time, but were still visible. As was a loose stone.

That was odd. In a section of solid stone, nonexistent joints of a brick shouldn't have been able to crumble.

Had someone purposefully defaced the building? Though it hadn't been Nicolas's home for centuries, the violation of the home he'd crafted infuriated me. Ignoring the sharp glare of a waiter smoking a cigarette on his break, I stepped onto the windowsill to see what was going on. The light backpack weighed heavily on my shoulders, reminding me how weak I still was.

On the loose stone was an alchemical carving. A real one. *Could this have been carved by Nicolas himself?*

The waiter muttered about uncivilized tourists as I tugged on the stone that bore the ouroboros. It didn't give. Then I thought about the symbol itself. The ouroboros—the serpent eating its own tail, representing the cyclical nature of alchemy. Following the meaning of the symbol, I gave the stone not an outward tug but a clockwise twist. That set it free.

Behind the ouroboros stone was a faded note on vellum.

Addressed to me.

My heart pounded in my ears and the voice of the aggrieved waiter faded away. The familiar hand of Nicolas Flamel had scrawled a note in old French: *Dearest Zoe. If you find this one day…*

The rest of the note was illegible. *No, no, no.* This couldn't be all there was! With shaking hands, I felt around behind the false brick. Nothing. I grabbed at the edges of the rough stone hole, getting nothing for my effort except a scrape across my knuckles.

I pulled my hand away, ran my fingertips over the soft, faded paper, and willed my eyes to see text that wasn't there. Was there anything left of the ink?

The waiter had brought a compatriot from inside the restaurant, a regal woman with leathery skin. She was at least twice my size and carried a rolling pin in her hand.

I could deal with the note later. I shoved the ouroboros brick back into place, making sure I heard a click, then jumped down from the windowsill and sped away from the house, the note from Nicolas in my pocket.

NINE

I WALKED TO THE university in a haze, passing elegant women expertly maneuvering cobblestones in perversely high heels, shopkeepers reminiscent of centuries past closing up shop for the day, and sidewalk cafés radiating the mingling scents of cigarettes, wine, and espresso.

What had Nicolas wanted to tell me? And when had he left the message? It wasn't before I left Paris during the war, was it? I'd visited his home then and hadn't noiced the carving. Yet the vellum looked old. I hadn't been in hiding while living in Paris before the war, so why hadn't he sought me out if he was alive and in Paris? And if he was angry with me for leaving my apprenticeship so abruptly centuries ago, before I completed my training, why reach out to me at all? It didn't make sense.

Reaching the Left Bank, I saw groups of college students dressed up for a night out on the town. Evening was quickly approaching. With my distracted thoughts, I bumped into a young couple with their arms draped around each other. They were stopped in the middle of the sidewalk, a map in their hands. They folded the map and nodded at each other, but instead of walking toward a metro station, café, or bar, they knelt down and pried open the manhole they were standing on. On any other occasion, I would have been curious about a young couple climbing into the sewers, but not today. With a note from my mentor in my pocket and a gargoyle to meet, I continued on my way.

I couldn't stop thinking about Nicolas. If he was still alive, would he be able to help me with Dorian's backward alchemy dilemma? No. Of that I was certain. He'd once warned me of backward alchemy. True alchemy is about personal transformation and requires a personal sacrifice to create the Philosopher's Stone and the Elixir of Life. Backward alchemy, in his eyes, was the antithesis of alchemy's purity. Nicolas wouldn't even speak of it, except to warn me away from it.

I stopped in front of a slanted Linden tree and steadied myself on its trunk. The bark was smooth and comforting under my raw fingers. Being with a small piece of nature in the loud and crowded city took the edge off of the troubling realization that even if I found Nicolas, he would fight me rather than help me if my quest involved backward alchemy. Being the purist that he was, I could imagine him insisting that Dorian was an unnatural creature who shouldn't be alive. He would also be furious that I'd been so careless as to be recognized by Madame Leblanc, who was threatening to expose alchemy.

I reached the university without walking into traffic or crashing into a light post, which was about as much as I could hope for at the moment. When I reached the professor's door, I took Dorian's book out of its three layers of taut plastic.

"*Bonjour, monsieur,*" I said from the doorway. "I was hoping to show you the architectural woodcuts in this antique book. I think when you see them, you'll understand why I'm so interested in seeing the gargoyle." I nodded toward the gargoyle standing in the corner of the office. More than a foot taller than Dorian, and with rougher edges, the gargoyle wore a pained expression on his stone face. Dorian had taken to calling him his "brother" ever since we learned of his existence the previous month.

"Chimera," the professor corrected me with a stern frown. "The sculpture is a chimera, not a gargoyle. Let me see this book."

I forced a smile and handed *Not Untrue Alchemy* to the professor. Technically, the term *gargoyle* only refers to a carving that serves as a water spout, with the stone creature's mouth and throat serving as the drainpipe. But the word *gargoyle* has become a general term for a range of stone creatures that perch on buildings. Even Dorian refers to himself as a gargoyle.

"Of course," I said. "The chimera. Do you mind if I open this window?" I moved to open it before he had a chance to reply.

He looked up from the book. "I'd prefer you did not—"

His words were drowned out by another sound. The buzzing of bees. The noise began softly, as a hum, but quickly rose to the level of a biblical swarm of locusts.

At least a dozen bees flew into the room. They circled the professor's hands. He dropped the book onto his desk and cried out as the stinging began. It took all of my willpower to stop myself from rushing to help him. *Deep breath, Zoe. He'll be fine.*

Professor Chevalier swore and rushed from the room. I donned gloves and whisked the book into a plastic bag with an airtight seal. Half a dozen bees were trapped inside with the book. The rest followed the professor.

I closed the office door and locked it. I knew I didn't have much time, so I'd make the most of it. First things first: I left a salve on the desk that would help with the bee stings.

Next I slid *Not Untrue Alchemy* from the bag, careful to keep the bees inside. The book fell open to the page it always fell open to. These were the words that had once accidentally brought Dorian to life, when Jean Eugène Robert-Houdin had read the words as a dramatic addition to his stage show.

I began to read the mysterious words aloud.

Here in Paris, I felt the power of the words so deeply that I was caught off guard. My body began to sway as strongly as when I'd been on a fishing boat during an unexpected typhoon. I braced myself against the wall with my free hand and looked at the gargoyle, hoping he wouldn't begin to shake as much as I was. Then he'd be sure to fall and shatter.

The gargoyle didn't move.

I sat down on a nearby chair and cradled the confounding book on my lap. Reading from an alchemy book alone shouldn't direct so much power toward myself. And certainly not this quickly. Alchemy involves practicing in solitude in one's own alchemy lab, going through the processes of calcination, dissolution, separation, fermentation, distillation, and coagulation.

But this book was *backward* alchemy, where shortcuts abound and one element is sacrificed for another. Alchemy can seem like magic, because we can't see the mechanism of the transfer of energy under a microscope. But it's not any different than theoretical physics. You don't have to see science to believe in it. Alchemists were early chemists, but because of "puffers"—the fools who only saw alchemy as a way to make money and sought favor with kings by transmuting lead into gold for political gains—alchemy was squashed, twisted, and discredited. Across time, whenever true alchemists have tried to come out from the shadows, it has ended badly.

Still feeling like I was seasick, I focused my breathing. *Think, Zoe.* I read the incantation again. The gargoyle again failed to come to life.

There was one more thing I wanted to try. I had a packet of tea with me, leftovers of the Tea of Ashes I'd made for Dorian before coming to Paris to stave off his backward transformation into stone.

I'd saved the remnants of the ash-like substance that I'd created from the living plants in my garden.

The gargoyle's mouth was frozen half open, revealing a dark gray tongue and sharp teeth. I rubbed the ashes onto his stone tongue. The gray powder coated the rough surface, disappearing into the stone pores.

I stepped back. Nothing.

The sound of a buzzing bee interrupted the silence. One of the bees inside the book's wrapping was frantically trying to escape. I shut the book and pushed it back inside. Let the bees have it. It wasn't doing me any good.

The buzzing subsided, but the room wasn't silent. There was now another sound.

Wheezing.

My eyes flew to the gargoyle's dark face. His gray eyes began to water. "*Peux-tu m'entendre?*" I asked. Can you hear me?

The gargoyle wasn't able to move his stone body, but his eyes were alive. I felt a jolt of pity as his sad eyes locked onto mine. Gray stone lips twitched. I wished I'd been wrong. I wished what the scholars believed was the truth, that this was simply a gargoyle carved by a stone carver with an offbeat sense of humor. Not this—a living soul trapped in stone.

I also wished I'd been wrong about Dorian's book. It had led me to the recipe for the Tea of Ashes and to Notre Dame, but it appeared to have served its purpose. It wasn't a miracle that could save the gargoyles from reverting to stone.

"*Aidez moi,*" the gargoyle croaked in a deep gravelly voice. "Help … Help me."

The last words were barely audible. The wheezing stopped. His lips froze, but for a moment longer his liquid gray eyes bore into mine. He blinked once more, then went still.

TEN

Dorian's black eyes opened wide and he blinked at me.

"*Mais c'est formidable!* It is true I have *un frère—a brother!*—and he is being held captive—" He broke off with a curse that had been popular a century ago and began to pace across the creaking hardwood floor. "*Mais attendez…* your visit to Notre Dame did not yet yield the answers we need, yet you are home."

I hadn't had trouble leaving Paris and my connecting flight had touched down in Portland shortly after midnight. Dorian and I sat in my Craftsman house's attic, which I'd half converted into an office for my online business, Elixir. I hadn't slept at all on the flight. Flying affects my body's natural rhythms more intensely than it does most people, because the planetary alignments go by too quickly. It scrambles my head. I much prefer to travel by car or boat, or on foot. I'd felt so alone on the long flights, fleeing both the country and the prospect of finding my mentor Nicolas, who I hadn't seen since I'd run away from alchemy.

"Did you fear they would arrest you for sending bees after the bad man who is keeping my brother captive?" Dorian asked.

I sat down on a hefty crate I'd pushed into the corner next to the sloping ceiling. How to explain what had happened? "Not exactly."

"She comes home speaking in riddles," Dorian muttered.

Home. That was exactly how I felt. Like I was returning home. I *was* home. I was again reminded that this was the first time in decades that I felt I had someplace besides my trailer to call home. I was simultaneously comforted and terrified. I loved the friends I'd made since moving to Portland several months ago. But if I failed to unlock the secrets of backward alchemy, my newfound best friend Dorian would suffer a fate worse than death. If I failed to convince a man who once believed in magic that believing in alchemy wasn't to be feared, I would lose my relationship with Max, my first chance at love in nearly a century. And now, if I dared return to Paris to finish what I'd started, I'd risk exposing my own secrets and the secrets of alchemy that the world wasn't yet ready for.

With Dorian in front of me, I couldn't bring myself to tell him about the complicated accusation of murder from 1942. Telling Dorian of my own entanglement in a disturbing death from so many years ago wouldn't help anyone. Nor could I tell him that I realized true alchemists like Nicolas Flamel might not understand that Dorian wasn't inherently evil. I didn't want to crush his hopes.

"How bad is your arm?" I asked, watching Dorian's awkward stance as he limped back and forth across the room, his clawed feet tapping on the floorboards with each step he took.

"*Ce n'est rien.*"

"In that case, move your left arm for me."

"I told you," he snapped, "it is nothing." He flapped his wings impatiently. "A kidnapped fellow gargoyle and the riddle of my book are much more important."

"I'll figure it out. I'm closer than ever before, Dorian."

Dorian stopped pacing and studied my face. "What else is wrong? What are you not telling me?"

"Why do you say that?"

He narrowed his liquidy black eyes. "I have known you for long enough to have learned your expressions, Zoe. When you are sad, your shoulders fall. When you are angry yet pretend you are not, you purse your lips. And when you are frightened, you tug at your hair. *You are frightened.*"

Apparently I would be a bad poker player. I put my hands into my lap.

"What has you so scared, *mon amie?*" Dorian asked. "I have faith you will help me. Help *us.*" He hopped up onto the crate next to me—he was only three-and-a-half feet tall—and patted my shoulder with his wing. His wings were heavy stone but simultaneously soft and malleable.

"I'm tired. That's all. I've got killer jet lag."

"For someone so old and wise, have you yet to learn you are a terrible actress?"

"You may recall I did fine on my own before you showed up in my living room."

"Yes. But you do much better when you do not lie."

I couldn't argue with that. Since one of the core tenets of alchemy is purity of intent, that's how I live my life. I don't feel comfortable lying. Whenever I can avoid it, I do. When I bought the crumbling Craftsman house in Portland, Oregon, earlier in the year, I didn't make up a story that I was a renovator or a house-flipper. When you act naturally, it's easier for people to believe what they want to. Real estate agents filled in the blanks that made sense to their worldview. They believed I was a young woman who wanted a bargain and didn't know what she was getting herself into. And my new neighbors assumed I was a good fit for the artsy Hawthorne neighborhood because I dyed my hair white to be trendy. In truth, I'm 340 years old, my hair turned naturally white nearly 300 years ago, and I wanted the falling-apart house so I could build myself an alchemy lab without people wondering what the construction was all about.

"You're an insightful gargoyle."

"*Oui*. I know this."

How could one refuse to answer an insightful, arrogant gargoyle?

"Something happened yesterday," I said.

I gave Dorian a brief overview of the unexpected turn of events that had driven me from Paris, telling him about Madame Leblanc, who'd known me when she was a child, and the murder of my old shop assistant. "Madame Leblanc said that her policeman grand-nephew would figure out what *I'd done*," I concluded, "and she'd figure out what *I am*."

Dorian's eyes grew wide with horror as I spoke. "*C'est terrible*. Of course you made the right decision to leave Paris. You could not risk yourself." He jumped down from the crate and began to shake. A seizure? This was a new development.

"Are you all right? Are you feeling yourself turn to stone all at once?"

He shook his head. "I have had a thought most *horrible*. This woman—she might have attempted to put a stake through your heart!"

I smiled for perhaps the first time since Madame Leblanc had confronted me at Notre Dame.

"It is not humorous, Zoe. If other people fail to take her seriously, she might resort to violent action. You are a pale woman who has been alive for centuries. What was she supposed to think?"

"I'm not that pale."

Dorian crinkled his forehead, causing his horns to wriggle. "All the hair on your body is white. People do not come much paler than you."

"You think she might think I'm a vampire? That's crazy. Vampires don't exist."

"Neither do alchemists, according to most people."

"Fair point. But what was I supposed to do? I couldn't tell her the truth. Besides, she already told me her mother thought I was a witch."

Dorian sputtered. "This is worse! Being burned at the stake would be even more painful. Fire takes longer to kill. Your skin would blister—"

"Hey," I cut in, "nobody is getting staked through the heart *or* burned alive."

"You are the one who said she was after the truth."

"Which isn't much better, I agree, but she doesn't want to kill me—only expose me."

"You did the only reasonable thing by leaving. You cannot help me if you are in prison. Or on the run in France. Or dying with a wooden stake in your chest."

"I get the point." I cringed at my unintended pun.

The gargoyle was right. He was a lovable and infuriating combination of adolescent puppy dog and wise old sage. Madame Leblanc was not someone to dismiss. I'd known people like her in different countries and different times. Women who were too easily dismissed when they should not have been. Some of them suffered in silence. Some of them formed communities of like-minded souls. And some of them took revenge.

"What are we to do?" Dorian asked.

"I've been thinking about that. I need to tell you about the other gargoyle—"

"My brother."

I hesitated.

"Why did you purse your pale lips?" Dorian asked. He tilted his head. "Perhaps you should buy some lipstick. That might squelch the vampire rumor."

"There's no vampire rumor."

"Whatever you say, ashen alchemist. Why were you pursing your pallid lips?"

"It's not good to think of him as a brother. You don't know him, Dorian."

"What is there to know? He is my brother."

He blinked at me so innocently that I felt tears welling in my eyes. "You shouldn't get too attached to the idea of another living gargoyle. We might not be able to bring him back from stone. When I saw him—"

"You *saw* him?" Dorian flapped his wings and wriggled his snout. "You did not tell me this! You said he was being held captive by a mad professor—"

"I'm fairly certain I didn't say that. But it's true, I did see him after I sent a swarm of bees after the professor so I could sneak into his office."

"*Bon.*" Dorian slapped his good hand against his knee. "Is my brother arriving later in a crate? I cannot believe you neglected to tell me of this upon your arrival."

"I didn't mention it first thing because I couldn't get him out of Paris, Dorian. He's more than a foot taller than you—there was no way I could carry him out of the university."

"Why did you go to see him without an escape plan? You caused harm to the professor but not so you could free my brother? This makes no sense. What were you thinking?" He flapped his wings.

"I'm most concerned about you. I needed to test what we thought we knew about your book and the Tea of Ashes."

"A test? You think *mon frère* is a test?" He harrumphed.

"If it worked, it would have helped him."

"Yet it failed." His wings folded around him.

"The Tea of Ashes transformed him for a brief moment. Only long enough for me to know he's still alive in there." I trembled at the memory of the gargoyle's pleading gray eyes.

Dorian peered intently at me. "The great Dorian Robert-Houdin knows what you need. I will bring food. Wait here. I will return shortly. Then you will tell me all about my brother."

I gave Dorian a hug. "I missed you, my friend."

"*Moi aussi, mon amie.*" He cleared his throat. This level of emotion was terribly undignified for a Frenchman born in 1860.

ELEVEN

MAYBE DORIAN WAS RIGHT that I'd have a clearer head after eating something. Especially Dorian's cooking.

Dorian had taken over my kitchen pretty much the day I moved into my crumbling Craftsman. Shortly before his death, Dorian's father, Jean Eugène Robert-Houdin, had the idea to serve as a reference for his adopted gargoyle son. Robert-Houdin explained that his "distant relative" Dorian was badly disfigured and did not feel comfortable being seen in public, but was a good man who would be a great help as a companion to a blind person. Dorian's first job was for the chef who'd lost his sight in a kitchen fire. Dorian learned to cook from the famous French chef. He took to it so well that he'd been a culinary snob ever since.

When Dorian followed me to Portland to seek my help last winter, he was horrified to learn that I eat only plant-based foods. Since alchemists aren't immortal, I learned long ago to take care of my body. I've been following a vegan diet since before the word was invented. I was a "Pythagorean" at one time—the mathematician also preached the merits of a plant-based diet. It's been a challenge at times to live in the United States, England, and France, which is why I always appreciated my sojourns to India. I was hopeful when Sylvester Graham's Grahamite diet caught on in the United States in the 1930s, but was dismayed that while he endorsed vegetarianism, he shunned spices. What good is a long life without some spice?

In the months since Dorian and I began sharing the house and the kitchen, he experimented with how to cook the decadent French foods he loved with vegan ingredients. Cashew cream replaced heavy cream made of dairy. Smoked salts and spices replaced bacon. Mushrooms replaced meat. Though it took him a while to admit it, he loved his new recipes more than his old ones. Before I left on this trip to Paris, he'd already declared himself to be the greatest vegan chef in all of Portland.

I smiled at the thought. Then yawned. The adrenaline that had kept me going was wearing off.

Dorian returned to the attic a minute later with a stack of three containers balanced in his right hand. I again noticed his inability to move his left arm, but I knew that bringing it up again before he was ready wouldn't get me anywhere.

The snacks he carried included a spread of morel mushrooms cooked simply in olive oil and spices, including a black salt sprinkled on top. I scooped up a mouthful with a piece of bread. It was exquisite, as expected. When I took care of myself, I ate well but far more simply than this.

"Brixton found you these mushrooms at the market?" I asked. Our fourteen-year-old neighbor, the only person in Portland besides me who knew of Dorian's existence, had been bringing Dorian groceries while I was out of town. Brixton was also tending to my backyard garden, which was the excuse he gave for coming over to the house while I was gone.

"Not Brixton," Dorian said.

"You promised you'd tell me if you were going to use my credit card again."

"This is what you think of me?" His snout twitched. "*Non*. I have my ways."

"Your ways?"

"A gentleman must keep his secrets."

"Dorian."

He shrugged. "While you were sick and then out of town, I was unable to cook for Blue Sky Teas, since they believe it is you who cooks there. I was bored. I wished to experiment with new recipes—ones that would work with only one good arm. You slept even more than usual while you were sick. It was quite tedious."

"That doesn't answer my question."

"No? Did you not taste the nut bread? It is superb. The perfect texture and the ultimate balance of sweet and savory. What else do you need to know? I have told you everything important that transpired last week—unlike *some* people. You still have not told me of my brother. *Bof.* I am so distracted thinking of my brother that I did not even remember *serviettes* with our snack. You are dripping oil and we have no napkins."

"It's not a long story," I said, grabbing a tissue to serve as a napkin. "Once I got into the office on my own, I read the backward alchemy incantation from the book." I glanced nervously at the book, its sweet scent of cloves and salty scent of the ocean filling the attic. "The words didn't affect him as they did you all those years ago, when Jean Eugène read from his 'prop.' But when I placed the Tea of Ashes in his mouth, he awakened and spoke—"

Dorian gasped.

"Only a few words," I whispered. The pleading terror in his eyes was something I'd never forget. I hoped Dorian couldn't see the horror on my face. "He was only awake for long enough to ask for help."

"*Alors*," Dorian said. "So it is true. This is the fate that awaits me."

"Not while there's an ounce of breath left in me."

Dorian frowned. "I am humbled by the sentiment. Yet you have already lost too much weight in this last month. Soon you will have completely wasted away." He pointed a clawed hand at the decadent snack that would have looked more natural at a sunny wedding reception than the silent shadows of an attic at three a.m. "Eat."

I obliged.

"How's Brixton?" I asked.

"Happy that it is now summer vacation. He is a good boy. He has been tending your garden, as you asked, and also bringing food to both me and Ivan."

"Ivan needs people to bring him meals? He said he was feeling better." I wondered if Ivan had told me that so I would answer his practical alchemy questions instead of telling him to rest.

Retired chemistry professor Ivan Danko had an interest in the history of alchemy as a precursor to modern chemistry. Like most modern-day scientists, he hadn't believed alchemy was real. Ivan suffered from a degenerative illness that left him with a weak immune system and a crushed spirit. His last wish was to finish writing his book before he died. At least, that was his wish before I'd been reckless. I'd accidentally shown Ivan that alchemy was real. I couldn't be a proper mentor to him (unlike Jasper Dubois, Ivan had asked), but because Ivan understood the need to be discreet about alchemy, I agreed to answer his questions as best I could when he set up his own alchemy lab. He was a good man and I wanted to help.

I was far from confident that Ivan would find the Elixir of Life that had consumed and eluded so many intelligent men over the centuries. I would have discouraged him from trying, save for one thing: it gave him *hope*. That hope gave him renewed energy for life. He might yet finish his book before he died.

"I do not trust that man," Dorian said.

"You don't trust anyone who knows the secret that alchemy is real."

"That is not so. I trust you and the boy."

"You trust me because you purposefully sought me out, and you didn't trust Brixton for months."

"This is true. But it is dangerous to trust others—as your trip to Paris proves. Brixton is young and naïve. So yes, the thoughtful boy brought Ivan a meal when he was recently home from the hospital, but this gave me an idea. Visiting Ivan was a perfect way for Brixton to keep him under surveillance during the daytime, when I could not watch him."

"Watch him?" I felt my eyes narrowing. "Why do you need to watch Ivan?"

"To see if he is up to nefarious deeds. Did I fail to mention we have been visiting Ivan?"

I rubbed my temples. "Are you trying to tell me that you and Brixton have been spying on Ivan?"

"*Spying* is a strong word. I prefer to call it gathering intelligence."

I closed my eyes and breathed deeply. "This is a bad idea."

"The boy can move about freely during the day—"

"He's fourteen."

"He did nothing unsafe. What is the harm? You are the one who believes we should trust Ivan."

I rolled my eyes at Dorian. "People don't generally react well when they learn they're being surveilled."

"Have you ever known us not to be careful?" he asked.

I opened my mouth to speak, but he cut me off by saying, "I withdraw the question."

TWELVE

In spite of the late night, I awoke with the sun, thinking of Jasper Dubois, who hadn't simply decided to move on from dangerous wartime Paris but had been killed.

My body is attuned to planetary alignments, so I always awaken with the first rays of sunlight. Alchemists have different strengths—some of us excel at transmuting corroded metals into pure gold, some of us feel the energy of gemstones, and some of us, like me, have a connection to plants—but all of us are affected by nature, from the scents that drift through the air to the rotations of the celestial planets above.

In the light of day, my immediate situation didn't seem as dire. I doubted the French authorities would spend limited resources to follow up on such an old crime, especially since I'd left France and the suspect was most likely dead. Ivan was a good man who would laugh if he learned Brixton was keeping an eye on him. An apprehensive feeling tickled at the edge of my consciousness, but with so many unanswered questions, that was to be expected. Jasper's death was an unsolved tragedy, but he was gone. Dorian was alive and needed me.

Since I'd arrived in the middle of the night, I hadn't yet seen my backyard garden. As a plant alchemist, the garden wasn't simply a hobby; it was an extension of my being and my salvation. Feeling the energy of the plants, from their roots in the earth to their soft, fuzzy, or prickly leaves, touched my soul. When my aptitude was discovered by an alchemist who assumed it was my brother's work, I learned that the alchemical term for creating healing medicines using the ashes of plants was spagyrics. I prefer to think of myself simply as a plant alchemist.

I was apprehensive as my bare feet touched the cool wood of the back porch. Breathing in the chilled air, I saw that Brixton had done a great job. Especially flourishing were the beets, parsley, and an assortment of salad greens. My young neighbor had more of an aptitude for gardening than I'd anticipated. I laughed as I noticed the plant that was doing the worst: nettles. Normally the tasty, healing plant that most people thought of as a pesky weed would grow under any circumstances, pushing out other plants. Brixton was afraid of the stinging leaves, so he must have ignored it. Now that I was home, I'd pour some extra energy into the nettles.

Simply stepping into the sanctuary helped calm my mind, which was still racing with all the confusing facts being thrown at me. The lavender made my head spin in a different way—it made me think of Max. I'd missed him more than I'd imagined I would. I shouldn't have been surprised. We shared so much in common, from our gardens to devoting our lives to helping people, and the chemistry between us was something I hadn't felt in decades. Was it enough to overcome the chasm in the foundation of our understanding of the world that made Max skeptical of anything he couldn't see?

After watering the garden and fixing myself a revitalizing green smoothie for breakfast, I came to a decision about what to do with the illegible vellum note from Nicolas Flamel. As much as I wished to learn what had become of the generous man who'd briefly been my mentor, I couldn't risk what he'd think of Dorian's connection to backward alchemy. I made sure the note was safely hidden away in an empty jar of Devil's Dung in my basement alchemy lab, where nobody would ever look, then climbed the stairs to the attic. The door was latched from the inside, so I knocked.

"I am at the denouement of a book that is giving me a *frisson*," Dorian called through the door. "Come back later, *s'il vous plaît*."

I wondered if it was true he was reading a thrilling novel, or if he didn't want me to see how poorly he was feeling. It distressed me to see my friend in so much pain, and it scared me to watch his body reverting to stone. Dorian used to shift between life and stone as easily as a person would move between standing up and sitting down. But now each time he transformed into stone, it was more and more difficult for him to regain movement. I needed answers. I hoped the bookseller would send me the book on backward alchemists as soon as promised.

Since the garden was thriving, I collected two buckets of parsley and beet greens, then went inside and unlocked the door to my basement alchemy lab. I hadn't had a chance to build a proper alchemy laboratory, just as I hadn't finished construction on my fixer-upper house, but both were holding their own. After things with my contractor didn't work out, my underemployed locksmith had made sure the house was in good enough shape that the neighbors wouldn't complain, and I'd cleaned the basement and made it my own. Both solutions were painfully close to the quick fixes I abhorred in backward alchemy. My imperfect alchemy lab served as my daily hypocrisy check. It was a good reminder that we do the best we can, but life isn't black and white.

I set the buckets of greens down on my work table, feeling an uneasiness creep over me as I did so. Something was amiss. There was nothing obvious, but I knew I wasn't wrong. The *energy* of the basement felt different. I glanced around.

I'd purposefully kept the room sparse, with two simple yet solid wooden tables, alchemy ingredients ranging from cinnabar to gold dust, and only candles and kerosene lanterns to light the space. Those sources of light served two purposes. First, they transported me to the right mental state to begin alchemical transformations. Second, they made sure that anyone snooping would have to take an extra step to cast light on their surroundings.

Had Dorian tidied the room in an attempt to be helpful? Though his body was failing him, he was a helpful little guy. I wanted to make another batch of Tea of Ashes for him. I knew if I told him what I was up to, he wouldn't let me go through with it. That's why I wasn't going to tell him in advance. Besides, this would be a small batch, not like the unwieldy batch that had backfired and made me so ill before going on my trip.

I followed the backward steps, beginning with fire. Extracting the essences of the fresh greens through this backward process left me with ash that wasn't alchemy's true salt, but mimicked it closely enough to work temporarily.

Two hours after beginning the Death Rotation, I had an ash-like substance to dissolve in hot water for Dorian to drink as medicine.

My joints ached as I climbed the steps leading out of the basement. At the top, it took a minute for me to catch my breath. It took all my energy to boil the water to make the tea for Dorian. Luckily, the scent was so pungent that he smelled it from the attic and came downstairs before I began dragging my tired legs up the stairs. He shook his head but accepted the tea.

"I'm going to rest for a little while now," I said. Dorian helped me to the couch. Between his limping gait and my wilting body, we were a sad sight. My eyes fluttered shut as soon as I hit the couch cushions. I felt Dorian place a blanket over me as I drifted off to sleep.

I woke up abruptly, with a gargoyle poking my arm with his claw and waving a bunch of fragrant roses under my nose.

"The roses worked!" he declared.

I rubbed my arm and sat up. My throat was so parched it took me a moment to speak. "I need sleep, Dorian."

"You have slept for many hours. You at least need to drink liquid." He set down the roses and handed me a glass of water. I sat up and drank it, then lay back down and pulled the blanket over me.

Dorian tapped me again.

"I'm serious, Dorian. I need more sleep."

"Zoe." The gargoyle gently tapped a claw on my forehead. "I do not wish to worry you, but you have been asleep for more than a day."

THIRTEEN

Against the will of my aching body, I sat up. "I slept for a whole twenty-four hours?"

"*Oui*. This is why I needed a strong scent to wake you." Dorian waved the roses in front of my face again. "Your phone rang many times, yet you did not awaken. It was Max."

"Max? Did you—"

"Of course I did not answer. He phoned many times. He must have missed you very much." Dorian frowned. "But the ringing was most distracting. I asked Brixton to tell him you had horrific jet lag and needed sleep."

"A *whole day*?" At least it was one day closer to receiving the book from Paris in the mail. I stretched my cramped neck. My velvet couch wasn't the most comfortable bed. "I slept for an entire day?"

"Is your hearing affected?" Dorian shouted into my ear. "Yes! A whole day!" He raised his arms above his horns to pantomime the rising and setting of the sun.

"My hearing is fine. At least it was until a moment ago."

"Ah, I understand. You were being incredulous at the amount of time you slept."

"Where's my phone?"

Dorian scampered across the room and brought it back to me. Ivan had left me a voicemail asking me to call him because he had something to show me, and my sort-of-maybe-boyfriend Max Liu had sent me several welcome home text messages. In spite of everything else going on, I couldn't wait to see Max. In his last message he said he was working on a case today, so unfortunately I wouldn't get to see him quite yet.

I looked up from the phone and felt a pang of guilt that I'd been thinking of Max and ignoring a problem right in front of me. "Your left arm and leg," I said, abandoning my phone on the coffee table. "The Tea of Ashes didn't work?"

Dorian hopped up onto the couch next to me. "Yes and no. They are easier to bend than before you returned home, yet I still cannot control them very well."

"I'm so sorry, Dorian." I groaned. "I know what must have gone wrong. Brixton was the one who's been keeping up the garden. The plants I sacrificed didn't have much of my own energy in them."

"*C'est rien*. The book will come and you will capture a backward alchemist. Then he will tell you what we need to know to save me and my poor brother."

"I don't know if it will be that easy."

"*Oui*. You will need assistance to get them to reveal their secrets. I have read many thrillers with ingenious methods of torture."

I gaped at Dorian. "We're *not* torturing anyone."

"It is not difficult. And your basement is perfect. Brixton has returned the books to the library, but I can ask him to check them out again."

"Absolutely not. No torture."

70

"But the professor is probably torturing my brother as we speak! Chipping away at his stone flesh. By the time we rescue him, there may be nothing left of him!"

"The professor doesn't want to destroy the statue—"

"Statue?" Dorian sniffed and stood tall. The dignified stance was only slightly marred by his limp and awkwardly hanging arm. "This is what you think of me? That I am nothing more than a piece of stone?"

"Of course not. All I meant is that the other gargoyle is in stone form right now. And yes, the professor will probably take small samples of stone to test—"

Dorian's good hand flew to his mouth and his black eyes opened wide with horror.

"He'll be fine," I added. "You were fine after your toe chipped off."

Dorian squirmed uncomfortably. "If you would be so good as to ship me to Paris in an express delivery crate, I could stage a hostage rescue."

"The book that I hope will lead us to a backward alchemist should be here any day now—"

"No books arrived in the mail while you slept. Only advertisements. These Americans and their advertisements . . ." He shook his head. "You are confident about this book?"

"It sounds like a good lead. If there are any practicing backward alchemists left."

Dorian narrowed his eyes. "You suspect there are."

"I do. But until we find one—"

"You are the smartest, bravest person I have ever met, Zoe Faust. Even more so than my father."

"Flattery won't convince me torture is okay."

"No?"

"No."

71

Dorian muttered something under his breath and hopped down from the couch. "It is almost eight o'clock in the morning. The market will be open. I have taken the liberty of drawing up a shopping list. Brixton was helpful, but he could only do so much."

Dorian used to slip meat products into his lists, hoping I wouldn't notice.

"No bacon?"

He pointed a claw. "Smoked salts are even better."

"No cream?"

"I have five pounds of raw cashews."

"Maybe my hearing was affected after all. I could have sworn you said *five pounds* of cashews."

He beamed at me. "Wait until you taste the new recipes I have created during your absence."

———

Three pints of lemon water, a mug of healing ginger and turmeric tea, and almond butter and sea salt drizzled on freshly picked fruit gave me the energy I needed to start a nettle infusion and pick up groceries.

Making a full alchemical preparation, with the steps that distill the core essence of a plant into ashes, takes time. To extract energy from my nettles more simply, I poured hot water over a tangle of nettles in a mason jar and left it to steep on the back porch.

I usually walked to the market, but the length of Dorian's list and the heaviness of my legs led me to the truck in my driveway. My 1942 Chevy took a couple of turns of the engine to get started, but I'd taken good care of it over the years and it repaid my love with reliability.

An hour later, I hauled in five bags of groceries. Dorian jumped up and down with glee. With his good arm, he pulled his stepping stool to the counter next to the bags.

"You're happier to see a kitchen full of food than you were to see me," I said.

He pulled his snout out of the bag containing grains and dried beans. "Would it offend you if I admitted to equal amounts of happiness?"

I left him to his food and went to the other room to make my phone calls in private. With the time difference I couldn't call the bookstore proprietor to check on the status of my book delivery, but I could call Max and Ivan. Max's cell went straight to voicemail, so I tried Ivan next.

Though Ivan knew alchemy was real, he didn't know that my interest in unlocking *Not Untrue Alchemy*'s secrets was to save Dorian's life. Everyone aside from Brixton and Tobias believed I owned a gargoyle statue that I liked to move around the house and had an interest in alchemy because of the business I used to run out of my Airstream trailer and now ran out of my attic. Ivan assumed I was passionate about understanding alchemy because I was an accidental alchemist who wanted to understand more. Ivan was a scholar, so that's what made sense to his own worldview. Alchemy was a quest for knowledge.

But I'd been *too* passionate in my attempts to understand the bizarre woodcut illustrations in Dorian's book. Approaching the problem from an academic angle, Ivan had insights that hadn't occurred to me. These insights had helped me understand some of the book's illustrations. I'd subsequently let my guard down and accidentally allowed Ivan to see that alchemy was real.

"*Dobrý den*," Ivan said when he picked up the phone.

"My friend, how are you?"

"Me? Never better." The enthusiasm in his voice came through over the phone. I knew what it was: hope. His realization that alchemy was real had given him hope.

"I'm glad to hear it."

"I have a newfound appreciation for alchemical riddles," Ivan said. "I'm so glad you called. I wish you were back from Paris so we could talk in person, but this will do."

"That's actually why I'm calling. I'm home."

Ivan paused for so long that I wondered if the connection had been dropped. "Where are you?" he rasped. "Can you come over?"

"Are you all right?" I waited for a reply that didn't come. "Do you need me to call a doctor?"

"No, no. I'm fine," he said. But the tone of his voice said otherwise. "Zoe, now that you are home, there's something you must see."

FOURTEEN

Books on chemistry, history, and alchemy filled the giant study in Ivan Danko's house. Had he bought more research books in the month since I'd been here? I didn't remember his library being so labyrinthine.

I maneuvered around a pile of books on Chinese traditions in alchemy that partially blocked the study doorway. I couldn't stop myself from straightening the precarious stack. It wasn't the quantity of books that had changed, I realized; it was their organization. The bookshelves were only half full. Books that were once shelved in a methodical way were now stacked in haphazard piles. I tensed as I stepped over a toppled stack of leather-bound books to enter the room. Pages ripped from a disassembled book lay on the desk.

"Ivan, what have you done?" My heart ached at the sight of the damaged books. As someone who collected antiques before they were antique, I hated to see so much knowledge and craftsmanship treated so poorly. "Practicing alchemy requires you to respect your materials. You've completely ruined this book." I picked up the skeletal remains of what had once been a museum-quality book from the sixteenth century.

He waved off my concern. "The opposite. Quite the opposite, I assure you."

My eyes fell from his sunken eyes to his scruffy beard. Ivan hadn't looked healthy for as long as I'd known him, but his eyes held a desperate tint I hadn't previously seen. His dress shirt and slacks were pressed and pristine as usual. It was only his surroundings that had changed.

Still, this wasn't like Ivan. Forced into early retirement from his job as a chemistry professor in Prague because of his illness, he liked to be in control of other things in his life, such as his library. He stressed the importance of order to properly organize his thoughts for his book on the history of early chemists—in other words, alchemists.

"Is everything all right, Ivan?"

"I'm so pleased you've returned. A photograph didn't capture the necessary nuance, so I thought it best to wait to show this to you." He took a labored breath but grinned as he lifted a hefty book with pages so dark they were nearly black. "Now that you can see it in person—"

"You *burned* this?" The memory of the fire at Elixir filled my mind. The fire that disguised the murder of Jasper Dubois.

"Not burned. I put ashes on the pages, as you did with *Not Untrue Alchemy* to reveal hidden meaning in the pages."

"That book is unique. I haven't come across anything like it in the centuries I've been an alchemist."

"But," Ivan said with fire in his eyes, "you were never looking." He pointed at the charred pages of the sad-looking book.

"What am I looking at?"

"Don't you see?" He jabbed a shaking finger at the blackened page. "The ashes reveal the page beneath, making the flying bees on this top page circle the dragon on the page below. That symbolizes—"

"It's a coincidence, Ivan. Alchemy books are filled with woodcut illustrations. Of course they'll end up on top of each other like that."

"You don't know that." His Czech accent became more prominent as he became agitated. How could I balance helping him feel like all his efforts hadn't been in vain with getting us back on track?

"When I left for Paris to do my own research there," I said, "you talked of reading your books in a new light as a first step on the path to alchemy, not experimenting on them in an attempt to replicate the bizarre codes from my backward alchemy book—"

"You don't have all the answers, Zoe. You said so yourself. You don't fully understand alchemy. If you did, you could help me find the Elixir of Life more quickly. I've done good work to help you understand the strange book in your possession and also to help my quest for the Elixir. What do I care if I ruin books? Even if you're right that I've destroyed them, what good are they to a dead man?"

"But your book—"

"I would rather live on than leave a book behind."

I squeezed Ivan's gaunt shoulder. When it comes to ideas about what's most important at the end of life, comfort is better than words. I've seen people deal with looming death in many ways. Some find consolation in what they leave behind for their children or the world, some wish to surround themselves with loved ones, and some push it from their mind altogether.

"I'd at least like a few years longer," Ivan continued softly, taking my hand. "At this rate, I might not have time to finish writing my book, even if I tried."

"I'm sorry, Ivan," I whispered.

"I know, Zoe. And I know why you have this drive to solve the riddle of this book."

I pulled my hand away.

"Don't be embarrassed, Zoe. I know you feel sorry for me. You wish me to be healthy again, as I do."

I bit my lip. Dorian's existence wasn't my secret to tell, and I *did* want Ivan to be healthy again. He was a good man and a rigorous scholar who could likely unlock alchemy's secrets. But that would take time—more time than Ivan had. The Elixir of Life was something each person had to discover for him or herself. I couldn't do it for him. And while I could play a small part in mentoring Ivan, saving Dorian was my first priority.

"I do, Ivan. I really do. But applying backward alchemy to your own practice isn't going to help you. It's not true alchemy. Backward alchemy takes life in order to give it. That's not right—"

"I understand that," he barked. "My books aren't backward alchemy. I only wish to learn from that book of yours, not to use it. You're the one who brought it to me in the first place."

"Ivan, I—"

"Forgive me. I'm sorry I snapped at you. We can figure it out together."

"*Without* backward alchemy's Death Rotation."

He smiled. "Let me show you the laboratory I set up in my garage."

To the average Portlander, it probably looked as if he was setting up a space to make home-brewed beer. Prominent on one table was a distillation vessel with an alembic retort to distill vapors, a round cucurbit for boiling, and a receiver to collect distilled liquids.

"I never imagined I'd be putting what I read into practice," he said, "so I'm sure I've got it all wrong."

"Not bad at all, Ivan. Not bad at all."

The doorbell chimed. Ivan went to answer it while I studied some handwritten notes in a notebook.

"Thank you, Max," I heard him say from the other room.

"Max?" I hurried from the garage. Max Liu stood in the doorway holding a bag of food truck takeout in one hand and a stainless steel thermos in the other. He dropped them onto the floor and swept me up in a hug. Everything else faded away. I'd missed his scent, his touch, and everything about him. He pulled back from the hug and cradled my face in his hands for a moment. His brown eyes held an intensity that combined delight, regret, and longing.

I'd thought about Max so many times while I was in Paris, wishing he could have been there with me. Even though I knew he wasn't ready to hear the whole truth about my past, I could be myself with him in so many important ways. I hoped he'd be ready to know the whole truth someday soon. But for now, it was easiest if I kept the alchemical part of my life separate. Max knew I was interested in alchemy, but he thought it was because of the alchemical artifacts I sold in my online store.

It had taken me a long time to realize an essential truth: I *could* have connections with people who didn't know I was a true alchemist. Thinking otherwise was a misguided idea born out of self-pity. Most human interaction doesn't take place on the spoken level. Before I'd come to realize that, I kept myself shut off from anything beyond the most superficial of friendships.

I'll never forget the moment I embraced that truth. It was a day that had started out without hope. I'd been lost and was suffering from heat exhaustion in the south of India. A young family took pity on the strange, pale foreigner. They invited me into their modest clay home for a meal. That scorching, dusty day, I learned to cook dosas and poori as people on the Indian subcontinent had done for millennia, grinding the flour by hand, adding spices that killed germs and healed the body, and watching the bread bubble on an open fire. I taught their toddler English nursery rhymes that made him laugh and squeal with delight. I don't think any of us under the thatched roof understood a single word we said to each other that day, other than our names. But I will always remember them.

Max stroked my cheek and drew me into a kiss. As I lost myself in the embrace, I remembered the special evenings we'd spent together that spring, sitting together in Max's backyard garden drinking tea, sometimes talking and sometimes simply reading in the twilight. The important thing wasn't what we talked about, but the feeling of togetherness, easy comfort, and electricity.

Ivan cleared his throat. I opened my eyes and saw him leaning in the doorway, shaking his head and smiling.

Max pulled back from his kiss, but he didn't blush. He kept his eyes locked on mine and his fingers entwined in mine.

"Since Ivan hasn't been feeling well," Max said, "I thought I'd bring him some lunch and tea while I've got a break. I'm so glad I caught you here too. I have to run, and today is going to be a long one for me, but how about dinner tomorrow night?"

"I'd love that."

Max gave me a quick kiss goodbye before departing.

"He brought more than enough for me," Ivan said after he shut the front door. "You're welcome to stay for lunch. Let me clear off the kitchen table."

I followed Ivan to the kitchen but stopped before stepping inside. The kitchen table was covered with more than a dozen alchemy books—each one of them destroyed.

Ivan hadn't experimented on only one book with questionable results. He'd obsessively taken apart at least fifteen antique books. Some had been soaked in water, some smeared with ashes, and some charred by fire.

Ivan had unnecessarily destroyed priceless history on a fool's errand. He was no longer simply a dedicated scholar. He was obsessed.

FIFTEEN

I GAVE IVAN AN excuse and made a hasty departure. I needed to think, and I knew the perfect place to do so. I went on a long slow ramble to Lone Fir Cemetery, named for the single tree growing in the cemetery when it was founded in the 1840s. Since then, nature has become as much a part of the graveyard as anything else, with hundreds of trees creating a serene atmosphere for contemplation.

The Victorians held many beliefs I disagreed with—such as the prevalence of dresses that made it nearly impossible to walk through a room without knocking things over let alone breathe—but their view on cemeteries mirrored my own. A calming atmosphere with well-tended landscapes and remembrances of loved ones provided a perfect setting for a thoughtful walk or picnic. In a cemetery, there was no rush. You could think about people past and present without the burdens of the outside world.

Ivan had clearly crossed the line from passion into obsession. I'd done that myself once, so I couldn't blame him. It was how I'd found the Elixir of Life without realizing I'd done so. I was obsessed with finding a cure for the plague that had afflicted my younger brother, and I'd foolishly wasted his last days. I hadn't listened to Nicolas or Pernelle about what was possible, nor did I heed their warning that I would regret it if I didn't spend time with Thomas making him more comfortable before he died.

I remembered that raw emotion well, so I knew there was nothing I could say to Ivan to make him believe he was approaching alchemy incorrectly and that his time would be better spent with his friends or writing his book.

Jasper Dubois had never listened to me either, but for different reasons. What had happened to him all those years ago?

I'd walked for only ten minutes, but the serene cemetery no longer felt peaceful. Death is one thing, but not knowing what happened to someone was another. Without consciously realizing where I was going, I walked out of the cemetery and found myself heading to Hawthorne Boulevard.

Blue Sky Teas was half full—much less crowded than it had been two months ago. Still the same was the weeping fig tree that stretched to the high ceiling in the center of the teashop, and the thick tree-ring tables that filled the cozy space.

It was partly my fault the teashop wasn't doing the brisk business it had been. I was Dorian's front, so while I was sick and then gone in Paris, he wasn't able to supply home-cooked treats for the teashop. Dorian baked vegan pastries in the teashop kitchen before dawn, but everyone thought it was me who was the chef who got up early to bake while they slept. I can transform herbs into healing remedies, but it's Dorian who's the culinary alchemist, transforming basic ingredients into decadent feasts. When "I" was unable to bake because of illness or travel, there was no way to explain fresh-baked treats showing up when the teashop opened.

The other reason for the drop in business was the fact that the owner, Blue Sky, was in jail for a past crime that we all wished hadn't resulted in prison time. Blue created teas and decoctions that rivaled anything I'd tasted in Munar, delighting the senses and healing the body and soul. She was due out soon, but in the meantime our friend Heather Taylor was running the teashop.

Heather stood behind the counter this morning. Her teenage son Brixton sat at a corner table next to a man with dark brown skin, long black hair, and a tattoo of interwoven metal bars winding up his neck. At first I wondered why Brixton wasn't at school, but then I remembered summer vacation had begun. His wealthy friend Ethan was organizing a fifteenth-birthday trip to London that summer, paying for his friends to attend.

"Zoe!" Heather called out. "Welcome home." The words warmed my soul. It wasn't a one-sided feeling that this was my home. "One second, then I'll introduce you to Abel." She turned back to the customer at the counter, but at the sound of his name, the dark-haired man sitting with Brixton looked up, as did Brixton. So this was Brixton's stepfather. He worked out of town a lot of the time, so I hadn't met him yet.

Abel stood and extended his hand. It was calloused and his handshake firm. "The famous Zoe Faust. Thanks for looking after Brix. He's been telling me all about your garden. I know he started helping you in the garden so you wouldn't press charges after he broke in, but it's been really good for him. Thank you."

Brixton rolled his eyes.

"How could anyone resist the lure of the neighborhood haunted house that someone was finally moving into?" I said. "I don't blame Brixton. If the tables had been turned, I might have broken into your house to see what was going on."

"So can we change the subject or something?" Brixton said. "I didn't think you were coming back so soon from your trip to visit your grandmother's friend in Paris."

I hoped Brixton wasn't paying enough attention to notice the flush I felt on my cheeks. I'd forgotten how close the lie I'd invented for my last-minute trip to Paris was to the truth I'd discovered, though Madame Leblanc couldn't rightly be called a "friend."

"The visit wasn't what I imagined it would be," I said truthfully.

"Well, I'm glad you're back," Abel said. "This way I get to meet you." He moved a banjo from a chair to make room for me.

"Pretty cool, huh?" Brixton said. "Abel brought it back for me. Did you bring me back something cool from Paris?"

Abel elbowed Brixton. "Manners."

"What?" Brixton said. "Isn't that what people do?"

I smiled. I could already tell that Abel was a good influence on Brixton. He wasn't Brixton's biological father, but they held themselves in a similar way. Abel actually looked like he could have been Brixton's half brother. He was in his twenties, a few years younger than Heather, who wasn't quite thirty. Without her then-boyfriend's support or her family's blessing, Heather had dropped out of high school when she became pregnant with Brixton at fifteen. Whenever Heather's flaky behavior frustrated me, I reminded myself that her father had left the family when she got pregnant, never to be seen again. I hadn't seen my own family since I was sixteen, so I knew how difficult that could be.

"Not hungry?" I asked, looking at the half-eaten sandwiches on the table.

"Mom thought of getting fresh herbs for tea," Brixton said, "but she forgot about making sandwiches at lunchtime. So she's making mint and basil baguette sandwiches." He rolled his eyes. "It's your fault, Zoe. Not only were you gone so we didn't get fresh food, but

84

now that I've eaten Dor—I mean, *your* cooking, I can't stand these premade sandwiches she picked up for behind the counter."

Able shifted his position so the weeping fig tree would block him from Heather's view. "We're going to get out of here in a little while to get some real lunch," he said quietly, a conspiratorial grin on his face.

Something was different about the setting. It wasn't just the people and food. Had the tree been trimmed? No. It was the paintings that now hung on the walls. I recognized the style.

"Heather's new art is remarkable," I said.

Brixton shrugged, and a look of pride spread across Abel's smiling face. "She sold two of them the day she hung the series on the wall," he said.

"I can see why," I murmured.

In contrast to Brixton's mom's bubbly personality, she used unusual colors of paint to create dark and deep images. In her latest series, she'd added metallic accents to black, brown, and green forest landscapes. The gold and silver peeked out of the trees like eyes watching the viewer.

These new paintings were close-up studies of women's faces, but there was more to them than portraiture. The reflections in the eyes and the wrinkles on the skin each told their own stories, as if transforming from one meaning to another as the viewer looked more closely. In the painting closest to me, the reflection showed a raven in flight, and a crease on the woman's cheek was two simple line figures dancing.

"I think Mom needs help with the lunch rush," Brixton said to Abel. "Would it be cool if you helped her so I can catch up with Zoe?"

It didn't look very crowded to me, but Heather was taking orders and grabbing premade sandwiches from the display cabinet. Abel tousled Brixton's hair and stood up. "Glad you're not too cool to think of your mom."

Once Abel made it to the counter, Brixton hunched his shoulders over the table and spoke softly. "I didn't really expect you to have brought me a gift from Paris, you know. That was just part of my cover, pretending like you were on vacation with your grandma's friend like you told everyone."

"That's what you wanted to tell me privately?" I whispered back.

"Nah. Did Dorian tell you what's up with Ivan?"

"Yes. About that, it's a terrible idea."

"Why? You don't care about what we learned?"

"I already know that Ivan is obsessed with alchemy. You need to distance yourself from him. Desperate people can change."

"Yeah. Whatever. Fine. But that's not what I'm talking about."

"It's not?"

"No. It's not just me and D keeping an eye on him. There's a creepy guy spying on Ivan."

SIXTEEN

SOMEONE WAS SPYING ON the alchemy scholar? I felt my temple twitching furiously.

"A creepy guy?" I repeated.

"Well, maybe *creepy* isn't the right word. But he was totally spying on Ivan yesterday."

"Dorian neglected to tell me that." Why hadn't he told me? The vein in my temple was now fully pulsating. I knew why Dorian hadn't told me himself: he knew I'd disapprove.

"You need to stop," I said. "Now."

Brixton rolled his eyes. "I have the daytime shift, so it's not like it's dangerous. What? You're friends with Ivan. He, like, helps you with stuff. You said so."

"There's so much going on right now that we don't understand. It's safest for you to stay away from anything that involves spying."

"Whatever. So do you want to hear about the guy I saw or what?"

I glanced at the counter. Abel and Heather had a good rhythm together. They weren't paying any attention to us. "Who was he?"

Brixton shrugged. "Just some boring-looking guy. He was spying on Ivan, like in a movie."

"Define *spying*," I said.

"Did you forget English while you were in France?"

I sighed. "I know what the word means. I want to know why you think someone is spying on Ivan, not visiting him. What exactly was he doing?"

"Looking in the windows. That totally counts as spying, right? When he first walked up to the house, I thought he was some professor Ivan knew. But then instead of knocking on the door, he looked in all the windows, and then flattened himself against the wall to make sure Ivan didn't see him."

That certainly sounded like spying.

My senses tingled. I was experiencing the feeling of being followed myself. Was it real or an overactive imagination? I scanned the tables and the sidewalk that was visible beyond the large front windows, half expecting to see Madame Leblanc hiding behind a potted plant, stealing a glance at me through her designer sunglasses. But that was crazy. The bushes on the sidewalk weren't big enough to conceal a person, even a small one. Besides, she didn't know where to find me. Still, I was uneasy as I watched several people walk past. None of them resembled the persistent Madame Leblanc or anyone else I knew.

"Without making obvious movements," I said to Brixton, "look around and see if you spot the man you saw spying."

"Wicked."

My pulse raced. "You see him?"

"No. He's not here. But we're totally in a spy movie."

"I'm being serious, Brix."

The eye roll. "I'm being serious too. There's seriously a guy spying on Ivan. That's why you need my help. Something is going on."

"When did your stepdad get back?" I asked Brixton.

"Yesterday." He scowled. "You don't think he—"

"No, that's the opposite of what I meant. You want to spend some time with him, right?"

"Yeah. That's not lame. He's really cool."

"I can tell. Spend the time with your family, and with Ethan and Veronica. Forget all about Ivan. Forget all about me and Dorian for the time being too."

"What's going on, Zoe?"

"I'm not sure. That's what worries me."

"You're kind of freaking me out."

"Sorry. Nothing freak-out worthy. You know me. I'm old. I worry."

"You're worried about saving Dorian, aren't you? Why did you leave Paris so soon if you hadn't figured stuff out?"

"I've got a lead." Would the book be in today's mail? "I should go check it out, actually. No more surveillance, okay?"

"Cool."

As I stood up, I fought the urge to tousle Brixton's hair as Abel had done.

On the sidewalk, my skin again prickled. There was no sign of anyone I didn't wish to see, but for a fraction of a second the profile of a man turning the corner reminded me of Ambrose. I felt for my locket. My encounter with Madame Leblanc had brought up too many painful memories. My long-ago lover who'd died by his own hand, my brother who'd been claimed by the plague, and Jasper Dubois, my assistant who'd met a murderous end. Death followed me. Why did I think I could save Dorian?

I hurried home. *Backward Alchemists of Notre Dame* hadn't arrived in the mail. I'd looked up the title after the bookshop proprietor told me of its existence, and I understood why I hadn't found it before. The only reference to it was a footnote in an obscure text I didn't own, according to the comments of one of the many blogs devoted to "the Secrets of Paris." In the modern age, people often assume they can find anything online. They don't realize how far from the truth that is.

I needed to get that book as soon as humanly possible. I'd already paid Lucien Augustin for the book, but it wouldn't hurt to reach out to rare book dealers I knew in the States.

I found Dorian standing on his stepping stool in front of the stove. With his right arm he stirred a fragrant pot of tomato sauce, heavy on the garlic. His left arm hung awkwardly at his side. It was even worse than it had been before my latest attempt at creating another batch of Tea of Ashes. I wondered if I should fix him a little sling.

I crossed my arms and stood over him. "You didn't tell me about the spy."

"Ah. You spoke to the boy." He continued stirring. "I wished to wait until we knew more. There was no sense speaking of it before I knew what was going on."

"I told you everything I know about the other gargoyle, about Jasper Dubois, and about all of my Notre Dame leads, even though I have no idea what's going on with any of those things."

"Using my little grey cells," Dorian said, setting down the wooden spoon and tapping his head with his index claw, "I have taken the liberty of diagraming a chart of possibilities for all of these problems—both yours and mine."

Dorian thought the famous Poirot expression "little grey cells" was especially appropriate to him because his body was gray.

"A chart," I repeated.

"*Un moment.*" He stepped down from the stool and opened the drawer with scratch paper and pens. He rummaged until he found the notepad he was after, then cleared his throat.

I sighed. "All right. What have you figured out?"

"*Bon*. We will begin with Ivan. He is Czech. He has defected, and therefore we can assume he is a spy—"

"Let me stop you right there. What was the last novel you read from the library?"

Dorian frowned. "Do not use the fact that it was a John Le Carré book against me."

"This isn't a spy novel," I said. "I'll let you finish cooking dinner, and then you can tell me what you think might be a realistic theory."

I left him grumbling in the kitchen and stepped through the back door to get the nettle infusion that was waiting for me on the porch. It was ready, so I strained the liquid into a clay mug and took it with me to the basement.

I sipped the energizing liquid as I descended the steps. When I reached the bottom, I nearly dropped the mug. Something was very wrong.

Someone had been inside my alchemy lab.

SEVENTEEN

A SWEEP OF THE room assured me there was nobody besides me in the room, but my heart refused to stop pounding. Because this time, I wasn't imagining that someone had been there. My dragon's blood had been moved from the front of a row of glass jars to the back. I twisted the lid, tilting the jar away from me as I eased it open. The contents were right, so nobody had added anything. I didn't keep a record of measurements, so I couldn't be certain if they'd taken any or simply looked.

Was this the same person who'd been spying on Ivan? How did they get in? And why look through my alchemy lab? Was someone spying on *alchemists*? Was I right after all that Madame Leblanc had tracked me down to expose me?

I abandoned my nettle infusion and raced up the stairs. "Dorian!"

"What is the matter? Is there news of my brother?"

"Someone has been in the house."

His horns twitched in horror. "*Mais non. C'est impossible.* You installed security locks on the doors and windows, and no human can enter via my rooftop entrance."

"You weren't doing anything in the basement alchemy lab, were you?"

"How can you think this of me? I know you do not wish it to be disturbed. What did you detect had been taken?"

I sighed. "Nothing is missing." But I hadn't imagined that the bottle had been moved, had I?

"You have not yet recovered from making the Tea of Ashes. It was foolish of you to make it again. But I forgive you. I will cook a satisfying early summer meal. That will help you think straight." He took my hand and dragged me back to the kitchen.

"*Alors*," he said, "no word of my brother?"

"I'm sorry," I said, wondering what Professor Chevalier's reaction would be if the woman who'd brought a swarm of bees to his office called for an update on his gargoyle—excuse me, his *chimera*—statue. I also wondered how soon a locksmith could get here to rekey the house. With so many unexplained mysteries circling me, I at least wanted to feel secure in my home. I stared at an unfamiliar basket on the kitchen counter.

"Where did these wild mushrooms come from?" I asked.

"The forest."

"You know how to safely forage mushrooms?" Eating poisonous mushrooms was a complication not worth risking. I'd seen the effects on people who'd eaten foraged mushrooms that looked nearly identical to safe varieties. Sometimes I'd been able to help the unlucky people who'd simply been trying to feed their families, but more often it was already too late once the first symptoms appeared.

"Do not worry," Dorian said. "They are safe."

I couldn't imagine a forager taking a gargoyle along with him on a forest walk. "How do you know?"

Dorian looked everywhere in the kitchen except at me. He coughed. "Did I neglect to mention I have a job?"

"A job? You? Without me as your cover?"

He sniffed. "I had many jobs before I met you. I have impeccable references."

"You brought your references to Portland?"

"It was not necessary. You remember Monsieur Julian Lake? Yes, of course you would. You may recall that the elderly gentleman is blind. What you may not have known is that he appreciates gourmet cooking. Unsurprising for someone from such a distinguished family. However, his housekeeper is a terrible cook." Dorian shook his head and pursed his lips. "After Monsieur Lake tasted my cooking, when I was pumping him for information earlier this year, he desired more meals cooked by the great Dorian Robert-Houdin. Monsieur Lake wished to employ the services of the disfigured Michelin-star chef who does not wish to be seen."

"You have a Michelin star?"

Dorian sniffed. "Not officially, no. One needs to be associated with a restaurant to receive the honor. May I continue?"

"Please."

"His invitation was so insistent that I could not refuse without being rude. He would have gone to extreme lengths to find me, had I not accepted. He is a man used to getting what he wants."

"I see. How long have you been secretly working for Julian Lake?"

"It is not a secret."

"You didn't tell me about it, and I had no other way to find out. That makes it a secret." Something seemed fishy.

"I did not wish you to worry."

I thought about that. "I'm not really worried. He's blind and you know how to hide from others. Why would you assume I'd worry?"

"No reason." Dorian became overly interested in brushing dirt from the mushrooms.

"Dorian."

"Yes, all right." He turned from the counter and looked up at me. His liquidy black eyes were imploring. "I did not wish you to think you had been replaced."

"Replaced?"

"*Bon.* I should have known you have a big enough ego that you would not feel threatened. One would hope so, after living for so long."

"You were worried about me being *jealous*?"

"It is a natural emotion, no? And Zoe, if you saw his kitchen! It is a thing of beauty. No, I shall never show it to you. For then you might succumb to a tremendous fit of jealousy. Modern stainless steel appliances including a subzero freezer, a five-burner gas range, and an island larger than your whole kitchen. Of that you *should* be jealous. And of the covered pizza oven near the backyard pool."

"There's nothing wrong with this kitchen. Or my backyard. Modern amenities and square footage are overrated."

Dorian waved his good hand in a dismissive manner. "Yes, yes, I know of Julia Child learning the art of French cooking in her closet-size kitchen. *Peutêtre.* I will grant that you might be right about space not being a necessity. Yet modernity has brought such wonders."

I pointed at the vintage blender that had been my travel companion in my Airstream trailer since 1950, up to the simple copper pots hanging from the ceiling in the cozy kitchen, and down to the glass bottles I'd filled with infused olive oils, vinegars, and salts. "This is the height of kitchen technology right here. Haven't you noticed the resurgence of young people embracing traditional methods?"

Dorian rolled his eyes. He and Brixton were a bad influence on each other. "I do not understand your resistance to modern food preparation techniques," he said. "You embrace modernity when it comes to language. You pick up modern vernacular like a house on fire."

"That's not quite the right idiom—"

"You have proven my point. You understand slang in ways I never could, yet you do not try to adapt your methods of preparing healing foods."

"Adapting to language lets me fit in without raising suspicions." At least it did when my worlds didn't collide. I tensed as I thought about my carelessness in Paris. The city had transported me back to a century ago, and I'd spoken the French that I'd spoken at that time, not thinking how it would sound. "But preparing foods, teas, and tinctures isn't something I do publicly. The old methods are what speak to me."

"*D'accord.* We shall agree to disagree, as always, *mon amie.*"

"How did Julian Lake find you in the first place?" I asked. "He didn't come over to the house, did he?" A worrisome thought.

"*Non.*" Dorian jumped off his stepping stool and opened the recycling bin under the counter. He pulled out a wrinkled newspaper dated earlier in the month. He opened the pages to the Classifieds section and shook it in front of me. "Modern technology has not completely replaced civilized communication."

"Stop shaking your fist. I can't read what you're trying to show me. Let me guess. Missed connection, seeking a Frenchman who'd visited him with vegan pastries this spring?"

"Close," Dorian said. "Very close. The newspaper advertisement is what caught my eye. Only I never told him the pastries I brought him were vegan. This advertisement offered a modest reward for anyone who put him in touch with the disabled French chef. When I called him, he remembered my voice." Dorian's snout twitched as he gave an indignant sniff. "Can you believe that he gave me a test before hiring me? A test! He did not trust that I had baked the food I brought him."

"Sounds like a smart man."

Dorian chuckled. "He would not accept my suggestion of plant-based cooking. I knew right away he was not a man to lose an argument, so I stopped arguing. Instead, I simply did not tell him I was not using the meats he purchased to use as starters in my soups and casseroles. He declares he has never eaten so well. Between smoked salts, infused oils, and creamy nut sauces, he never had a chance."

"With Julian Lake's setup, I'm surprised you're still doing any cooking in my kitchen at all."

Dorian pointed a clawed fingertip at my midsection. "You are skin and bones, Zoe. What would you do without me cooking for you? When I met you, though you did not cook feasts on par with mine, you ate well. You took care of yourself by fixing yourself smoothies with vegetables from your garden, soups with oils and salts you infused yourself, and an assortment of healing teas you created with the power of the sun and moon."

I twirled my hair around my finger. "I still do those things." Did I, though? I'd let Dorian bring me food while I was sick before leaving for Paris. While in Paris, I'd bought fresh food daily, like other Parisians, but I didn't have my blender, which is what allowed me to make healthy meals easily. And since returning, I hadn't followed my usual morning practice of starting the day with a glass of lemon water, tending to my garden, and fixing either a smoothie of fruits, vegetables, and nut butter or a bowl of slow-cooked porridge with dried fruits, nuts, cinnamon, and sea salt.

"You have not noticed that we are out of half of the flavored salts in the cabinet," Dorian said, "nor that I used the last of your favorite cayenne-infused olive oil."

"We have enough left. My first priority is finding a cure for you."

"*Food is life*, Zoe. I appreciate the sentiment, but you must first slow down and take care of yourself."

A faint buzzing sounded. My shoulders tensed for a fraction of a second before I realized it was my phone. Not bees. I went in search of my phone and found that I'd missed a string of text messages from Brixton, as well as two voicemails.

A fist banged on the front door so loudly that I dropped the phone.

I opened it to find a trembling Brixton. When he spoke, his voice shook as well. "He's dead, Zoe. He's dead."

EIGHTEEN

THE FRAZZLED TEENAGER PUSHED his way past me into the house. He ran his hands through disheveled hair and took several deep breaths. "I've never seen a dead body before."

"Who—"

"It's not like it is in the movies, or even photos of real corpses."

"Brix—"

"I tried calling you, Zoe." He shoved his hands deep into the pockets of his jeans and paced the length of the living room. "When you didn't answer, I called Max. I didn't know what else to do! I didn't want the killer to get away."

Killer? "You *saw* someone murdered? Oh, God, Brixton. Who—"

"I didn't see the actual killing, just the dead guy with a gash in his head." Brixton broke off and flung himself onto the green velvet couch. He put his head in his hands. He brushed off my attempt to put my hand on his shoulder, so I gave him space.

When he looked up at me, his face was calm. So was his voice. "I screwed up, Zoe. I was far enough away that the killer slipped out without me seeing where he went." He punched the coffee table.

I cringed. So much for forced calmness. I'd get him a poultice later to help with the inevitable bruise. For now, an injury was the least of my concerns for Brixton. If a killer had seen him, he'd have suffered a lot worse than a sore hand. "You did the right thing getting away and calling the police. You should have called them first. Why did you call me?"

I dreaded the answer I expected: that it was someone I knew.

"Didn't I say? It wasn't a random dead body I saw. The killer was the same man who Dorian and me saw spying on Ivan."

"Ivan." I sank onto the couch, my legs no longer steady enough to support me. "He killed Ivan?"

Brixton swore. "I didn't mean it's Ivan who's dead. Sorry to scare you. I don't know who the dead guy is. I mean, I kinda thought he looked familiar, but I probably just saw him around somewhere. But Ivan is probably in danger now, right? Since the spy who was spying on him killed someone?"

I desperately hoped Brixton truly had been far enough away that the killer hadn't seen him, otherwise he'd be the one in danger. "You told all this to the police?"

"Yeah, Max was on some other case and said he couldn't just assign himself to whatever case he wanted. But he made sure some cops showed up real fast. I told them everything. They made me call my mom too. Not cool. She totally freaked."

I could imagine. "Brixton. Back up a sec. *How* did you find the dead body?"

"You know we've been following Ivan, right? How Dorian had the idea to figure out what Ivan was doing now that he knows alchemy is real—in case he was going to expose you and D." Brixton's voice shook as he spoke. "So, this dude we saw at Ivan's, we didn't have a clue who he was." Brixton hit the coffee table with his fist again. At least it wasn't as hard a punch this time. "It doesn't matter, really, cuz we know the important thing now—that he's a killer."

"We should get Dorian," I said, surprised he hadn't heard us and come downstairs already. I ran up to the first flight of stairs and called to him. He had to have heard me, but he didn't reply. "Hang on one second, Brix." I continued up to the attic, slowing only on the narrow steps leading up from the second floor to the attic. The attic door was closed. I turned the handle, but it was locked. "Dorian, let me in." I shook the handle. "Dorian?"

"He's not there?" Brixton startled me from the landing below me. "Weird."

"He must have snuck out just now. Now that he has my cape, I think he's getting more brazen." I whirled around. "Don't follow his example."

He rolled his eyes. "Like I'd imitate a gargoyle."

A perfectly sensible response. "Let's go back downstairs. You were telling me how you found the man."

The detour to look for Dorian seemed to have given Brixton the time he needed to collect his thoughts. He was more relaxed when he continued.

"There's this cabin that looks like an old shack. It's in the woods past Ivan's house, in one of those greenbelts in between housing developments. The cabin is boarded up and there are signs saying to keep out. It's where Dorian saw this guy go a couple of nights ago. So I went to check it out during the day today."

"And you stayed, even after you saw there was a dead body? You stayed in the woods with a killer out there?"

"I went far enough away." Brixton rubbed his hand.

Brixton's temper worried me. He was a teenage boy, so some outbursts were to be expected, but I hoped he would grow out of the uncensored temper that had already given him a juvenile record. "All that matters is that you're safe. Next time you see something like that, you get the hell out of there. No, there's not going to be a *next time*, because you're not going to be involved in this. Or anything like this. Ever. Again. Is that clear?"

Brixton rolled his eyes. "I had to see what was going to happen."

"I know a crime scene can seem intriguing—"

"That's not what this is about! The shed, Zoe. God, aren't you listening to me? It wasn't a normal shed. The stuff inside—" He broke off and shook his head. "It's why the killer was following Ivan. What they have in common. It's what *you* have in common with them too."

I felt a cold shiver tickle its way down my spine. The look on his face terrified me.

"It was an alchemy lab, Zoe. The dead guy and the killer, they were practicing *alchemy* in the woods."

I stared at Brixton. This wasn't a joke. "You're sure?"

He nodded "What's going on? I mean, I thought there weren't hardly any of you guys around. There are more alchemists here in Portland?"

"I didn't think so," I said, but I wasn't so sure. My head swam. Had I been drawn to Portland on a subconscious level not because of its welcoming people, splendid food options, and lush greenery—but because alchemists were here? Could that have been the reason Portland felt immediately like home? As a female alchemist, I'd always been an outsider. Only Nicolas Flamel, who thought of his wife as an equal, had deemed me worthy of an apprenticeship. But I'd left abruptly, after a personal tragedy, and had lost touch with him.

"Tell me what you saw." My throat was so dry that my voice cracked.

"Do you need some water or something?" Brixton took me by the hand and led me to the kitchen. His hands were clammy but strong.

I was still in a daze as he poured me a glass of water. It was the people that drew me here to Portland—normal, everyday people like Brixton, Max, and Blue. Alchemists aren't drawn to each other like that. We're not magical beings. We're simply people who've tapped into different energies, performing different experiments than mainstream science.

There was another explanation, but I didn't like it one bit: that alchemists were here in Portland because of me, Dorian, and his backward alchemy book.

I accepted the glass of water from Brixton and drank it in five gulps. The liquid revived me. "I'm the one who's supposed to be taking care of you, kiddo."

Brixton shrugged.

"I'm all right," I said. "I don't know what came over me. Go ahead and tell me what you saw."

"I don't know how to describe it exactly." The frustration was clear in every aspect of the boy in front of me. The expression on his face hovered between innocence and angst, between boyhood and adulthood. "Stuff like in your alchemy lab."

"You haven't taken chemistry yet, have you?"

"No, I just finished freshman year. Chemistry is later. Why?"

I grabbed my phone and looked up a photo of a chemistry lab. I handed the phone to Brixton. As he hesitated, I relaxed. "You've only seen my alchemy lab a couple of times. Come with me."

I unlocked the door to the basement and lit the candles that illuminated the room.

"I still think it looked more like this than the photo you showed me," Brixton said.

"Have you been inside a chem lab?"

"I saw that meth lab before it got shut down."

"And that's it?"

"I'm not making this up. I'm not."

Was he trying to convince me or himself? "I didn't say you were. It must have been really upsetting to see a dead body."

"I'm not a kid, Zoe. I'm not imagining things." His voice broke and he swallowed hard. "I know what I saw."

That's what worried me. If Brixton had seen a murderer, that meant the murderer might have seen him too.

NINETEEN

I made sure Brixton had told the police everything he'd seen and extracted a promise that he wouldn't investigate further. I wasn't sure how much good that promise would do, so I insisted on tossing his bike in the back of my pickup truck and driving him home.

From my seat I watched Abel open the door and give Brixton a bear hug in the doorway. Abel mouthed "thank you" to me and waved. I drove home in silence, save for the sound of the engine I'd tended for more than half a century.

I turned off the engine once I reached the driveway in front of my Craftsman house. I sat there for a few minutes, unsure of what to think, feel, or do. This couldn't be Madame Leblanc's revenge on me, could it? It wasn't impossible that she could have tracked me to Portland. But this was far too subtle a way for her to frame me through alchemy. This murder wasn't meant to be discovered so quickly. The discovery in the remote area had occurred because Brixton had been following the killer.

Gripping my keys, I walked over to the Airstream trailer that had sat in the other half of the driveway since I'd moved in. I unlocked the creaking door that needed oil, then lay down on the built-in couch.

Though I'd cleaned out most of the contents of the trailer when I moved into the house, subtle scents from years of love and life lingered. The musty postcards I'd sold at flea markets across the country for decades. The fresh, uplifting mint from the tendrils of lemon balm and peppermint plants that had lived in my traveling window box garden. And the salty scent of the sea—a combination of the flavored salts I used to flavor simple meals and the trailer's long stretches driving across snow-covered country roads and through sandy beach towns.

I wasn't maudlin enough to truly believe that death followed me wherever I went, but I was at a loss to explain the deaths surrounding me. Jasper's death in my Paris shop couldn't be connected to a dead body found in a shack in the woods in Portland—yet they were both connected to alchemy.

I closed my eyes and let the fragrance of salty, musty mint carry me back to a time when life had been simpler. Only that was a false memory. My life had never been simple. From the time I'd been driven from Massachusetts for having an "unnatural" aptitude with plants, to ignoring Nicolas Flamel's warnings about how to study alchemy, to finding love with a man who'd killed himself after his son failed to find the Elixir of Life along with him. Those hadn't been simple times.

The years I'd spent traveling across the United States in my truck and trailer were simple on the surface, but if I was honest with myself, I knew I'd been running away. There was always a cloud lingering over my head, even when I would park my trailer in a nice town and settle down for a year or two at a time.

The quirky friendliness of Portland's residents and the greenery the city insisted on maintaining was an inviting combination that made me think I might finally have a simple life, at least for a little while. Though that illusion had been shattered the day I moved in, I still held onto hope. If I could figure out the last piece of the puzzle to save Dorian, put these unsolved deaths behind me, and spend time with Max—

My eyes popped open.

I was having dinner with Max that evening. The thought filled me with a mix of emotions, ranging from desire to comfort to apprehension. Part of me wanted to cancel, because how could I possibly think of enjoying myself with everything that was going on? But life has always been complicated. I'd seen too many people regret spending their time worrying instead of living. With one last look around my empty trailer, I went inside the house and picked out a dress to wear that night.

———

I walked to the restaurant on Hawthorne with the sun high in the sky above me. It was the start of summer, but it was also an early dinner. Max knew I wasn't a night owl. Even though he didn't know how closely my body's reactions were tied to the cycle of the sun and the planets, he understood that I felt most comfortable in the earliest hours of the evening.

Max had suggested this restaurant because it served organic vegan food, and as I looked through the front windows, I realized the restaurant was even closer to my own way of eating than I'd imagined. Patrons were being served on wooden plates.

Even as the world moves towards progress, a pendulum is also in play, swinging between different ideas that societies embrace at different times. When I was growing up in Salem Village—not to be confused with wealthier Salem Town—in the late 1600s, we grew our own food and ate off of shared wooden plates called trenchers.

Today's young people had embraced much of what I remembered from my childhood, going back to the land and appreciating slow food, the idea that food should be locally sourced and respected for its traditions and transformative processes rather than thoughtless calories that immediately appear out of thin air at a takeout counter. As a bearded man in the window took a sip of dark beer from a mason jar, I smiled at another parallel. In my day, beer was often drunk for breakfast with porridge. I'm sure today's hipsters would have approved.

A heavily tattooed couple stepped past me. The one with an intricate black dragon wound around his elbow and a fedora on his head held the restaurant door open for me.

Max was already in the lobby. He was dressed in a slim-fitting charcoal suit and skinny silver tie that made me want to reach out and touch it. I resisted the temptation, but Max didn't. He greeted me with a brief kiss that tasted of lemon and rose hips. I pulled back but left our noses touching for a moment. That made him smile.

"I'm glad you're home from visiting your grandmother's friend," he whispered.

If you want a lie to be believable, stick as close to the truth as possible. When I left for Paris, I told Max and most of my Portland friends a believable lie: that my grandmother's dear friend was quite elderly and wanted to see me before she died.

"I'm glad to be home too. Thanks for making sure Brixton was taken care of today. He came to see me after he was done talking to the police."

"Poor kid. He seemed really shaken."

"Does he need protection?"

Max pursed his lips. "Why would he need protection? People used to deal drugs out of that place, but not since it's been boarded up."

The hostess interrupted Max's strange answer and led us to a corner table.

"Are we talking about the same thing?" I asked once we were seated. "He told me he found a dead body and saw the killer. I know he says he hung back far enough and the guy didn't see him, but what if he was wrong? I'm still worried he'll be in danger."

"Brix either let his imagination get the better of him or he was trying to get a rise out of you. I can see him doing that." Max's deep brown eyes softened. I wished I hadn't brought up the murder.

"He wasn't acting, Max."

"The body is at least a decade old, Zoe."

"But Brixton said—"

"I don't know what Brixton was playing at when he talked to you, but the victim has been dead for quite some time. For whatever reason, Brixton lied to you."

TWENTY

"Maybe it wasn't a deliberate lie," Max continued. "Brixton loves dark things, like how he's into Portland's murderous history."

"Not so much anymore," I murmured, thinking of where that interest had led us earlier that year.

"His imagination probably got the best of him. But I'd have thought he'd find it exciting to find a mummified dead body."

"*Mummified?*"

"That's not exactly the right word, but I'd rather not talk about decomposition over dinner. Brix really didn't tell you that? Maybe he was trying to tell a macabre joke that backfired and he didn't know how to talk his way out of it."

I shook my head. Something wasn't right here.

"I'm surprised you kept our date if you thought Brixton was in danger," Max said. "I'm glad you came, and that I could put your mind at ease."

My mind was far from at ease, though. Brixton could be immature, but this wasn't right. "Brixton told me there were alchemical items like the things I sell." I took a moment to take a sip of the water placed on the table, deciding how much I should say to Max. "I suppose you're going to tell me that was Brixton's imagination, too, since he knows I collect healing and alchemical artifacts for Elixir?"

Max swore softly and shook his head. "I'd have thought the guys would tell him not to talk about the case. Don't you want to talk about something else? How was your trip? How was the visit with your grandmother's old friend? Did the boxes she found in her attic belong to your grandmother like you thought?"

"Yes. No. I mean, I don't want to change the subject yet."

Max rested his elbows on the table. "What can I tell you so we can properly begin this meal? At first the guys thought it was a drug lab, but it turns out Brixton got the part about alchemy right."

"*He did?*" Brixton was right about alchemists being in Portland, but not about the state of the dead body?

"It wasn't exactly like the stuff in your shop, though," Max said. "Someone was using it as a lab to practice alchemy. Can you believe in the twenty-first century there are still people who believe in that nonsense?"

My shoulders tensed, and I instinctively reached for the gold locket hanging around my neck. A waitress came to take our orders, so I was saved from saying something I'd regret. If cayenne-spiced bean burgers with a seasonal early summer salad and white wine didn't make me feel better, I didn't know what would.

"I'm glad you ordered some wine," Max said, his eyes lingering on my locket. "You still look tense. Don't worry about Brixton. He'll be all right."

"Your grandmother wouldn't have called alchemy nonsense, Max."

"Being an apothecary is different." He crossed his arms defensively. "That's about healing people. It's like the herbal remedies we both use, but with a different name."

"That's not how you talked about it before." Sometimes it seemed like Max was so close to being open to the ideas I wanted to share with him, but other times he was closed off, as if two sides of himself were fighting with each other.

"I can get fanciful when I think about my childhood. False memories from photographs." He gave me a shy smile and relaxed his arms. "I hope you like the guy in front of you more than eight-year-old Maximilian."

"Not Maxwell?"

"Nope. Now you know everything about me."

I couldn't help but smile. "I doubt that."

The waitress dropped off our glasses of wine, and we raised them in a toast. "To eight-year-old Maximilian," I said, "who saw the world as full of wonder, and who believed anything was possible. May we find him once again."

Instead of laughing, Max frowned. What had gone wrong with my date?

———

On my walk home—alone—I replayed Max's words again and again. Someone had been practicing alchemy in the woods. That was the relevant fact. But what I couldn't stop thinking about was that Max thought my beliefs were idiotic. Of course, he didn't know they were my beliefs. Not exactly. How could I tell him, especially now? But I had more urgent things to worry about.

I still couldn't quite believe that Brixton had been right. I had to see that shed in the woods.

I climbed the stairs to my attic. The door was locked from the inside.

"Dorian?"

"*Un moment!*"

The door swung open a minute later. A gargoyle with one of his arms hanging limp at his side looked up at me. "I thought you were out on a date."

"I was. It ended. Why did you have the door locked?"

He flapped his wings defensively. "You are the one who says I must be careful."

"Tonight isn't a night to be careful," I said. "It's a night for action. I need you to show me the cabin in the woods."

While we waited for it to be late enough for Dorian to safely venture outside, I made myself a chocolate elixir in the blender, which I needed for energy to stay awake so late into the night.

Two hours later, I doubted the caffeine had been necessary. Adrenaline was more than enough to keep my eyes wide open as Dorian and I snuck across the grass in the no-man's land between two neighborhoods.

From the outside, the cabin in the overgrown section of woods looked abandoned. Though a public path cut across this narrow swath of forest, a sign nailed to the cabin's door marked it as private property. Holes and broken pieces of wood indicated the front door had once been nailed shut, but jagged pieces of wood now hung loosely around the door frame. The door itself, musty and half decayed from years of neglect, pushed open easily.

Stepping through the crime scene tape across the rickety threshold, it became obvious that the disrepair was only an outward disguise. Though the police had taken most of the objects from inside the cabin—presumably why they hadn't left an officer to guard the shack—enough remained to assure me that Max and Brixton were right. This was the workspace of practicing alchemists.

It was the scent that hit me hardest. Honey, charred salt, and ash. It smelled like Dorian's Tea of Ashes.

This wasn't simply an alchemical lab. *This was backward alchemy.*

A branch snapped in the distance.

Dorian's horns twitched. He'd heard it too.

I turned off the flashlight and felt my way to the window on the far side of the cabin. I tensed as a weak floorboard moaned under my foot, but I needed to get to that window. That was the direction from which the sound had come. Dorian shushed me, but I had no choice. I had to see what was out there. Like the door, the window had been boarded shut long ago. Unlike the door, the window hadn't recently been opened. My only view was through the uneven spaces between rotted boards.

Only a small sliver of moon hung in the sky, leaving our surroundings nearly pitch black. But it wasn't too dark for me to make out the shadow of a figure, perhaps fifty feet from the cabin. A man.

"We need to leave," I whispered. "*Now.*"

"What do you see?"

"There's someone out there."

"Let me see. You know I see better in the dark."

"Cover yourself in your cape."

Dorian didn't fight me. I heard the sound of cloth flapping as he flipped the cloak around his wings. He took my hand and remained mute. Thank heaven for small favors.

My eyes hadn't adjusted to the darkness, but Dorian could guide us. He led the way out the front door.

"*Un moment,*" he whispered.

"Don't—"

But it was too late. He'd already let go of my hand.

It couldn't have been more than a minute that I stood alone in the crisp darkness of the cabin porch in the sinister woods, willing my eyes to adjust and for Dorian to return. But it felt like an hour. Every sound made by nocturnal creatures and plants blowing under the pressure of the gentle wind set my senses on edge.

I jumped as a familiar hand took mine. My eyes had adjusted to the dim moonlight enough for me to make out Dorian's cape-shrouded form.

"A man," he whispered. "With my leg, I cannot risk getting a closer look. But you are right. A man is out there. Watching."

Dorian tugged at my hand, pulling me away from the cabin. "If we go this way, the cabin should block us from his view. As long as he cannot see in the darkness as I can, this path should be safe."

I followed Dorian's lead, creeping between the thick groupings of trees on our way out of the woods, hoping the man out there didn't have night vision goggles. At the edge of the greenbelt, we waited in silence for a few more minutes before walking to where my old truck was parked. We didn't need to speak. Both of us understood we had to be sure we hadn't been followed.

"This is bad, Dorian." I turned the ignition, cringing at the sharp sound of the engine revving. No sense in keeping quiet now. I opted for speed instead. The tires screeched as I peeled onto the street and pointed us homeward.

"It will be worse if you are given a speeding ticket."

I gripped the gear shift.

"I wish to hear 'Accidental Life,'" Dorian said.

The cassette was already in the player, so I hit the play button. Tobias Freeman's booming voice filled the car. He'd written the song for his 100th birthday, in the 1950s. After I'd nursed him back to health when I met him in my work on the Underground Railroad, Tobias had discovered the Elixir of Life. His loved ones had not. One by one, he had watched them age and die. It was a lot to grapple with, as I knew well. He'd recorded the track under the moniker The Philosopher. The soulful song by my friend immediately made me feel calmer.

"*Bon*," Dorian said with a grin.

"You asked me to play the song so I'd feel better, didn't you?"

"*Oui.* I know you wish Tobias could be here. Now he is."

Careful to drive the speed limit, I watched the nighttime greenery bounce off my headlights, then give way to houses. "What's going on, Dorian? A long-dead man was found in a backward alchemy lab. Another man, 'creepy guy,' who must have known about the dead body, was following Ivan—possibly the same person followed us back there by the cabin."

Dorian peeked out from the folds of the cape. He was sitting on the floor of the passenger side of the truck. "Do not forget the woman in Paris who wishes to expose you."

The brakes screeched as I came to a stop at a red light. Dorian bumped into the glove compartment. "How," I said, looking down at the scowling gargoyle, "could I possibly forget her?"

"You are upset," Dorian said. "Perhaps we should continue our discussion in the morning."

Feeling the effects of being awake so late at night, I had to agree with Dorian. Talk could wait for tomorrow. But I had one more thing to do before I could sleep.

I dialed the Paris bookseller's shop to check again on the book he was sending. It was early afternoon in Paris, yet there was no answer at the bookshop. As the phone continued to ring, a disturbing thought tickled my brain. Someone was following alchemists. They'd spied on Ivan and they'd broken into my house. Had they also been following me in Paris when I'd visited the bookshop? Had they done something to the bookseller?

What had become of the bookshop proprietor?

TWENTY-ONE

I DREAMT OF A fierce sea.

Dressed in a feedsack dress with scratchy fibers that bore into my skin, I watched from a rocking boat as water serpents gracefully spun their lean bodies through the water, circling each other in an underwater dance. What at first looked like a benevolent action morphed into a scene of battle. The creatures curled their bodies around one another and bit into each other's flesh. Above them, bees circled and toads fell from a dark sky.

A pelican swooped from the air and caught a toad that was about to fall on my head. She nodded at me, then flew back to her nest, where she would give the toad to her offspring. I watched her flapping wings until the bird disappeared in the clouds. These dream clouds weren't the clouds of reality. They were faces of women.

These were the faces from Heather's new paintings, with reflections in the women's eyes. One of the reflections was of a man. Was it her father who'd fled? No, I recognized this man. It was the Frenchman who owned the bookshop, Lucien Augustin. His body was bound in thick ropes, and he'd been lashed to the mast of a ship. The ship that I was on. The raven I remembered from one of Heather's paintings appeared behind him, only the bird was no reflection. The black bird flew out of the clouds and dove straight for me. The ominous feathered being would have crashed into me had it not been for a toad I had assumed dead. The amphibian jumped from the boat at the last moment and caught the bird in its mouth.

I woke up.

The cotton sheets of my bed were tangled around me like tentacles. I was drenched in salty sweat. If I'd been fanciful, I would have sworn the salt came from the sea of my dream.

Sometimes I really hated that Freud was right about our subconscious speaking to us in our dreams. I'd found him to be a terribly arrogant man, but I grudgingly admitted he was a smart one. In alchemy, serpents represent the life force that's exchanged in each transformation, pelicans represent sacrifice, and toads represent the First Matter that both begins and ends the creation of the Philosopher's Stone. My subconscious was definitely trying to work out the confusing events around me.

A sweet aroma brought me back to reality. The scent of fresh apricot tarts told me that Dorian was back from his predawn baking at Blue Sky Teas and had brought back misshapen pastries, as usual. The treats tasted as good, but customers were less likely to buy a lopsided tart, so he brought these malformed treats back to the house … if he didn't eat them first.

I made myself a cup of jasmine green tea from tea leaves Max had given me and sat down with Dorian at the dining table. Built by a craftsman I met in the south of France shortly after the turn of the twentieth century, the table had been in storage during the years I'd lived out of a trailer. It was nice to have a home again, even if I always made sure to keep the curtains drawn tightly so that Dorian could have the run of the house.

Even at the familiar table that had brought me joy from the moment it was handcrafted, with a perfect breakfast and my best friend at my side, I couldn't relax. I was plagued by the troubling idea that the bookseller had been harmed by whoever was following me and Ivan. Could the book he found be more important than either of us thought? Could *Backward Alchemists of Notre Dame* hold a real clue to finding a backward alchemist? And if so, was someone trying to stop me from getting it?

"Breakfast is unsatisfactory?" Dorian asked, his horns twitching in alarm. "I will cook fresh food. I suspected I had gone too far trusting the malformed atrocities. This scone resembles your Richard Nixon, no? It is the chin." Dorian frowned at the scone. "What would you like? Buckwheat crepes? Chickpea pancakes? Almond milk porridge?" He jumped down from his chair, falling onto the creaky hardwood floor in the process. His left ankle was now unbending, solid stone.

"These pastries taste perfect, Dorian." I helped him back into his chair and held my tongue about his stone lower leg. "I simply didn't sleep well."

"If you are certain."

"I am." I took a huge bite of a heavenly apricot tart to prove my point.

"*Bon.* Then we can get to work. My little grey cells have been mulling over this most unusual problem: not one but *two* old alchemy murders. Both of which are distracting you from helping me and my brother." He tapped his claws on the wooden tabletop. "When we have eliminated the impossible, the only thing that remains, however improbable, is the truth to which I will apply my little grey cells."

"I'm pretty sure you're mixing your fictional detectives."

"I am being most serious, Zoe. Murders across time and location, yet they have one thing in common: *you*."

"The connection," I said emphatically, "is alchemy."

Dorian shook his head even more emphatically. "This week has stirred up two alchemical murders relating to you. You cannot think this is a coincidence."

"Jasper was killed in France seventy-five years ago. The unknown man in the cabin was killed in Oregon around a decade ago. I was careless in Paris and Brixton was snooping in Portland because we want to get alchemical answers to help you. In that sense, you're right: they're connected. But only because of dangers we both stepped into."

"You miss the logical next step, *mon amie*. You being recognized in Paris could have set forces in motion—"

"I can't think straight. Everything seems connected right now. Even Heather's paintings remind me of alchemy."

"*Oui*. She has a vivid imagination. I can see why the themes of transformation remind you of alchemy."

"You've seen the paintings?"

"When I arrive in the café's kitchen at three a.m., before removing my cape I look around to make sure there is nobody there."

"Now you think Heather is an alchemist? *Heather?* The woman who dropped out of high school at sixteen, who can't be bothered to wear shoes for half the year, who's more interested in weaving daisy chains in her hair and finding the perfect shade of green paint than making sure where her son is?"

"I agree, it does not make sense that all of Portland is overflowing with alchemists. I have explored enough to know that is not the case. There is something else at play, Zoe. *You*. You must investigate the unknown dead man to find out his connection to you—"

"The police are already doing that."

Dorian flapped his wings at his side. "But there is a connection to the man who has been spying on Ivan!"

"The only thing I have to investigate is the alchemy that will save you. I'm so close to understanding what's going on, Dorian. So close to saving you." I swallowed hard, willing my eyes not to fill with tears. "As soon as that book from Paris arrives, I'll be able to find a backward alchemist and have the last piece of the puzzle."

"And in the meantime?"

"The book will be arriving soon. Maybe even later today." If someone hadn't gotten to Lucien first.

"*Alors*, the meantime? We are well equipped to solve these past mysteries, you and I."

"I know you're careful, but you can't move your left arm. And your foot … " I let the words trail off as I looked at his poor foot. His stone ankle was frozen at an awkward angle. Was it painful?

Instead of protesting, as I suspected he would, Dorian's wings folded as he nodded sadly. "I nearly fell from the roof the other day. No, no. Do not worry. I have since compensated and know how to hold on with one hand and foot. But you are right that I cannot investigate as I once could. Yet I have other skills to assist you. In addition to reading the entire Christie canon, I read Tey's *Daughter of Time*. Twice."

I crossed my arms and stared down at the gargoyle. "Then you should stay in the attic instead of following phantoms. If memory serves, the hero in that novel about solving a centuries-old mystery didn't leave his hospital bed the entire time."

Dorian's snout twitched. "Well played, Alchemist. Well played."

"If you want to play armchair detective, why don't you help me look through online archives of newspaper accounts from 1942 Paris?" I didn't think learning more about Jasper Dubois's death would help, but it couldn't hurt, and it was a safe line of investigation for Dorian. I handed him my laptop.

"I have already done this."

"You have?"

"You thought I would not use my little grey cells to help you?" His shoulders and wings fell. "I searched for clues for many hours, while you slept. Alas, I have not discovered any new facts, only theories. This is why I have not spoken of my findings. As for my brother—"

"The other gargoyle," I corrected.

Dorian narrowed his eyes.

"I should run to the market," I continued. "There's a farmer's market today."

"You are a *très intelligent* woman, Zoe. You knew the one thing you could say that would not cause me to object to ending this conversation."

———

Though it was early summer, an unexpected rainstorm had blown in that morning, though I probably shouldn't have called it "unexpected" since this was Portland. I grabbed my silver rain coat and walked to a local farmer's market. I found myself looking over my shoulder the entire way. Could Dorian be right that the two murders were connected to me? It wasn't possible. Jasper's death might have been connected to me, but I wasn't in Portland a decade ago.

I was so distracted I barely noticed the early-summer fruits and vegetables. I was vaguely aware of a pyramid-shaped stack of apricots, but didn't stop wandering until I reached a stall that sent me back to another century.

The farmer had freekeh, a preparation of durum wheat in which the young green stalks are set afire to stop the process of the wheat aging and to give the grain a smoky flavor. It would be a perfect complement to the green onions from my garden. And I knew Dorian would love it. For a brief time he'd missed the smoky flavor of cured meats, but he'd been delighted to discover a whole other world of smoky spices and grains.

The more I got to know Portland, the more I loved my new home. A stab of frustration overcame me. I was *so close* to having a happy life here. If only I could solve the riddle of Dorian's alchemy book to save him and rid myself of the murderous mysteries that had followed me, I knew that life was within reach.

I was almost hopeful on my walk home. I let myself appreciate the moment, taking in the scents of the smoky freekeh and sweet summer peas in the bag over my shoulder, and the roses and pine from the nature that surrounded me.

I quickened my pace as I approached the house. A package was sticking out of the mailbox. I'd let my imagination run wild in thinking something bad had happened to the bookseller. I tore into the package.

It wasn't the book from Paris.

The book-shaped package contained a bound stack of magazines. I flipped through the pages. All back issues of a vegan magazine Dorian had recently discovered.

It was probably still true that I was jumping to conclusions about the bookseller. An unsettling thought about Lucien crossed my mind: The French police could have tracked me down to the bookshop. If they told the bookseller about Jasper's murder in 1942, Lucien might have decided that he didn't want to help a criminal.

Or worse. If the authorities had traced my movements in Paris, could they have traced me back to my house in Portland?

Dorian had an escape-hatch in the roof of the house; if anyone entered the house with a search warrant, he could make an easy escape. What did it say about my life that I'd already had to think about such matters multiple times this year?

Being traced here didn't seem especially likely, though. The supposed granddaughter of a possible criminal who was most likely long dead wouldn't merit the French authorities sending their American counterparts to follow up with me. But Madame Leblanc cared enough. I tensed as I remembered her high-end clothing. She could very well have the resources to hire a private investigator to look into anything related to alchemy in Portland.

I couldn't sit at home doing nothing, so I walked to Blue Sky Teas. It was early afternoon, but as I drew near I saw that the teashop was dark and the sign set to CLOSED. A little rain never stopped a Portlander. I peeked in the windows but saw nothing amiss.

Is EVERYTHING ALL RIGHT? I texted Brixton.

WHERE ARE YOU? he texted back.

TEASHOP.

MEET ME AT THE MORGUE.

The morgue? This couldn't be good.

TWENTY-TWO

"MOM IS SUPPOSED TO identify the body," Brixton said. "They think it might be her dad."

"Oh God, Brix. I'm so sorry." In the sterile hallway outside the morgue, the astringent scent in the air was stifling. It didn't help that none of this made any sense. *Brixton's grandfather?* Brixton and his mom didn't have anything to do with alchemy.

"Why do they think this man—"

"Unsolved missing persons cases from that time. Mom's dad was one of them. Her mom filed a report after he disappeared."

"I didn't realize. I thought he ... " What was a nice way to say his grandfather fled instead of sticking around to support his young daughter and grandson?

Brixton shrugged. "Yeah, Mom thought he ran out on the family. You don't have to look so uncomfortable, Zoe. I never knew him." He shrugged again, trying to look aloof but fooling nobody. "Looks like he might have been killed right here in Portland."

And Brixton was the one who found the body.

"All these years we hated him," Brixton whispered.

Abel tried to give him a hug, but the kid shrugged him off, opting instead to shove his hands into the pockets of his hoodie. Abel tapped his foot nervously. Brixton fidgeted and began to bite his fingernails.

Abel straightened and put his hands on Brixton's shoulders. I followed his gaze. Heather was walking down the hallway toward us. Her blonde braids were a mess, her face set in a stoic mask unlike any expression I'd seen on her before.

Heather could be an immature flake, but she was always full of vitality and hope. Until now. This was the first time I'd seen her with a cloud over her face. Even when Brixton had been in trouble in the past, she met the challenge with energy and love. The woman in front of me wasn't the same person. Her face was cold. Defeated. When she reached us, I could see her arms were shaking.

"Was it him?" Abel whispered.

For a fraction of a second, I could have sworn she stared at him as if he was a stranger who had no business talking to her. When she recovered, her reaction wasn't much better. "How could I tell? Tell me, Abel, how am I supposed to know what that *thing* was?"

I cringed. The body had been decomposing for more than a decade.

Abel's muscles tensed. "They showed him to you, even though he was beyond recognition?"

"They thought I might recognize identifying markings."

I would have expected her to shudder or break down. Instead she was emotionally distant.

"Let's get you home," Abel said.

"The teashop," she said. "I have to open Blue's teashop."

"It's okay for it to be closed for a day."

"But there's no need. I don't know who that poor man is." She paused, and I saw the first hint of emotion cross her face. "He didn't have any teeth—they'd all been removed." She shuddered. "Dental records won't work, so they might have to do a DNA test to identify him. They're sure to get an answer. A real answer. Oh, God, Abel. What am I going to do if it's him? All this time, I thought he hated me. But what if, what if he went off and did something dumb, trying to get money for me? What if that's why he never came home? He might have sacrificed himself for us, and I never knew it."

———————

I left the morgue understanding far less than I'd known going in.

Had Brixton and the police been wrong about the old cabin in the woods being an alchemy lab? The person Brixton had seen leaving the shack had been spying on Ivan, and possibly on me, but that man wasn't necessarily here in Portland years ago when the murder took place.

Did we even know it was murder, and not just a recluse who'd died of natural causes? That would be a less gruesome answer for why he didn't have any teeth. Why hadn't anyone found the body before? Had it been hidden until now? Had the man spying on Ivan moved the body?

The more I thought about my unanswered questions, the more my theories fell apart. Was I being narrow-minded to think these deaths were connected to me? Or, at the very least, to alchemy? Guilt at being so self-absorbed replaced my confusion. Heather's dad, Brixton's grandfather, might have been cruelly taken away from his family. Was it him in the morgue? Did he die with regrets, or was he happy to have died trying to provide for his family?

I drove home past the combination of parks and forests, bridges stretching across the river and urban neighborhoods, wondering what secrets were hiding beyond what I could see. The brief summer storm had felled an old tree that had crumpled a small car, and a detour rerouted me onto a different street. If I were to be killed by a falling tree branch, would I die with regrets? I was doing everything I could to help those I cared about. But what about my own life? I was pushing Max away for stupid reasons.

When I got back to my house, a bouquet of amaryllis was waiting for me on the porch in a simple hourglass vase. The red flowers streaked with white were the perfect choice, for the scent was beautiful but subtle. It struck the right balance: heartfelt but not too pushy.

The card read *Peace Offering. I'm cooking a veg curry for an early dinner tonight. There's plenty.* The card wasn't signed, but it was Max's handwriting.

I brought the flowers inside and placed them in the center of my beloved dining table, then picked out a bottle of wine to bring to Max's house. I would have asked Dorian's opinion, because he was the one who created our wine list, but he wasn't home that I could see. Was he cooking at his new employer Julian Lake's house? I couldn't help worrying that he would struggle with his arm and foot while away from home.

I was used to living on my own, so the stillness of an empty house didn't usually bother me. But with the unexplained deaths surrounding us, being in the house alone filled me with apprehension. I walked through my basement alchemy lab and watered my plants, then methodically checked the locks on all of the windows and doors. My locksmith friend had come over as soon as I'd called him. The house was secure. I checked again. And maybe one last time. Third time's a charm, right?

I picked up the bottle of organic Zinfandel and walked to Max's house.

Max opened the door with his black hair spikier than usual, wearing a once-white apron over his black clothes. He grinned sheepishly as he wiped his hands on a clean corner of the apron and accepted the bottle of wine.

I knew a fair amount about wine from when I lived in France, but it was Dorian who forced me to get caught up to the twenty-first century. He didn't believe in using cooking wine or table wine. According to the little chef, the wine used in cooking had to be every bit as good as a wine you'd order to drink. Since Dorian couldn't come to the local markets with me, I photographed the wine shelves and he gave me lessons on which ones to buy for different dishes. I wasn't completely convinced it mattered as much as he thought it did, but there was something to the idea of pairing.

"This wine goes well with spicy food," I said. "From the smell of sizzling cumin seeds and cayenne, I think I chose wisely."

Max sniffed the air and bolted for the kitchen. His modern kitchen was sparsely decorated but simultaneously full of character. Teacups and a kettle from his grandmother gave the room an elegant simplicity that embodied Max. A philosophically decorated room.

"I didn't know I was getting in over my head when I started this curry," he said as he stirred the pot with a bamboo spoon. "It always looked so easy when I watched it being prepared."

"Thanks for the flowers, Max. And for inviting me over."

"When I heard about Heather's dad, it made me realize how stupid our fight was. I mean, it wasn't even a *fight* fight. But I didn't like it."

"I don't even know what we were fighting about anymore." I felt for my locket. My security blanket.

His eyes dropped from my eyes to my neck, where I held my gold locket between my fingertips. "You're holding me at arm's length, as usual. Your actions speak louder than words. I know you're not completely over your ex."

I stopped fiddling with the locket. *That's* what this was about? Jealousy?

"It's supposed to be a difficult thing to work through," Max continued. "We each have our baggage. Plus I'm too old for you."

"What are you saying?" Had I misinterpreted the flowers, and this whole invitation? "Is this a break-up dinner?"

"I said it's *supposed to be* difficult." He set the wooden spoon on the counter and took my hands in his. "But it's not. When I'm with you, the hours pass like minutes. I like being with you. So much. Can we forget about all that other stuff? And just be here in the present?"

Ever since I'd met Max, that's what I'd been hoping for. I was about to verbalize my answer, but as soon as I smiled, Max drew me into a kiss spicier than the curry cooking next to us.

The coconut milk curry and basmati rice pilaf ended up slightly burned, but neither of us cared. The hours passed without me realizing where the time had gone or feeling tired.

When I helped Max clean up the kitchen after dinner, I noticed the recipe. In a wrought iron cookbook holder sat a three-ring binder of recipes. Facing forward was a hand-written notecard behind a plastic sleeve. The handwriting wasn't Max's. Was it his grandmother's? I set down the dish rag in my hand and flipped through the binder. More than half of the recipes were for Indian foods. This binder had belonged to Max's dead wife, Chadna.

I felt my cheeks burn with a small pang of jealousy. I willed myself to push away the baseless feeling. Why was I being so silly? I'd been in love before, too, and it didn't change my feelings for Max.

I set the binder down as Max placed the last dishes into the cabinets.

"That was perfect," I said.

"When did you learn how to lie?"

"I mean it. You make it so easy to relax and enjoy life, even if I only get a few hours' break from it. Thank you for the perfect evening. But I should go. I've got an early day."

"I've gotta be up early too."

I hoped I didn't show my disappointment. Part of me had hoped Max would try to convince me to stay. A big part of me.

"But the thing is," Max continued, "I don't seem to care."

I didn't either.

———————

I crawled out of Max's bed at 4 a.m. I'd remembered to set my phone alarm for the time everyone thought I got up to bake for Blue Sky Teas. I glanced back at Max, who was sound asleep. I sent Dorian an email that he shouldn't worry if he didn't see me when he came home, then crawled back into bed.

My locket felt cool on my chest. I realized I hadn't thought of it all night. That hadn't happened in ... I couldn't remember how long. I fell back asleep with a contented smile on my face.

I woke up next as the sun rose shortly after 5:30. I rolled over onto my stomach, enjoying the comfortable warmth of Max's bed. Thin rays of sunlight pushed their way through breaks in the curtains. The top of Max's head poked out from the duvet. He was always so put-together that I smiled at the sight of his sleek black hair askew on his forehead.

I was so contented that I must have dozed off again, because I awoke to the sensation of kisses on my bare shoulder.

"I'm glad you came back after baking," Max said.

"I wanted to be here with you when you woke up."

"I'm glad." He propped himself up on one elbow and ran his hand through my hair. "I always assumed you dyed your hair. I mean, the bright white suits you. It adds to your beauty. But ... " He ran his finger down my arm. "*What happened*, Zoe? Every hair on your body is white."

"Life," I said. Honesty is the best policy.

"You told me about the stuff you went through losing your family so young, and I've heard of people getting streaks of white hair from stressful encounters. But *all* of your hair?"

"We all experience life differently, Max." I put a finger to his lips as he tried to speak. "I'm glad I'm experiencing mine here with you. What's up with the skeleton at the end of the hallway?"

"You're changing the subject."

"It's a fair question, considering I spent the night with a detective who might moonlight as a homicidal maniac."

Max laughed and covered his face with a pillow. "I'm not very good at disposing of bodies, though, am I?" he mumbled.

I pulled the pillow from his handsome head. "Maybe you're just a body snatcher."

He grinned and grabbed me. "You caught me. I'm a body snatcher." He ran his hands over my hips. "You're not too tired after getting up in the middle of the night?"

I shook my head. "I'm a morning person."

"Good."

An hour later, I stepped out of the bathroom, drying my hair with a towel, and found Max putting on his shoes.

"I really do have to get to the office to finish the paperwork on this case," Max said. "Want to grab a cup of tea at Blue's before I head on to work?"

Max and I both lived in the Hawthorne neighborhood within walking distance to Blue Sky Teas. The storm from the previous day had passed, and we walked to the teashop under a bright blue sky.

Heather stood behind the counter and waved at me as we walked through the welcoming door of the teashop.

"Here she is," Heather said to a man who stood at the counter.

He turned around. My balance gave way. It felt as if the world was spinning out of control. Max steadied me. My heart raced and

132

my limbs went numb. I grasped the locket hanging around my neck, but I could barely feel it between my fingers.

Though I hadn't seen him in nearly a hundred years, I knew the man. Or at least, I had known my beloved a century ago. Before he died.

Ambrose.

TWENTY-THREE

NOISY VOICES SWIRLED AROUND me. I blinked and saw blue sky and clouds above me. No, that wasn't right. It wasn't real sky. A dream? No, I was awake. I was looking up at the painted ceiling of Blue Sky Teas. I was lying on my back. A group of people stared at me from above. I struggled to focus on the blurry faces.

"She's coming to," Heather said. "You guys, give her some room."

Max and another man helped me up. A familiar man I'd known a century ago.

"Hello, Zoe," he said in an English accent. "So sorry to have startled you."

Could it really be Ambrose? I clutched my locket as my eyes focused on the handsome face in front of mine. No. This wasn't Ambrose.

"Percy?"

It was Ambrose's *son*.

The Old English accent was more refined than I remembered, as was the man. Gone was the plump insolent man suffering from gout, replaced by a younger, fitter man with a humbler tone of voice.

"It's been a long time," he said.

That was an understatement. Percy had died in 1935.

I closed my eyes. This wasn't real. I was hallucinating. I must have fainted and hit my head after seeing a man who reminded me of the great love of my life. Percy had the same black hair, distinctive nose, and striking eyes as his father. The similarity hadn't been as strong when I'd known them, because Percy's fondness for beer and overindulgence in rich foods had given him a pudgy layer and a ruddy tinge.

Max put his arm around me and pressed a glass of water to my lips. "Do you want me to take you to a doctor? Work can wait."

"I'm all right. I usually eat first thing. Must be low blood sugar."

"Help her to a chair," Heather suggested.

Max and Percy lifted me to a chair. Much more forcefully than was necessary, I thought. I looked sharply at them both as they lifted me off my feet. Were they each trying to prove they were stronger than the other? Percy's flab had been replaced by lean muscle. He wore a leather jacket over a white dress shirt and trendy fitted jeans.

"Let me get you one of your carrot cake muffins," Heather said. "Lot of natural sugars."

I nodded. Even though I was pretty sure it was shock that had caused me to faint, one of Dorian's treats couldn't hurt.

"Max Liu," Max said to Percy, extending his hand.

"Percival Smythe."

I raised an eyebrow involuntarily and hoped Max didn't catch the gesture. I wondered how long Percy had been using that surname. Though the last name he gave was false, he was very real. Rage and regret swirled inside me, feeding each other. Ambrose and I had been told Percy was dead, and Ambrose had bitterly mourned the loss of his son. Our lives would have been more different than I could fathom had we believed otherwise. Ambrose might still be alive today.

Percy had never had the patience and demeanor to become an alchemist. It had been painful for him that both I and his father had found the Elixir of Life while he continued to age, so he'd moved far away from us. Ambrose and I hadn't seen Percy's body, but we had no reason to doubt the news of his death. If only we'd known it had been a lie, Ambrose would never have killed himself.

"So you're an old friend of Zoe's?" Max asked, pulling up a chair protectively close to me.

"Percy is Ambrose's son," I said.

"Ambrose?" Max said. He knew I'd traveled across the US in my Airstream trailer after the man I was involved with died. Max didn't know those travels had stretched over decades rather than just a few years. I could see the unspoken question on his lips. Percy looked like he was in his mid-twenties, the same age I claimed—far too old to be the son of a man I'd been involved with.

"I was hoping we could get caught up," Percy said.

Heather saved me from answering by setting a carrot cake muffin in front of me. "I've gotta get back to the counter, but give me a holler if you need anything else."

I didn't feel hungry, but I forced myself to take a bite. Pecans and cranberries, salt and dates, a sweet and savory blend to awaken my senses while feeding my lightheaded body. Dorian continued to outdo himself.

"You want me to leave so you can get caught up with him?" Max asked. His voice was sharp, and I recognized the emotion. Jealousy. It was a stronger version of the same feeling I'd experienced the previous night when I realized the recipe I'd just enjoyed had come from Max's dead wife. I couldn't worry about Max's jealousy now. My unfinished past trumped my love life.

Percy lowered his eyelids, giving me a hint of the petulant man I remembered.

I had never liked Percy, but I had to talk to him in private, without Max looking on.

"Go file your paperwork," I said to Max. "I'm all right. I'll stay here and catch up with Percy."

His lips set in a frown, Max nodded and left.

"I really am sorry about all this," Percy said. "I—"

"You *died*," I whispered sharply.

"Rumors of my death were greatly exaggerated."

"Very funny. While you were *not dead*, I see you've had more time to become well read. I can't remember you opening the pages of a single book when you stayed with me and Ambrose."

Percy was already a young adult when I met Ambrose. His mother had died in childbirth, and Ambrose had done the best he could. It was far better than most men had been able to do at the time, even the ones who'd been able to maintain custody of their children. But Ambrose had spoiled the boy.

Percy sighed. "I deserve that. But I'm a different man than when you knew me, Zoe. I've turned my life around."

"Where have you been all these years? You discovered the Elixir but didn't tell us? And now, all of a sudden, you decided it was time for a reunion? This isn't the best time—"

"That's not why I came. I'm here because I need to warn you. A dangerous alchemist followed you here to Portland. I believe you met him at a bookshop in Paris."

The plain man from the bookshop? "Lucien? He's an alchemist?"

Percy nodded. "Not just an alchemist. A backward alchemist."

TWENTY-FOUR

I'D FOUND A BACKWARD alchemist and hadn't even known it.

Worse yet, the backward alchemist had turned the tables. While I'd been blindly seeking someone like Lucien, he knew exactly who I was. And he'd followed me to Portland. But why? He'd taken the time to lead me on with talk of the obscure book that could have helped me locate backward alchemists, but it now seemed he never meant to send the book at all.

"Why?" I croaked. "Why is he here?"

Percy seemed surprised by my expression of horror. Had he expected me to be surprised or disbelieving instead?

"I take it you know what that means, to be a backward alchemist," he said, his gaze unwavering. "I didn't figure you for the type to know about that kind of thing."

"What kind of thing?"

"Not untrue alchemy."

Not Untrue Alchemy. The translated name of Dorian's book.

"That's what they call it these days, you know," Percy continued. "'Backward alchemy' is so passé."

"What they practice isn't true alchemy," I murmured mostly to myself. "But it's not completely false either. So they practice not untrue alchemy." He was talking about a *phrase*, I realized, not the name of Dorian's book itself.

Percy nodded. "Lucien Augustin is a very dangerous man."

"Percy, what the devil is going on? A backward alchemist is following me—and you! You let us think you were dead."

"I didn't have a choice—" He started to raise his voice but glanced around the café and broke off. "I know you've got no reason to trust me," he continued in an earnest whisper, "but I want to help you."

"Why? You never made a secret of the fact you despised me."

"Half a century can do a lot for one's maturity. It took me awhile, Zoe, but I've grown up. I may look nearly as young as the day you last saw me, but I've had a lot of time to think. You and I may not have always gotten along—"

"An understatement."

"—but you're the only family I've got."

I, too, had lost my entire family long ago. Aside from my beloved brother Thomas, I hadn't been close with my immediate family. They didn't question the ways of Salem Village and were quick to judge when I was accused of witchcraft simply because I had an "unnaturally good" way with plants. My connection to plants and aptitude for plant alchemy weren't witchcraft. My only "crimes" were helping the vegetables and grains on my family's plot of land grow more robustly than our neighbors.

My brother and I fled the village instead of waiting for me to be condemned to death as a witch, but Thomas died only a few years later. It wasn't until I met Ambrose that I felt like I had a family again.

I looked straight into Percy's eyes. "Ambrose would want me to hear you out," I said. "His love of you was so great." My voice broke. Of all the unexpected things life had thrown my way, I never thought I'd see *Percy* again. And looking so much like his father.

"Once, that didn't mean as much to me as it should have," Percy said. "I know I took Father for granted. And you too. Like I said, I've grown up." He gave me an embarrassed smile before his eyes darted around the teashop again. "Look, is there somewhere we can talk in private? I'll tell you everything, but I'm worried about Lucien. I don't know where he is, and I don't want him to find me here in Portland."

"Stay here. I'll be right back."

"But—"

"Stay inside and I'll be right back."

I rushed outside to call Dorian. My hands shook as I dialed, but I relaxed slightly after getting a good look at the people on the sidewalk near Blue Sky Teas. They were all far too hip to be Lucien, even in disguise.

So Lucien had followed me to Portland. That explained why he hadn't answered the phone at the bookshop. It also meant there was probably no book that would give me the answers to save Dorian. Well, maybe there *was* a book that held answers about people who'd died at the hands of backward alchemists practicing at Notre Dame, but not one that he'd share with me. But why had Lucien followed me here?

I thought that if I could find a backward alchemist he could answer my questions, but I hadn't thought through the reality of the situation. Lucien must have known what I was to follow me to Portland, but he didn't reveal himself to me. He wasn't going to let go of his secrets easily. My grand plan was in shambles.

After completing our special sequence of coded rings, Dorian picked up the phone.

"I'm bringing someone over to the house who shouldn't see you," I said. "Get whatever you need to stay in the attic for a couple of hours."

"Max is moving in?" an indignant gargoyle replied.

"What? No. Why would you say that?"

"He is why you did not come home last night, was it not? Yet you do not sound happy, like people in the movies after they have—"

"Max has nothing to do with what's going on this morning. Ambrose's son Percy is here."

A pause on the other end of the line. "I thought he died many years ago."

"I thought so too. I need to talk to him in private, so I'm bringing him over to the house."

"You can trust him?"

I hesitated before answering. "Not completely. That's why I want you—and *Non Degenera Alchemia*—out of sight."

"Why is there such fear in your voice?"

"I'll explain everything as soon as I understand it myself."

"No matter. I will simply listen through the pipes."

"Fine. Wait, *what*?"

"From the attic, there is a way to access the audio qualities of the plumbing in the house."

"You're telling me you've been able to listen in on downstairs conversations all this time?"

"I only recently discovered it, during the party. And you have been away—"

"What party?"

Dorian cleared his throat. "I misspoke. My English, it is not so good."

"Your English is perfect, Dorian. What party?"

Dorian sighed. "Brixton and his friends wanted to have an end-of-the-school-year party. They were supposed to have it at Ethan's home, while the boy's parents were out of town, but his parents came home unexpectedly. Brixton asked me if they could have the party at your house. He already had a key … "

"Do you realize all the dangerous elements in my alchemy lab—" Was that the reason the items in my basement alchemy lab had been askew when I arrived home? Oh God, if *kids* had gotten in there …

Dorian clicked his tongue. "You think I did not consider this? The basement and the attic were securely locked. The children were only allowed on the first floor. I listened through the pipes to make sure they did not get into trouble."

"How could you—"

"If I had not allowed them use of the house, they would have gone somewhere else—perhaps somewhere more dangerous, like those Shanghai Tunnels they used to sneak into. But … *qu'est-ce que* a 'jello shot' I heard them speak of while giggling? When I cleaned up the last mess that Brixton made, I did not see a dessert mold."

I groaned, but I had more important things to worry about than unchaperoned fourteen- and fifteen-year-olds getting drunk off jello shots. Even though he could be infuriating, Dorian would take care of Brixton and his friends. A trustworthy gargoyle chaperone was better than no adult oversight in the dangerous tunnels under the city.

"Percy and I will be there in a few minutes," I said.

In front of Blue Sky Teas, I looked through the large windows to where Percy sat under the weeping fig tree, with his hands wrapped gently around a mug of tea. My throat tightened. He looked so much like his father.

Were my feelings for Ambrose getting in the way of a rational decision? Was I fooling myself that I could trust a word Percy spoke?

TWENTY-FIVE

"The twenty-first century suits you well," Percy said, resting his elbows on my dining table and tapping his manicured fingertips together. Like his diction, the way he carried himself was more refined than the slovenly man I'd known. "Vegan restaurants are everywhere in this strange new century, you can buy unusual herbs and minerals without being hunted as a witch, and your white hair looks good in this short, modern hairstyle."

"You look good too, Percy. For a dead man."

"I'm sure you've guessed that I found the Elixir."

"Mmm. What I can't guess is how you found *me*."

"This is where things get tricky." Percy pushed the chair back from the table and began to fidget. He tapped his breast pocket, and for a moment seemed surprised to find it empty.

"Recently gave up a smoking habit?"

"Something like that."

"Nobody followed us back to the house. You don't have to be so nervous."

"If you knew what I know, you'd be nervous too."

"You're stalling, Percy. Why don't you tell me what it is you know?"

"You have to hear me out—the whole story—before you pass judgment. Will you do that for me?"

I didn't answer for a moment. What was his game?

Percy jerked backward as my phone beeped, nearly toppling the chair. What was he so frightened of?

The phone was set to only make a noise if one of a few people contacted me. I reached for the phone while keeping one eye on Percy. The phone notification was an email from Dorian. I expected he was in the attic along with my laptop, listening to us through the pipes.

Hear Percy out, Dorian's message said.

"I owe it to Ambrose to give you the benefit of the doubt," I said.

Percy's lip quivered, giving his face the humanity of his father. "I never meant for any of this to happen. I didn't know what I was getting myself into. When I found Lucien, he told me so many wondrous things about not untrue alchemy. Things you and Father never told me."

"Oh, God, Percy." The skin on my cheeks prickled, my mouth went dry, and I felt like I was looking through a tunnel. "What have you done? You found the Elixir through backward alchemy?"

I should have realized it as soon as I saw him. Both because he didn't have the temperament for true alchemy and also because he was *younger* than he was the last time I'd seen him. He hadn't simply stopped aging; he'd reversed the clock. I hadn't seen it at once because of my feelings for Ambrose. I hadn't wanted to believe Percy capable of such evil; I was already subconsciously giving Percy the benefit of the doubt. Ambrose and I had tried to teach alchemy to Percy and failed. But because Ambrose always held out hope, I did too.

"You said you'd hear me out," Percy said, a flash of the petulance surfacing. There was the young man I remembered. "I told you it wasn't an easy story to tell. Please, Zoe. Please let me tell you. Maybe then you'll understand."

I bit my lip and nodded. This was what I'd wanted: a backward alchemist who could explain to me how it worked. What was he going to tell me? Would it be possible to save Dorian's life?

But now that I had a backward alchemist right in front of me, I was frightened of what he might say.

"Go ahead," I said through trembling lips. "I'm listening."

"I know now," Percy said, "that there was a reason you didn't speak of not untrue alchemy. But I couldn't see it then, could I? I never had the same sense of discipline as you and my father. Back then, I blamed Father for spoiling me. Lucien told me I could be more. And that I could achieve it without the years of effort that might not ever pay off. He was so charismatic in how he talked about it—"

"Lucien? Are we talking about the same man? The bookseller at *Bossu Livres*?"

"He might not be charismatic now, but that's only because he's been alive so long that he's begun to lose his humanity. He was different back then."

It was one of the dangers of any type of alchemy. The longer you lived, the easier it was to disassociate from normal people, to begin thinking you were something more. I wondered if that was one of the reasons I hadn't searched as hard as I could have for Nicholas Flamel. He'd been alive since the fourteenth century. If I found him and Pernelle again, I wasn't sure I'd like what I found.

But something wasn't quite right about Percy's analysis of Lucien's change. If an alchemist lost a firm grip on human emotions, it wouldn't have made him less charismatic. Could it be that Lucien wasn't the man I'd met?

"I was young and foolish," Percy continued. "He told me my sacrifice would be cutting ties with the people I knew. Lucien was the one who arranged for the plot in the cemetery and a telegram with news of my death. I didn't want to do it, but he insisted. That's how we've lived without being found out."

"How many of you are there?"

"Not many. Around a dozen at the time of my transformation, but only three of us left that I know of. It seems like a lonely existence, I know. But I believed the stories Lucien told me." He broke off and shook his head.

"How does it work?" I asked. "How do you get a life force back?" This was the moment I'd been waiting for. The last pieces of the puzzle.

"There was a book, and we followed the formulas in the illustrations."

My heart raced. "What's the code?"

Percy blinked at me. "There's no code."

"There's always a code, Percy. We're alchemists."

He shook his head and smiled. "The whole point of backward alchemy is *shortcuts*, Zoe. The founders were lazy, lazy men. Lucien and Olav."

"Who's Olav?"

"A Viking. Exceptionally strong, but very stupid. Like the Vikings were."

I reminded myself this wasn't the time to combat Percy's stereotypes.

"The two of them were complementary," Percy continued. "With Lucien's brains and Olav's brawn, they bullied alchemists into sharing the codes of true alchemy, then used the Death Rotation to cut through the clutter and skip straight to the Elixir."

"But if there's no code in backward alchemy, then what's the secret?"

Percy swallowed hard. He sat back down at the table and reached for his water. After drinking it in one gulp, he slammed the glass down and met my gaze. "Are you going to make me say it? You're a smart woman. You already know, don't you?"

"Sacrifices," I said without realizing I was speaking out loud. "You're talking about the necessary sacrifices. It was *people* you sacrificed, wasn't it?"

Percy nodded gravely.

I'd suspected as much, but I hadn't let myself believe it because I was terrified about what that would mean for Dorian. I'd been able to keep him relatively healthy through *plant* sacrifices that also drained my own energy, but that wasn't enough. Even with the knowledge a backward alchemist could give me, I would still have to go through with a sacrifice.

It was an impossible situation. I could never purposefully take a life. There was no way I could convince myself it was right to sacrifice a life, even if it was to save another.

My phone buzzed. I scooped it into my hand so Percy wouldn't see Dorian's message.

No sacrifice, Dorian's email read. *If it is my fate to live trapped in unmoving stone, so be it.*

I swallowed a sob as I set the phone facedown on the table. Even if Dorian was ready to accept his fate, I wasn't.

TWENTY-SIX

"LUCIEN DIDN'T TELL ME about the sacrifices." Percy's chest rose and fell. He wiped sweat from his forehead with a handkerchief. "Not at first. It wasn't my fault. I was already in too deep when I found out. He started me off performing processes that weren't so different from the alchemy you and Father practiced—except that these processes involve counterclockwise Death Rotations shown in a book, skipping the long, boring steps. So it's not necessary to use a long-burning athanor furnace to cook the vessel that becomes the Philosopher's Stone. Only fire is needed, just like the book illustrations showed. The result is an ash-like substance."

"The Tea of Ashes," I whispered.

"What did you say?"

"Nothing. I'm thinking aloud. Go on."

"The result is Alchemical Ashes." Percy cleared his throat. "Could I get some more water?"

I filled Percy's glass with more water from the kitchen. It gave me a moment to think. Now I knew the real term the backward alchemists

148

used: Alchemical Ashes. But it was the same substance as in the tea I'd been making Dorian: ashes. I'd followed the coded instructions successfully. I *wasn't* missing anything. Only the sacrifice.

"And the sacrifice?" I said as I handed the glass to Percy. I remained standing over him as he accepted the water with shaking hands.

"It's the sacrifice who stirs the transformation that results in Alchemical Ashes." Percy lowered his voice and his gaze. When he continued, he whispered his words to the table. "That's how the energy gets transferred: through an apprentice who gives his life."

"An apprentice 'gives his life.' As in gives *up* his life?"

"Or *her* life, I guess I'm supposed to say, now that it's the twenty-first century." Percy forced a laugh as he again wiped sweat from his forehead. "But as far as I know, it's only been men."

And I thought *my* alchemy apprenticeship with Nicolas Flamel had been difficult. Staying awake through the night to watch the fire burning steadily in the athanor furnace was nothing compared to an apprenticeship that ends with losing your life. "Apprentices *willingly* sign up for this?"

"Well, the thing is ... "

"They don't know what they're signing up for, do they?"

"I didn't either," was Percy's indignant reply.

"You killed someone to be here today."

Percy wouldn't look up at me. "*Not* directly."

"That's splitting hairs, Percy."

"It's not, you know." His gaze snapped to mine. "I *couldn't have* killed anyone directly. The boy signed up for it himself."

"Have you ever taken responsibility for anything in your life, Percy?"

"I didn't mean to, Zoe! Please forgive me. I've never forgiven myself, but if you could forgive a child's mistake—"

"You were far from a child."

"When nobody ever treated me like an adult, how was I supposed to grow up?"

I tried to steady my breathing. "I don't want to fight with you, Percy. I want to know why you came to me. I want to know what Lucien is doing here."

"I'm getting there. I told you, you need the whole story if you're going to understand." He nervously tapped his fingers on the table. "I broke off contact with Lucien years ago, once I knew what he was. I was able to stay young through my plant sacrifices—never hurting another person, I swear. You were so good with gardening. I paid attention to that. I learned from you. I've got a garden now, so I make my own Alchemical Ashes every year or so, whenever my life force begins to fade. It's only that first transformation that requires an external sacrifice."

"It doesn't hurt you to do that?"

"To do what?"

"Make the Alchemical Ashes."

"Why would it hurt me?"

I didn't want him to know I had the backward alchemy book and had made the Alchemical Ashes for Dorian, so I had to choose my words carefully. "Based on how alchemy works, I would assume it would be extremely draining."

"It's not so bad."

"No?"

"Well," Percy continued, "it's not so bad as long as you only need to do it once a year. More frequently and you're looking for trouble."

"How do you know?"

"That's what I'm getting to." The petulant boy was back. "It's why I'm here. Even though I broke off contact with Lucien, he kept tabs on me. Several months ago, there was a change that caused our backward alchemy to become unstable. Lucien got in touch with me to see what I knew."

"Wait, you mean he *didn't know* what the change was?"

"I don't know either. That's the problem. None of us know. Several of us have already died."

This wasn't how I imagined things would go when I found a backward alchemist. They were supposed to know what was going on. "Nobody knows?" I echoed.

He shook his head. "I don't have the answers. That's what we're looking for. The book I mentioned, it's called *Non Degenera Alchemia*."

I held my tongue, even though part of me wanted to confide everything I knew. I was so close to answers. But I was also close to an unknown danger. Could I trust Percy?

"The book spelled out the secrets of not untrue alchemy," Percy continued. "It was lost or stolen ages ago, but it didn't really matter, because we had other practicing not untrue alchemists to pass down the knowledge. Lucien and Olav created the book at Notre Dame, and after that, a small secret society followed their work, meeting at Notre Dame."

That explained the book's connection to Notre Dame. And how Dorian had been brought to life by accident. He'd been created specifically for Notre Dame. Life forces were linked.

"Why did Lucien need the information in the book if he's the one who created it?" I asked.

Percy shrugged. "Maybe he forgot. That's the reason he wrote the information down, right? So he wouldn't have to remember it."

"But you just said he, Olav, and others passed down the knowledge."

Another shrug. "Maybe there's something special about the book itself."

"You don't know what's special about it, though?"

"I already said that, didn't I?"

I called upon every ounce of my will power to avoid strangling, or at least slapping, the lazy man in front of me. "If you had this book, would it save you? Is there something in there that would stop the shift? Something that doesn't involve another sacrifice?"

"It doesn't matter, because how would we find it? It's been gone forever."

"Nobody looked for it?"

Percy shrugged yet again. "Why would we? We'd already gotten what we needed from it."

I shook with frustration. Backward alchemists and their shortcuts! They didn't see the power of true knowledge. I circled the table. Clockwise. Was I subconsciously trying to counteract the backward Death Rotation?

"But now," Percy said, "our energy is fading. It's fading at different speeds, but fading all the same. Even mine."

"You could have saved yourself a lot of my skepticism if you'd come right out and said you wanted help. That's your real motivation for coming here, isn't it?"

"Lucien really did follow you here from Paris. I'm not making this up."

"I didn't say you made it up. I believe you want to help me too. But it's not your main focus. You want to save yourself."

"Is that so bad? For all of time, man has been interested in self-preservation."

"I'm all for self-preservation. Just not when it involves murdering others."

"I didn't kill anyone on purpose, I swear. And I stepped back from it once I knew. I'm not a bad guy. I didn't have it in me to do it again. It was only Lucien. After the inexplicable shift, he made another sacrifice—"

I gasped. "He killed someone else? Now? This year?"

"The sacrifice didn't work, though. He's still aging rapidly. All of us who are left have been aging quickly for the past few months."

"That doesn't make sense, Percy. That would mean you were, what, twelve years old last month? Or ten?"

Percy smiled. I couldn't believe he actually smiled moments after telling me a man he knew had recently murdered someone. "It's thanks to you that I'm spared, Zoe. I was a few years younger a few months ago, and because of my thriving *potager* garden, I've been able to keep myself relatively young." His smile faltered. "But I've run out of plants. We're all desperate to discover what changed. Lucien thinks the answer is in *Non Degenera Alchemia*."

"What does that have to do with me?"

Percy stood up and crossed his arms confidently. Several inches taller than me, he positioned himself to look down his nose at me. "Why were you in Paris, Zoe?"

"I used to live there, you know."

Percy stood so close to me I could feel his stale breath on my face. Yet I refused to back away.

"You went to Lucien's bookshop in Paris," Percy said, "asking questions about alchemy. You made him suspicious. Lucien now believes you have this book. That's why he's here. He wants that book, and he won't stop until he gets it."

TWENTY-SEVEN

"IT'S RIDICULOUS OF LUCIEN to think you've got the book," Percy continued. "*Zoe Faust* in possession of a backward alchemy book?"

"Absurd," I murmured. It was my turn to avoid his gaze.

I thought back on all of my interactions with Lucien. I couldn't imagine him as the charismatic leader Percy had described. What had I said to Lucien to arouse his suspicions that I was a true alchemist, let alone that I had his backward alchemy book? It couldn't simply be the interest I expressed in alchemy. There were many people out there like Ivan, who weren't true alchemists but who had an interest in alchemy. That's why there were so many modern books on the subject.

"Why would Lucien even think I have this book?" I asked as casually as I could.

Percy shrugged. "Something you said made him suspect it. He mentioned that you two talked about the Cabaret de L'Enfer, but I don't know why that would mean you had *Non Degenera Alchemia*."

I groaned. "I do. Or rather, I bet I know why he suspected me of being an alchemist. He saw me looking at a photo of a Hell-mouth door that led into the nightclub I once knew well—a hundred years ago. He asked if I knew it. I said I'd read about it, but I'm sure my face revealed the truth." Caught up in those memories, I also might have slipped into colloquial French. Not a problem in and of itself, since many Americans speak fluent French, but my conversational French is from a century ago.

"Lucien didn't realize you were someone I cared about," Percy said, "or he wouldn't have told me he was going to get the book *by any means necessary*. I didn't like the tone in his voice when he said it. I didn't like it one bit."

"He admitted that to you?"

Percy's eyes darted nervously around the house. "He, uh, might have thought I was on his side. Because I, uh, told him who you were. Don't get angry! I didn't mean to do it. He caught me off guard. I hadn't seen him in ages, and he showed up on my doorstep with a photograph of you. He took it on his mobile phone while you were browsing at his crummy little bookshop. I asked him why he had a photo of Zoe Faust … He'd heard of you because you're one of the few women alchemists taken on as apprentices with a master. You can't blame me for that, can you?"

"It's not your fault, Percy," I said, half believing my words.

"I'm glad you can see that. Lucien said you left Paris abruptly. Otherwise I bet he would have stolen the book from you in Paris."

"The book I don't have, you mean."

"I meant he would have *attempted* to steal it from you in Paris. I don't know how he found you in Portland, though."

I put my head in my hands. "I gave him my address."

"I know he can be a charmer, Zoe, but giving a strange man your address—"

"For him to send me a *book*, Percy. He's a bookseller."

"Oh."

"How did *you* find me?" I asked.

"I knew the name of your apothecary shop." He pulled out a cell phone and scrolled for a minute. He held up the web page to my online business, now an "antiques" store as opposed to an apothecary. Brixton's friend Veronica Chen-Mendoza had overhauled the website. The bottom listed my home address. Veronica didn't know I was hiding.

"I came to your house this morning but nobody was home," Percy said. "I peeked into the recycling bin outside and saw a takeaway cup with a stamp that said Blue Sky Teas." He said it like riffling through someone's trash was the most natural thing in the world. "I knew I had the right house, because you've got the oldest car on the block. Is it from the forties? I don't know how you keep it running."

"It's called hard work."

The dig was lost on Percy. "Aren't you worried you might give yourself away with the alchemical artifacts you sell through Elixir and that old truck?"

"Apothecary wares are cool again, hadn't you heard? Hiding in plain sight has been working well for me." *Until last week.* "Let's get back on track, Percy, since there's a madman out there."

"God, I could use a beer."

"It's ten o'clock in the morning."

"It's six o'clock in the evening in England. Seven in France."

"No beer." My phone buzzed. I ignored it. I'd forgotten Dorian was listening to our conversation through the pipes, but I knew perfectly well there was beer in the kitchen for a beer-battered vegetable tempura recipe. "I think it would be helpful for me to understand more about this book."

"You've never come across it over the years, have you? You sell so many antique books. If you and I find it before Lucien, we could use it to help us. Not sacrificing anyone again, of course. But I'm already immortal; I only need to figure out how to stop whatever change happened."

"We're not immortal, Percy."

"Speak for yourself." He flexed his muscles, clearly pleased he had the toned body of a twenty-five-year-old.

"Your cells have stopped aging, but we can both die. You realize that, don't you?"

Percy frowned. In denial, as always.

I weighed my options and made a decision on instinct. I trusted that Percy didn't wish to harm me, but I didn't trust him to keep my secrets under pressure.

"I came across photographs of the book you spoke of," I said. "That's what sent me to Paris to research alchemy's connection to the cathedral of Notre Dame. When overlaid, the woodcut illustrations pointed to the cathedral." Everything I said was true except that I possessed the original book, not only photographs. And that it was fire that had shown me how the illustrations fit together.

Percy nodded vigorously. "That's where the not untrue alchemists used to meet. Where did you find the photos? Do you have them?"

"Not here. They're at a friend's house. He's an alchemy scholar—" I swore.

"What is it?"

"Someone was seen spying on my friend Ivan—the alchemy scholar I mentioned. I'm sure it was Lucien. And you don't know about the murder victim who may have been an alchemist, do you?"

"*Murder*?" Percy flipped his head around. Was he making sure Lucien wasn't hiding behind the couch?

"It's an old murder. A decade old, something like that. But the odd thing is that the body was found in a cabin in the woods with alchemy supplies, and I think Lucien was seen there too. What was he doing there?"

157

"He's after the bloody book, Zoe. Your friend is in danger, as are we. Even though Lucien can't kill you directly—"

"Of course he could kill me. Especially if he's as bad a guy as you're making him out to be."

"You don't know?" Percy blinked at me. "Of course you wouldn't, since you've never killed anyone." Percy shook his head and spoke as if addressing a toddler. "The Elixir of Life is a transformation of the life force. If an alchemist kills a living being directly, their own life force is taken away. That's what I was talking about earlier, how the sacrifice has to be volunteered. You understand?"

Was he attempting to lecture me on alchemy? Not only was he condescending, but he was completely wrong.

"Percy, that's an old wives' tale. There's nothing stopping anyone on earth from killing another person. Aside from their moral compass. Or fear of being caught."

"No, it's true. That's why Lucien hasn't killed the rest of us. He's a very bad man, Zoe, but he's afraid he'll die if he goes too far. The sacrifices are different, because they're *willing* participants. Unwitting, but it's still their choice to sacrifice themselves."

"Then why do you think Lucien is so dangerous?"

Percy bit his lip. "There are many things that can be done to a person without killing them."

I shivered. It was an absurd theory, but if Lucien and Percy believed it …

"Give me a minute," I said.

I stepped into the living room, keeping my eyes on Percy while I called Ivan. Thankfully he picked up the phone immediately. "This is going to sound strange," I said, "but I need you to take what I'm going to say seriously."

"With you, Zoe, I've ceased thinking of anything as strange."

"There's a man called Lucien who's stalking people and places related to alchemy."

"This man is harassing you? How can I help?"

"Yes, and he might harass you too. And he could be dangerous."

"I'll be careful. What does he look like?"

"He looks like … " I closed my eyes and tried to think about how to describe such a nondescript man. "Average-looking guy, but don't underestimate him."

When I opened my eyes, Percy was gone.

"I can take care of myself," Ivan was saying, "but I thank you for your concern. I'll be careful."

Percy was a bigger concern, so I ended the call with Ivan. The kitchen door swung open a moment later. Percy emerged with a platter of misshapen vegan pastries.

"God these are good," he said. "Why didn't you cook like this when I knew you? I'm starving after that long flight."

"Where are you staying?"

"Nowhere yet." He indicated the small satchel he'd dropped inside the door.

"That's the entirety of your luggage?"

"I've never understood why people in this century feel the need to travel with so many possessions."

"In some ways you're very much your father's son."

"I'm so sorry about what happened to him, you know." His face was filled with such sincerity that my eyes welled with tears. "I wish—I wish I could take it all back."

I didn't completely trust Percy, but I wondered … Could we help each other?

TWENTY-EIGHT

DORIAN STOMPED ACROSS THE tiled kitchen floor. "How could you do it? How could you let him stay here?"

Percy had gone to a restaurant for lunch, so Dorian and I were alone in the house. As tasty as Dorian's pastries were, Percy had insisted there was no way he would eat a vegan lunch. Dorian and I were in the kitchen with the curtains drawn, as always. I was making a summer salad with a bounty from the backyard garden that Brixton had been keeping up, and Dorian was slicing freshly baked French bread for sandwiches.

"You keep talking about the perfection of Julian Lake's kitchen," I said, "and the delicacies he'll order for you. Why don't you stay there for a few days—and take your book with you. I want to keep Percy close and the book far away."

"*Je ne comprend pas.* Do you or do you not trust him?"

"I haven't yet made up my mind. But he's a backward alchemist. We need the information he can give us."

"You do not need to pretend with me, Zoe. I heard every word. I know there is no hope. I will not stand for the sacrifice of an innocent to save me."

"We don't know that's the only way."

Dorian didn't answer. Instead, he selected a paprika-infused sea salt and handed it to me. "This one will be good with the salad."

Though I'm not the cook Dorian is, I've always been intrigued by how salt can bring out the flavors of the simplest foods. Unlike some unnecessary culinary flourishes, salt fulfills a body's basic needs. Throughout history, salt has played an important role in society and culture because of how essential it is for the body. It's why salt, along with sulfur and mercury, is one of the three essentials in alchemy. In that *tria prima*, salt represents the body, and is the child of sulfur and mercury.

As Dorian skillfully tossed a salad using only one hand, my phone buzzed. It was a text message from Brixton, asking if Dorian could prepare a feast for two dozen people—tonight. I called Brixton back to tell him it was bad timing. To my surprise, he picked up his phone.

"I got your message, Brix, but that's awfully short notice. We can't just—"

"Blue's home," he said. "She's out of jail."

I could hear the joy in his voice. It was so innocent and blissful that I nearly forgot the tragedies swirling around me. "That's wonderful. I didn't know she was being released so soon."

"She didn't want to tell any of us in advance. I guess she didn't really believe it was going to happen, until she was actually out. Isn't it wicked awesome news? Especially with Mom so upset about her dad maybe being dead. Blue's sure to cheer her up. Have you noticed she has a way of doing that?"

I smiled even though neither the teenager on the other end of the line nor the gargoyle absorbed in his cooking could see me.

"She definitely does have a way about her," I agreed.

"She showed up at her cottage today. Mom and Abel thought having a welcome home party for all of her friends would be even better than keeping her to ourselves. Is Dorian there? Can I talk to him?"

"He's busy. But I'm sure he'd be happy to cook."

"I am not busy," Dorian called out behind me. He hopped down from his stepping stool and snatched the phone from me. "Allo? *Oui. Oui.*" He nodded thoughtfully. "This is a superb idea. If only Zoe had not banished me from my home—"

"I didn't banish you." I tried to grab the phone back. Dorian shushed me and scurried away. "I'll keep Percy out of the house this afternoon, so you can cook before you move into Julian Lake's house for a few days."

"*Merci.*" He handed the phone back to me.

"I'll make sure Dorian has everything he needs to cook," I told Brixton, "then bring the food to the teashop tonight."

"Cool. This is going to be wicked."

"You're going to be with Blue and your parents the whole afternoon, right?"

I swear I could hear the sound of his eyes rolling. "Sure, probably."

"I'm serious. There's a killer—"

"No, there's not. Those cops told me I was wrong and the guy had been there for years. That's why they think my grandfather—"

"I know. I'm sorry, Brix. But the man you saw spying on Ivan is a very dangerous man. I don't know what he has to do with the man who was found, but he's killed before."

A pause came from the other end of the line, then a swear word I chose to ignore. "Seriously?"

"Seriously. You need to stay far away from him. Don't go anywhere on your own."

After I hung up the phone, I had to figure out how to keep Percy out of the house all day. He was expecting me to pick him up in a little over an hour, so I had time to figure it out.

I drove to the market to get the ingredients on Dorian's shopping list. Usually I walked to local shops or farmer's markets every few days, to supplement the vegetables from the garden and the staples in the pantry, but today I was both in a hurry and needed to buy in bulk. After surviving the fluorescent lights at the supermarket, I dropped off four bags of groceries with Dorian. I was about to head back out to pick up Percy, but Dorian stopped me as he looked through the sacks of food.

"Where is the garlic?" he asked.

"We already have plenty of garlic." I pointed to four heads of garlic, Purple Stripe hardneck, and Western Rose softneck.

Dorian narrowed his black eyes. "I need more for this tomato sauce recipe."

"Are you sure garlic pasta is the way to go for a party?"

He chuckled. "If everyone eats the garlic, they will not mind."

"Remind me to pick some parsley from the backyard to mute the effects."

"Garlic will welcome your friend home with luck."

I paused at the swinging kitchen door. "I didn't realize you were superstitious."

He clicked his tongue. "Not superstitious. Food has cultural significance, as you of all people should understand. It feeds both the body and the soul. Everything I am creating for tonight will welcome Blue Sky home."

I leaned in the door frame and looked over the left half of Dorian's body that was rapidly turning to stone. He didn't dwell on his limitations. "Thank you. That's so thoughtful."

Dorian waved off the comment, and moved his stepping stool to unpack the last bag of groceries. The simple task took longer than usual, since he could only use his right arm to lift the stool.

"I can help when I get back," I said.

"It is unnecessary. I have selected recipes that only require the use of one good arm." Dorian said the words casually, but he didn't look at me. He peered into the grocery bag containing the first tomatoes of the season and shook his head. "I will make do," he muttered, dismissing me with a wave of his clawed hand.

I smiled and left Dorian to the feast preparations. I did a quick walk-through of the house, making sure it was tightly secured and thinking about how different my life had been six months ago. I used to eat for healing and nourishment, with pleasure coming in last on my list of priorities. Since Dorian had come into my life, he'd shown me that delectable foods didn't have to be unhealthy. Which was an accidental discovery.

When Dorian showed up on my doorstep—or, in a moving crate in my living room, to be more accurate—he learned I didn't keep bacon, butter, or cream in the house. Dorian respected my eating habits, but he refused to eat the same "boring" food I ate. I used my flavored oils, salts, and vinegars to season simple soups, stews, and salads, but in cooking with what I had on hand, he showed me how easy it was to turn simple meals into mouthwatering feasts.

I knew why I was thinking so much about food. I was starving. I'd been feeling so anxious I hadn't stopped to take care of myself. I knew better than to disregard my body. I stuck my head back into the kitchen to grab a snack to take with me. The thoughtful gargoyle was one step ahead of me. He handed me a toasted baguette sandwich wrapped in parchment paper.

My friend and I were so alike but also worlds apart.

And that gave me the perfect idea for what to do with Percy. I slipped up to the attic before leaving the house.

———————

I picked up Percy from a local brewery where he was enjoying an extended lunch accompanied by beer and a pretty young woman. She wasn't happy to see me, but she perked up when Percy whispered something in her ear before paying the bill.

"Not too worried about Lucien after all?" I said once we were on the sidewalk.

"I was in a darkened back booth, so I knew I'd see him before he saw me."

I led Percy to the truck. My myrrh air freshener was no match for the scent of batch brewed beer that had ensconced itself in Percy's clothing.

"I thought you lived in the other direction," he said as I pulled onto the highway.

"I need the house to myself to cook for a good friend's welcome home party tonight, so I've got another idea—"

Percy gaped at me. "I'm dying and you're having a party?"

The words bristled. Percy was in much better shape than Dorian. And one of the lessons I'd learned after being alive for so long was that you need to slow down and enjoy the small moments in life. Not only did they make existence more meaningful, but they helped you see things more clearly. I was going to give myself this evening to celebrate life with Blue, Brixton, and Max. I didn't know what would happen the next day, but time with them tonight was a gift I could give all of us.

"I'm going to help you help yourself," I said. "I found the photocopied pages of that book we were talking about." I pointed to my purse that lay at Percy's feet. He lunged for it and greedily scooped up the pages.

"You have it," he said. "You have it! Where did you find these?"

"I used to do a lot of research. I found those pages years ago. You're the one who's the backward alchemist. I'm going to leave you at a library."

"A library? Zoe, are you serious? I can stay out of the way at your house."

"I need to concentrate, and so do you. You can read these pages and see what they tell you."

"But—"

"I'll pick you up in four hours. You can come to the party with me."

"Can we have dinner first?"

"Didn't you hear me? I'm going home to cook for the party."

"But you're cooking vegan food."

Family.

TWENTY-NINE

Long before I saw her, I knew Blue was there. The fragrance of her homemade teas filled the cozy space. I'm sure it was my imagination, but even the weeping fig tree in the center of the cafe appeared to have perked up that night. The illusion was created because the tree-ring tables that normally circled the living tree had been moved aside to make room for the crowd that had gathered to welcome Blue home.

I'd dropped off Dorian's feast before picking up Percy from the library. Unsurprisingly, Percy hadn't gleaned anything useful from the hours surrounded by information.

As Percy and I walked into the party in full swing, everyone was facing the back of the café. The sound of two acoustic guitars strumming with two voices harmonizing echoed through the teashop. Abel and Brixton were performing "Imagine," a perfect choice for the occasion. Their voices blended to create perfectly imperfect harmony. Their arms moved in rhythm on their guitars.

The song concluded. Heather whistled and the crowd applauded. I caught a glimpse of wild gray hair moving stealthily through the crowd, toward Brixton. My heart skipped a beat as I thought about how easy it would be for someone to get to Brixton if they wanted to. Blue snuck up behind Brixton and gave him a hug. He turned nearly as red as the beets in my garden but hugged her back.

I saw another smiling face in the crowd. Max Liu. He must have felt my eyes on him, because his gaze met mine. I felt my stomach give a little flip-flop as his smile grew wider.

"These two are way too good," Blue said to the crowd. "I'm calling for a forced break so you'll all eat this wonderful spread of food Zoe prepared for the occasion. Eat!" She caught my eye and winked.

"First," Max said, "a toast to the heart of the neighborhood." He raised a clay mug of tea. "Blue, you were here for me during a rough time in my life, and you made me feel at home. I can confidently say that every person here feels the same way. Thank you, Blue."

"Hear, hear!" several voices chimed in.

Blue wiped a tear from her eye. "I'm only crying because the food is getting cold." She laughed and cleared her throat. "This is the first place that's ever truly felt like home."

I knew the feeling more acutely than she or anyone else in that room knew. I wished I could have told Blue how much I related.

We all knew Blue Sky as the owner of Blue Sky Teas, the woman who knew how to brew exquisite teas, who'd helped Brixton with his homework at the teashop since he was in elementary school, and who brightened any room with her infectiously relaxed demeanor.

But the woman who let her curly gray hair run wild and lived in baggy jeans also had a past that nobody knew about until earlier that year.

"Thanks for welcoming me back," Blue concluded. "Now eat!" I could barely imagine blissfully chubby and exuberant Blue Sky as Brenda Skyler, a stick-thin workaholic who wore power suits, dieted, and worked for her husband's legal practice, where she unknowingly helped him with illegal schemes. She wasn't culpable for the crimes she didn't know about, but she was guilty of forging documents and faking her own death to begin her new life.

The woman in the teashop that evening was a mix of the two. She'd lost weight in jail, and her radiant face, usually full of natural color from the time she spent wildcrafting outside, was pale.

The party guest list included me, Brixton, Heather, Abel, Brixton's best friends Veronica and Ethan, Max, and a dozen of Blue's friends who I hadn't previously met, as well as Percy, who I'd brought along with me. Ivan wasn't feeling well enough to attend.

The teashop usually closed at seven o'clock in the evening, but tonight it was open for this private party. Two of the tree-ring tables had been pushed together for the spread of food prepared by Dorian in my kitchen that afternoon. I needn't have worried about his infirmity. He'd outdone himself with a freekeh and parsley salad , freshly baked bread with garlic tomato sauce for dipping, bowls of nuts, each home-roasted with a different spice mix, plus a dessert tray of miniature tarts and mousses. Everyone congratulated me on the food.

"How did you get the tomato sauce so creamy?" Heather asked, popping a bite of sauce-dipped bread into her mouth.

"A chef never reveals her secrets," I said. I'd have to ask Dorian later. She was right. A delicate flavor I couldn't place added depth and balance to the flavorful garlic.

Heather had woven a banner out of wildflowers that was supposed to read WELCOME HOME BLUE. But some of the flowers refused to be tamed, so by the time the party started the string of letters read EL ME HOME BLUE. Blue loved it.

The teenagers took photographs of people standing under the sign to share on social media. Percy and I ducked out of the way as photos were snapped.

"It was so much easier before every bloody man, woman, and child had a damn mobile phone," Percy whispered.

During a short break for everyone to fill their plates, I introduced Percy to my friends. Brixton and Abel resumed the live music, with Brixton still on his acoustic guitar, and Abel switching to a banjo. I wished Tobias could have been there to sing, but I knew he was exactly where he needed to be, spending precious last moments with his beloved Rosa.

Max brought me a lemon tart. "Penny for your thoughts."

I took a bite of the tart, giving myself a few moments to think. "The tart is more tart than I expected," I said. *Smooth, Zoe.*

"You didn't taste them at home?"

Damn. "Too many things to sample. I trusted the recipe." *Please don't ask what's in it*, I thought to myself. Although from the flavors dancing on my tongue, I could guess most of the ingredients, the two dominant ones being coconut oil and lemon.

Max nodded and bit into a chocolate mousse tart.

The connection between us from the day before was missing, and I knew why. He kept glancing distractedly at Percy.

"You asked what I was thinking about," I said. "I was thinking about how beautiful it is that so many people came to celebrate with Blue at the very last minute."

"It's lovely," Max said. Unlike our generic conversation. Max stole another glance at Percy, who was on the outskirts of a small group with Blue.

"You never told me the story of the plastic skeleton in your house," I prompted.

"It was Chadna's during med school."

Great. He was jealous of Percy and I'd asked about his dead ex-wife. But instead of the reaction I was expecting, a grin spread across Max's face.

"She refused to tell me why she kept it so long. On each of my birthdays, she'd tell me a little bit more of the story. That way she said I'd be forced to live a long life with her, to hear the end of the story."

"That's beautiful."

The smile on Max's face faded as I felt a tap at my elbow. Percy.

"I'm going to get more food," Max said.

"What's up, Percy?" I asked.

"I'm tired. I thought I'd go back to the house for an early night. Could I have the key?"

"You don't have to lie to me," I said.

"Fair enough." Percy shrugged. "I was trying to be sly about giving you some time with your beau and letting you have fun at the fete."

Maybe Percy had grown up, after all. I gave Percy a key and made sure he remembered how to walk back to the house.

"GPS," he said, shaking his phone at me.

Brixton and Abel amped up the music. Blue began to dance with her friends. I was reminded of my love for Portland when I couldn't tell the difference between Blue's forager friends and the group of lawyers who'd come to her aid. Perhaps they were one and the same. Brixton was busy playing guitar and his friend Ethan was too cool for dancing, so Veronica joined the group of older women and let loose. At fourteen, she was already the tallest woman in the group. Her cascading black hair tossed from side to side in rhythm with the music. The awkward young woman I'd met six months before was slipping away, innocent adolescence sacrificed for a more fully formed young adulthood.

Max pulled me from the corner in which I was hiding to dance with him. Looking into his eyes, my stomach fluttered. Things were starting to feel like they had before Percy arrived in Portland—until Max abruptly stopped dancing.

His eyes narrowed and he walked to the door of the teashop without a word.

Two men in suits stood at the door. Even though they weren't dressed in policemen's uniforms, their stance and Max's interaction with them suggested they were detectives. With the volume of the music, from across the teashop I couldn't hear what they were saying, but Max was shaking his head. *No no no.* Had I dismissed the French police too soon?

The two men were insistent. Max shook his head one last time, then led them around the weeping fig tree in the center of the teashop. Not to me.

To Heather.

With an abrupt jerk of his arm, Abel broke off strumming his guitar. He smiled as he stood and whispered to Brixton to continue playing. I knew that look of bravado on Abel's face was a mask applied for the benefit of his stepson. Brixton tried to argue but ultimately listened to his stepfather.

As soon as the music resumed, people forgot about the interruption. They went back to dancing and eating. Nobody else seemed to notice that the newcomers weren't welcome guests. I followed Max and Abel to the corner where the detectives were talking with Heather.

"It'll be easier if we talk to you both down at the station," one of them was saying to her.

"What's this about?" Abel asked. "Did you confirm the identity of the man Brix found?"

"You are?"

"Her husband."

"It's okay, hon," Heather said, stroking Abel's arm.

"Please step aside, sir," the detective said. I hoped Brixton was too busy on the guitar to see the look the detective directed at Abel, or I feared the impetuous teenager might try to punch the detective.

"You have no right to interrupt this private party," Abel said, his voice rising. Brixton's guitar riff ended with a discordant crash. He flung the instrument aside and ran to his mom. All eyes followed him.

"It's okay, Brix," Heather said. "They only want to talk to us."

"Us?" Brixton asked.

Heather linked her arm through Brixton's, stood on her tiptoes to kiss him on the side of his head, then nodded to the detectives.

"Now?" Brixton said, pulling away from his mom. "They can't just—"

"It's okay, sweetie," Heather said softly.

Brixton looked to his stepfather. With a clenched jaw, Abel nodded at Brixton. Then Max, Abel, and Brixton followed the detectives out the door.

Blue tried to assure everyone that it was a private family matter and nothing to worry about, but the party broke up after that.

I walked home alone, wondering what the detectives had found out about Heather's father. Why wouldn't they answer Abel's question? It seemed simple enough.

Walking up my driveway, my senses tingled. I haven't survived as long as I have without listening to the subtle cues surrounding us that we pick up as intuition. Something was different, but what? I chastised myself. I had a house guest. I must have noticed the subtle movement of him moving behind a closed curtain. I continued walking, but stopped as soon as I passed my Chevy truck and Airstream trailer.

The front door was ajar.

I ran to the door and pushed it open. The living room had been ransacked.

"Percy?" I called out.

No answer.

I ran through the house. The lock to my basement alchemy lab had been broken open. I grabbed a heavy flashlight and crept down the stairs. With each step, my heart pounded more loudly in my ears.

At the base of the basement stairs, Percy lay unconscious on the concrete floor, his hair wet with blood.

THIRTY

"I'm all right," Percy croaked. But he clearly wasn't. Blood covered the side of his head.

"I'll call an ambulance."

"No." He grabbed my wrist. "Too many questions. You know that."

He was right. But he was also in bad shape. In worse shape than my natural remedies could fix.

"All right," I said as Percy struggled to sit up. "Let go of my arm and I promise I'll get supplies, not call an ambulance."

He obliged then sank back to the floor. I rushed upstairs to get supplies.

After I'd cleaned his head wound, I saw he wasn't as badly off as I'd feared. Head wounds tend to bleed a lot, but the gash itself wouldn't need my sloppy stitches after all. I led him to the bedroom he was using, exchanged his bloody shirt for a fresh one, and applied a healing salve that would serve as a natural antibiotic.

"Was it Lucien?" I asked, holding an ice pack to the side of his head.

He nodded and winced in pain.

175

"I don't suppose you have any Paracetamol? No, I didn't think you would."

"He was after *Non Degenera Alchemia*?"

"It appears that way. I'm so sorry I couldn't stop him—"

"I'm sorry I left you alone. Neither of us should be on our own right now."

A knock on the door sounded from below.

"You'll be all right." I tucked him into bed before running downstairs.

At the front door I found Max. He looked infinitely more frazzled than he had an hour before. Brixton sat on the porch steps behind him, a banjo slung over his back.

"Abel is with Heather at the police station," Max said. "I thought I could look after Brix—"

"I'm almost fifteen," Brixton cut in. "Nobody needs to look after me."

"But I was called into the station," Max continued. "So I can't keep an eye on him. I hate to impose upon Blue the day she's out of jail. Can he hang out here until his mom can pick him up?"

I hesitated for long enough that Max picked up on the delay. At the sound of creaking floorboards overhead, he stepped in front of Brixton and shifted into a combative stance.

"It's fine," I said. "Everything is fine. I just have a visitor. Ambrose's son Percy is staying here."

"Oh," Max said, his voice curt. "I didn't realize he'd be staying with you. We can go. Sorry to have bothered you. I'll figure out something else."

"It's no bother," I said. "Brix, since the party got cut short and you were busy making music, I bet you're hungry. There's a lot of food in the fridge."

"I'm not hungry." Brixton glared at me. "But I'll pretend to eat something so you two can talk." He pushed past us and disappeared through the kitchen's swinging door.

"Smart kid," Max said.

"I don't think he likes being treated like a kid. Come inside. What did you want to talk about?" I took a step toward Max, but he turned away. He strode across the living room and gripped the back of a dining room chair.

"What's going on, Max? Is the man Brixton's grandfather? Why the secrecy?"

The sound of scales being played on a banjo came from the kitchen.

"This case keeps getting stranger," Max said. "The lab guys got things wrong. This isn't an old case after all. Some of those chemicals we found in the shack's laboratory messed with the speed of decomposition. The man Brixton found was killed *this past week*."

Oh no . . . "That means Brixton *is* a witness to a murder." Had Lucien killed a new apprentice in a makeshift alchemy lab here in Portland? Was that what Percy was hinting at?

Max swallowed hard and nodded.

"Then why," I asked, "were the detectives interested in Heather and Brixton, if it's not Brix's grandfather after all?"

"I didn't say that."

"So it *is* Heather's father? That's why they're questioning her?"

"Not exactly."

"What does that mean, *not exactly*? It's both her dad and *not* her dad?"

"He hasn't been identified yet. There are no teeth to test for dental records, and DNA testing doesn't work that quickly. But now that we know it's a new death, it's unlikely to be Heather's father."

"Then why—"

"Those guys don't have the best social skills. Because of the new information about the probable timing of death, they wanted to get more details from Brixton about what he saw. As a minor, they needed his mom present."

"So it was Brixton they wanted?"

"At first." Max rubbed his eyes. "But Heather's manner made them suspicious."

"So now they're talking more with her alone."

Max nodded. "She wasn't doing herself any favors. The first time they talked with her, she wouldn't agree to a voluntary DNA swab when they thought it was her dad, which could prove or disprove a familial match, since there weren't teeth for a dental match."

"She had every right to refuse an invasive test."

"It's a swab across her cheek, Zoe."

"Which you said was *voluntary*. Of course she'd decline." I feared the day when modern technology would make it impossible for me to keep my privacy. I'd already avoided many educational and job opportunities because I didn't want to be in more databases than necessary.

"Even when it could have helped her learn if it was her dad?" Max said. "Look, never mind. I don't want to have a stupid fight. I get it that privacy rights are important. *I* don't think she behaved suspiciously. But it's not my case."

"Meaning you're going to let them—"

"They're good cops, Zoe. We all want the truth."

"How's Brixton doing with all this?"

"Not great. If he was okay, he'd be fine on his own at home." He glanced at his phone. "Look, I've gotta run. You sure it's okay for Brixton to be here with you while your houseguest is here?"

"Positive." With Lucien on the loose, I wanted Brixton close.

"You two aren't ... " He cleared his throat. "You sure you don't need privacy?"

"He's Ambrose's son, Max."

"Yeah, but he's a lot closer to your age."

"Age is meaningless." I took his hands in mine. I believed the words I spoke, and he must have seen it in my eyes. He squeezed my hand and gave me a slow kiss on the cheek before departing. The fresh scent of citrus lingered even after he was gone. A small piece of his comforting presence remained with me.

———

In spite of his claims that he wasn't hungry, I found Brixton eating a sweet potato pie straight from the pan.

"I thought you and Max were a couple," Brixton said through a mouthful.

"We are." Maybe. I hoped.

"Then who's the guy singing in the shower?"

"Percy. You met him tonight." From the kitchen, if I listened carefully, I could hear the singing coming from the bathroom above us.

"Your ex's kid? No offense, but he's kind of a tool."

I tried not to laugh.

"See?" Brixton said. "I'm totally right, aren't I?"

"I wouldn't say you're wrong."

"So is alchemy, like, hereditary?"

"It's easier to find out about alchemy if you know an alchemist," I said, "but it's not inherited."

Brixton nodded thoughtfully. He set down the half-empty pan of pie and hopped up onto the counter. Dorian hated it when he did that, but I liked how it made the house feel more like a home.

"I don't want you to teach me, Zoe. I don't want to learn alchemy." He picked up a sprig of spearmint from the kitchen's window box and twirled it in his fingers, looking at the spinning green pinwheel in his fingertips as he spoke. "I know Ivan wants to learn, since he's dying. But I think it would suck to outlive Veronica and Ethan, and anyone else I'll ever care about. I'll probably already outlive Abel and Mom." He squished the mint in his hand, releasing the scent into the air.

"Max told me what the police discovered."

"About the skin under his fingernails?"

"I meant how long the man had been dead. They found skin under his fingernails?" Was that the real reason they wanted Heather to voluntarily give her DNA? I decided now wasn't the time to worry Brixton about his mom. It wouldn't be her DNA under his fingernails regardless.

"I told you I wasn't lying about the body being new."

"We need to talk about something else serious." I lowered my voice. "Quickly, in case Percy is feeling better and comes downstairs. I hate to do this right now, when I know you've got so much else on your mind."

"It's cool."

"Percy came to Portland because he knows the man you saw spying on Ivan. The man's name is Lucien, and he's a dangerous backward alchemist. Percy fell in with him a century ago, and got caught up in backward alchemy, but Lucien is after Dorian's book, so Percy wanted to warn me."

"Whoa. He doesn't seem like the kind of guy who'd look out for other people."

"With everything that's happening around here, I'm glad you've got good intuition." Even though I could hear Percy still singing Spice Girls songs in the shower, I kept my voice low. "You're right. I don't trust him completely, so I haven't told him about Dorian or that I have Dorian's book. He's not the most altruistic of men. He also wants my help. He's suffering the same alchemical fate as Dorian,"

"His body is returning to its original form?" Brixton asked.

I groaned. Brixton's concise summation made me realize I'd made a significant oversight. I knew that with his life force deteriorating, Dorian would be alive but trapped in stone *because he was originally made of stone*. With a *human* backward alchemist's life force quickly deteriorating, they'd transform into their original flesh and bone—as their flesh and bones would have with age.

"Zoe, are you okay? You look like you've seen a ghost or something."

"Something much worse. I think I've seen the truth about a backward alchemist."

"Wicked. What is it?"

"I need you to tell me exactly what happened when you saw Lucien go into the shack in the woods."

"I told you, I saw that Lucien guy, who'd been spying on Ivan, go into the shack and then kill some guy."

"But you didn't see him do the actual killing."

"No."

"You saw Lucien sneak out?"

Brixton hesitated, and I knew I was right.

"I might not have actually seen him," Brixton said. "But it was all loud, like a fight, and then it was quiet."

"You didn't see anyone else coming near the shed?"

"No. I waited a while, and after it was quiet for a really long time, I looked inside. That's when I saw the dead guy."

"A dead man who didn't look like Lucien."

"No, this guy was way older. That's how I knew Lucien must have slipped out the back when I was too far away to see him."

"You didn't see the body until a few minutes after he died."

"So?"

"That means," I said, "that the dead man is Lucien."

"I saw the guy, Zoe. He's not—"

"Lucien was a backward alchemist. His life force was reversing, so once he died, his body would wither much more quickly than that of a normal person. That's what's confused this whole situation. You saw him shortly after he died and thought he was an old man. The police saw him a short time later and thought he'd been dead for a decade."

Brixton kicked a kitchen cabinet. "And the police don't know about alchemy, so once they figured out the body was changing they thought it was the chemicals from the alchemy lab. So, he did an experiment wrong or something?"

I gripped the edge of the counter. "I don't think so. Percy isn't here to warn me. He fooled me, making me think he was being thoughtful tonight when really he wanted time alone in my house. Percy followed Lucien here to kill him and to steal Dorian's book for himself."

And by telling him I had a copy of the contents of the book, I'd pretty much admitted to him that I had it.

THIRTY-ONE

"Whoa." Brixton looked from me to the kitchen ceiling. The singing from overhead had stopped.

"We're leaving," I said. "Now."

I scribbled a note to Percy about having to go to the police station for Heather, so he wouldn't think I'd discovered his secret, grabbed my silver coat, and shoved Brixton out the door.

"The scent in this truck is always so weird," Brixton mumbled as he climbed inside.

"It's not weird," I said as I put the key in the ignition of the truck. "Myrrh is a great air freshener. It works well in toothpaste too."

"I remember. Like frankincense, from the Bible. My life is too weird."

"Frankincense is too strong for an air freshener. Seatbelt."

Brixton rolled his eyes but obliged.

"Is it possible that Lucien was already injured when he made his way to his alchemy supplies in the shed?" I asked, trying the engine again. That's what I got for having a 1942 Chevy. I hated to think that Percy was stealthy enough to get into and out of the cabin without Brixton seeing him.

"Yeah. He was kind of disoriented, but I figured it was because he'd forgotten exactly where the shack was. It's pretty overgrown out there. You think that could explain why I didn't see Percy or anyone else?"

"Because Percy had already dealt him a fatal blow."

The engine of my truck turned over three times before finally starting, just long enough that I wondered if Percy had disabled it. I gave silent thanks as we peeled out of the driveway.

How could I have been so stupid as to think Percy believed the old wives' tale about alchemists not being able to kill people? He'd been trying to misdirect me this whole time. Had I fallen for it because he looked so much like Ambrose? Or because I'd wanted so badly to believe him because of my love for his father? Or maybe it was simply because I wanted to believe in the goodness of humanity.

Percy must have knocked himself out to cover his tracks after he searched my house for Dorian's book. A superficial head wound was a good choice. Even a minor wound in that location would bleed profusely and could easily look more serious than it was. He hadn't left the party to give me and Max space; he left so he'd have time alone to search my house. And I'd sent Dorian away, so I had no way to prove it. At least I'd asked Dorian to take *Not Untrue Alchemy* with him.

"Where are we going?" Brixton asked, gripping the dashboard as I turned a corner faster than was prudent. He winced.

"Is your hand still hurting?" I glanced at Brixton, expecting to see a bruise forming. Instead, I saw a bleeding scrape. "You didn't tell me you cut yourself on the table."

"It's nothing." He wrapped his sleeve around his hand. "And you didn't say where we're going."

"Your mom didn't do anything, so I'm guessing they're going to let her go soon."

"We're going to hang out at the police station?" Brixton rolled his eyes. "I should have brought the rest of that pie with me."

"How can you be so relaxed?"

"That guy Percy doesn't seem like an evil mastermind. You and I could totally take him on. And with Dorian in the mix, he wouldn't stand a chance."

I pictured Dorian clawing at Percy's perfect hair and burst out laughing. It was nervous laughter, brought on by the stress, but it was a welcome release of tension.

"See?" Brixton said. "You sure he could really be the killer?"

"I'm not taking any chances."

———————

I left Brixton with Abel, apologizing for not being able to hang out with Brixton because my houseguest was unwell.

When I got back to the house, Percy had his feet up on the couch with an icepack on his head and a tray of ginger cookies on his lap, watching a sitcom on his phone. He'd found the beer in the fridge. Two empty bottles sat on the coffee table, and a third was open on the floor next to the couch.

"How's your friend?" he asked.

I was done playing things safe. I had to find out what was going on.

"Lucien is dead," I said.

The platter of cookies dropped to the floor, as did Percy's phone. The screen cracked as it struck the hardwood floor. He left it where it lay.

I could have sworn Percy's reaction was genuine. Unlike his sincere expressions of regret from earlier that day, this was true shock.

"You saw him? Where?"

"He's the dead body they found in the woods."

185

The color drained from Percy's face. "But you said—I mean, how—?"

"I know you lied about Lucien being the one to ransack my attic and basement in search of *Non Degenera Alchemia*. It was you." I yanked the icepack from his head and pulled back his hair.

He howled with pain.

"It's only a scratch," I said. "It stopped bleeding right away. You didn't even bother reapplying bandages after your shower. You also didn't back up your lie by breaking down the door to get inside. You unlocked the door with the key I lent you—which you're going to give back to me. Now. Did you think keeping track of your lies wasn't necessary because I trusted you?"

"How can you—"

"Your most convincing lie was that you believe that silly legend about alchemists not being able to kill anyone." I let go of his hair and let him sink back onto the couch.

"It's true!"

"How can it possibly be true when you're the one who killed Lucien?"

"I would never. I *could* never. It was awful with Father—" Percy stopped himself.

Ambrose? My heart beat furiously in my throat. "What did you say?"

"Nothing." He clutched his head in his hands. "I'm in shock over hearing that Lucien is dead. I don't know what I'm saying."

"*What* was awful with Ambrose?"

"Nothing. Truly. I didn't mean anything."

"Yes, you did. When you tell the truth, you lose the cocky tilt of your head. You did it a moment ago. That means you didn't know Lucien was dead—I stand corrected there. I believe you about that."

"Why are you looking at me like that, Zoe? You're scaring me."

"You believe that old wives' tale from *personal experience*." My pulse raced. "Did Ambrose find out you had turned to backward alchemy, and that's the real reason he killed himself? No ... Oh God, Percy, was your father's suicide the death you needed?" With Percy providing no answers, my imagination began running wild with horrible thoughts. The room spun. I couldn't catch my breath.

"You're unbalanced, Zoe. You always were."

My focus snapped to Percy. The spoiled little man who only superficially resembled his father. The physical similarities were striking, but not their souls. "I've never been more clear-headed," I said. "I've always worked to protect the people I love."

"What does that have to do with—"

"You don't understand everything that's going on, Percy. I'm someone with nothing left to lose."

Percy tried to stand. I pushed him back onto the couch and stood over him. His beautiful eyes, so like his father's in appearance but not spirit, opened wide with fear.

"This is how it's going to go," I said. "You're going to tell me the truth about what happened to Ambrose."

Percy's eyes filled with tears. "I never meant to hurt either of you. I only wanted what you had. Can't you understand that? It was so easy for you. Not for me."

"What happened with your father? And what does it have to do with that stupid superstition?"

"You don't know that it's stupid, Zoe. You didn't believe backward alchemy was real at first either."

"That's different. The death rotation makes sense. It's sacrificing one element for another, or even one living being's energy for another's." I thought of how creating Dorian's Tea of Ashes depleted my own energy. "If anything, killing should make a backward alchemist *stronger*, not kill

187

him." I regretted the words as soon as they left my mouth. But alchemy is science, and that's what made sense scientifically.

"How would you know?" Percy snapped. "Have you ever killed anyone?"

"Of course not."

"Then you don't know. It would kill you—or, if you're strong, only bring you to the brink of death." Percy's lower lip trembled. The shaking spread to his whole body. He truly believed what he was saying; he truly was afraid of something.

"Oh God, Percy. What did you do?"

"Nothing," he said too quickly. "I'm not talking about myself." His eyes didn't meet mine.

"What did you do?"

"I told you—nothing! I didn't mean to do it. It was Father's fault. And yours. The more I think about it, it *was* your fault. You put him in that awful place. That's why it happened."

"Why *what* happened?" I'd had no choice about sending Ambrose to Charenton Asylum. I was worried he would harm himself. The psychiatric hospital was known for its humanitarian treatment of patients, unlike so many other "lunatic asylums" of the time. It had been good for him, even though in the end they hadn't been able to stop him from taking his own life. But that couldn't have been what Percy was talking about.

"I don't want to talk to you anymore. You're a bully. You always were."

I stared at the stranger in front of me; funny how the resemblance to his father faded more with every passing moment. Ambrose had been generous to a fault, never petulant or petty. "I've always showed you kindness, Percy. Always."

"By rubbing my nose in your own perfection? By stealing my father from me?"

"Is that what you think I did?"

"He didn't tell you everything, Zoe. My father is the one who told me about Lucien and Olav. He's the one who told me how I could find the backward alchemists." In my stunned silence, Percy rose and pushed past me.

"No, he would never—"

"You don't know everything." Percy rolled onto his heels and thrust his chin out, the same spoiled mannerism he'd had when he was twenty. Yet, he hadn't regained control of his quivering body. He wasn't nearly as confident as he wanted to appear.

"Sit down, Percival," I said in my most commanding voice. "You're going to tell me exactly what you've been dancing around. What do you know about Ambrose being in the asylum?"

He snorted. "Why would I tell you anything?"

I drew a deep breath and took a huge gamble. I could have played more on his superstitions, but there was a seed of a good man in Percy that I hoped I wasn't mistaken about.

"Because you're not a bad man, Percy. You never were. You're weak, though. Whatever you're holding in is what's killing you even more quickly. The weight is crushing your soul."

"I'm dying anyway, Zoe." Percy closed his eyes. His lips moved, but no sound came out. Was he praying? When he opened his eyes, I caught a glimmer of humility in them.

"I might as well die with a clean conscience," Percy said. "My father didn't kill himself."

THIRTY-TWO

"THE STORY BEGINS," PERCY said, "when I came back to Paris to see someone. A woman."

Of course, I thought to myself.

"I didn't visit you and Father," he continued, "because you believed me dead. I had no choice but to let you believe that. They forced me—"

"Stop with the excuses. If you want to die with a clear conscience, you need to own up to your actions."

Percy nodded, but the motion was erratic, as if he was battling himself. "Lucien kept an eye on you and Father when you were in Paris," he said with a trembling voice. "He knew that Father was raving about alchemy after *you* put him in Charenton Asylum. He was going to ruin alchemy for all of us. He shouldn't have been in that asylum."

"I believed it to be for the best," I said through my tightly clenched jaw. "He was distraught when he thought you'd died. He thought he'd failed you as a father, that it was his fault you were so unhappy, even though he'd given you everything he possibly could. He was talking about hurting himself."

"Instead," Percy said, "his actions threatened to hurt all of us."

"They believed him a mad man, Percy. Nobody took his ravings about alchemy seriously. He also talked about how he'd opened the gates of Hell at the *Cabaret de L'Enfer*. Which obviously wasn't true."

Percy grunted. "You thought you were so much better than him because you hated nightclubs."

I clenched my teeth. Percy was the type of man who thought he understood everything, even if he only had a small sliver of the truth.

I had rarely accompanied Ambrose when he went to *le Cabaret de L'Enfer* nightclub. Not because I didn't appreciate the macabre beauty or the dancing, but because staying awake late into the night has always been a challenge for me. Ambrose understood that, and he went out of his way to bring me the joys of the nighttime I otherwise would have missed.

The memory washed over me. One winter morning, nearly a century ago, Ambrose had awakened me a few minutes before dawn with a wicked grin on his face. "I have something to show you," he'd said. "Put on your dancing shoes." He'd discovered how to sneak into the nightclub while it was closed. While most of Paris slept but my own energy was surging, he lifted me onto his shoulders and helped me squeeze through a narrow window with a faulty latch. Once inside, I let him in through a larger door. He lifted two glasses from behind the bar and poured us drinks from the bottle of claret he'd brought with him. Carvings of devils and imps hung from the walls. Like the debated purpose of gargoyles, it was unclear whether the inhuman creatures were there to warn revelers or to tempt them. As the sun rose above Paris, Ambrose spun me around and around on the dance floor we had to ourselves.

"They could have believed his rantings," Percy said, shattering the memory. "He could have revealed everything. That's why Lucien asked me to visit Father and talk sense into him."

I bit back tears. I didn't want to hear the rest of the story.

"We looked alike, he and I," Percy continued. "That's what made it possible. I approached the gates of Charenton, pretending that I was Father and that I'd escaped. I couldn't very well walk in as a visitor, as I was supposed to be dead." Percy ran a shaking hand through his dark hair that was so like his father's. "As I expected, a nurse opened the gates for me, letting me inside. She was such a tiny thing, with a fragile heart-shaped face, I don't know how she could work in such a place. It was easy to administer the chloroform. I didn't hurt her. She was asleep before she knew what was happening. With her keys, I let myself into Father's room. *He* was the one who became violent. Not me. I only meant to talk sense into him."

Percy was pacing furiously now and knocked over the coffee table, but he didn't seem to notice. I barely noticed either. This couldn't be happening. This couldn't have been how my beloved Ambrose spent his last moments on earth.

"He must have been forced to take drugs or something that made him crazed. It wasn't my fault. I did only what I had to do to save myself. He said I was a hallucination sent there by God, telling him to reveal alchemy to the world." Percy's voice shook. His eyes darted around the room, looking everywhere but at me. "It was the exact opposite of what I meant to achieve. I didn't know what I was doing. It was an accident. I was only trying to stop him shouting, blurting out our secrets. My hands went around his neck—"

He broke off in a sob as I felt myself crumpling onto the velvet couch. Instead of feeling soft and comforting, the texture was like razor blades. The asylum had found Ambrose with a broken neck. They told me he'd hung himself.

"When I stopped," Percy whispered, "it was too late. He was dead, and I was nearly dead myself." He continued through hiccupping sobs. "It took all the strength I had to get myself out of there. Lucien had to take care of me while I recovered. I w-w-was lucky to survive."

192

Percy was bawling by now. My normal instincts to comfort and heal were absent. I couldn't find it in me to forgive the man who'd killed Ambrose. He'd felt such guilt that it sickened him to the point of feeling like he was going to die. He wasn't an evil man, but I couldn't look at him for one more second.

"Get out," I said. "I never want to see you again."

THIRTY-THREE

I was shaking so much that I could barely shove Percy's bag into his arms and lock the door behind him. I somehow got the door bolted before sliding down onto the floor.

I didn't cry. I couldn't. I was too numb from shock. I'd grieved for Ambrose, but this was different. Yet strangely, along with my horror, I also felt a sliver of *peace*.

Ambrose had grieved for his son. He'd lost himself in his guilt over finding the Elixir of Life when his only son could not, and he found it difficult to move on in the months that followed Percy's supposed death. But he *hadn't* been so lost that he'd taken his own life.

I gripped the wallet in my hand. As I'd shoved Percy's bag into his arms, I'd also lifted his wallet. It was done sloppily with shaking hands, but he'd been too upset to notice. There were still many blanks about Percy's current situation, but I couldn't bear to keep asking him questions. I hoped the wallet would provide some answers.

I took several deep breaths and picked up the coffee table Percy had knocked over. The simple action gave me a measure of reality to focus on. By the time I'd collected the books and newspapers that had fallen to the floor, I had mostly stopped shaking. I sat down on the couch and opened the wallet. Percival Smythe had a driver's license from Britain with an address in London, a membership card for a gym in a town in a suburb of Paris, and a library card from Edinburgh. A black credit card and several hundred dollars in cash indicated he was living well.

Two photographs were tucked inside the wallet. The first photograph was of Percy and a glamorous young woman. They sat together at a Parisian café, a cigarette in her hand and a pipe in his. They weren't looking at the camera, but at each other. She looked like a movie star. She reminded me of an actress from a 1930s Charlie Chan movie.

The other photograph was a faded black-and-white picture of Ambrose. The print was nearly worn through in the center, as if fingers had run over its surface many times. Percy had saved the photograph of his father and looked at it countless times. Damn. I couldn't dismiss him as completely heartless.

A tentative knock sounded on the front door.

"Zoe?" The voice was hesitant. "You don't have to look at me again, but I think my wallet fell out. Could you check the couch cushions?"

If it hadn't been for that well-loved photo of Ambrose, I wouldn't have opened the door. But now . . .

I opened the door and pressed the wallet into Percy's hands. "I hope you find peace before you die, Percy. But never show your face here again."

"I'm sorry," he said softly. "For everything."

By the time I locked the door again, my anger hadn't subsided, but it was a calmer rage. Clarity washed over me, showing me an important fact.

Percy was either one of the world's greatest actors, or he truly felt remorse over killing his father. He wholeheartedly believed the myth that alchemists can't kill one another without suffering grave consequences, and thought it was this old wives' tale that had brought him to death's door, not his own guilt. I would have bet my gold locket that he sincerely believed he'd nearly died from the wrath of a magical legend.

Meaning he couldn't have killed Lucien.

———————

Filled with a confusing mix of fury and anticipation, I couldn't stand to be indoors. I went out to the backyard and stepped into the garden. It was a clear, crisp night. Pinpricks of stars dotted the indigo sky above. Amidst the sorrel, garlic, and nasturtiums, I breathed in the early-summer scents.

A desperate sound escaped my lips, half laughter and half sob. Finding a backward alchemist had been a distraction, not Dorian's salvation. An experienced backward alchemist had died because he came to Portland in search of *Non Degenera Alchemia*, and a less experienced one wasn't able to tell me anything truly helpful. All Percy had done was devastate me.

I lay down in the garden, not bothering to look at which plants were beneath me. I didn't mind that I happened to be in the midst of blackberry brambles. I took pleasure in the pain of the thorns pricking my skin. It was a distraction from the mess of a situation I had to climb out of. I stared up at the star-filled sky.

I'd wasted too much of my life wallowing. Five minutes was enough time to compose myself. I had a gargoyle to save.

I brushed the brambles from my hair and clothes and went back inside to climb the stairs to the attic. There, surrounded by my alchemical and healing artifacts, I emailed Dorian to tell him I'd kicked Percy out.

I can come home? he emailed back immediately. *Tres bién. Julian Lake's housekeeper does not like me. She is suspicious that I will not let her see my visage. I believe she will try to sneak into my bedchamber tonight—little does she know I do not sleep!*

It's not late enough for you to walk across town, I wrote back. *I'll pick you up at the end of his driveway in 20 minutes.*

On the drive across town, I second-guessed everything I'd done not only that day, but since deciding to leave Paris several days ago. If I had stayed in Paris, how would things have played out with Lucien?

I pulled up in front of Julian Lake's estate. *House* wasn't a big enough word to describe the castle-like mansion, complete with stone lions standing guard. I didn't plan on walking up to the house and ringing the doorbell, so I idled the engine and waited with my thoughts.

A hunched figure in a black cape carrying a small satchel sprinted across the lawn. His bad leg gave him a limp, but it didn't slow him much. He looked rather like a hunchbacked Little Red Riding Hood with a book-shaped picnic basket.

Dorian climbed into the truck with *Non Degenera Alchemia* tucked under his arm. On the drive home, I filled Dorian in on what had happened with Percy. He replied with a string of profanities.

"I am so sorry, my friend," he said once he'd exhausted all the profane words he knew in both French and English, some of which I'd never heard. "Never fear. Dorian Robert-Houdin is on the case. I will put my little grey cells to work."

That's what worried me.

THIRTY-FOUR

I COULDN'T FALL ASLEEP that night. My mind was racing and refused to calm down enough for my body to get the sleep it craved. I got out of bed and lit a candle. The natural light of the flame was better to get into the mindset of alchemy, and that's exactly what I needed to do. Through Percy, my life had been connected to backward alchemy for far longer than I'd realized. I rubbed my gold locket, smooth for the decades it had comforted me.

How was everything connected?

The sulfurous scent of the candle and a mug of cashew milk cocoa calmed my nerves and awakened my senses. I unlocked the basement door and followed the stairs to my alchemy lab. As I lit a kerosene lantern and sat down at the solid wooden table I'd used for countless alchemical transformations, I thought through the confusing backward alchemy events that had happened.

I reached for my cell phone. My fingers hesitated for a moment before I sent Tobias a text message. I couldn't help chuckling to myself. When I was nursing Tobias back to health over 150 years ago, hiding in plain sight on a farm that was part of the Underground Railroad network, neither of us ever imagined a future when people could communicate instantly from hundreds of miles away, let alone without wires on a tiny device that fit in the palm of my hand.

It was the middle of the night, so I wasn't expecting him to answer. The very act of sending a message to my oldest living friend was comforting. I gave a start when my phone rang.

"Sitting up with Rosa?" I asked. I thought of Max, allowing myself a brief moment of the hope that that might one day be me and Max. It was a false hope, I knew. But that didn't mean I didn't want it.

"Is mind reading an alchemical skill I should be trying to hone?" Tobias replied good-naturedly.

"No supernatural skills required to know how much you love her. How is she?"

"Why don't you let me take care of you for a change. Are things not going well in Paris?"

"I had to leave."

A pause. "You're back in Portland? But that means it's the middle of the night for you too. You don't do nighttime, Zoe."

"I know." I hadn't thought Tobias would reply, much less call me. Where did I begin?

"I've seen you after you stayed up all night." His voice transformed from concern to anger. "You were no good to anyone after that."

"That night we had to run," I whispered, staring into the flames of the kerosene lantern and remembering the wretched night that left me with scars from harsh thorns and brambles.

"Are you in physical danger right now?"

"Not exactly."

"Then hang up and get some sleep."

"Please, Toby."

A long sigh sounded over the phone line. "What is it that has you reaching out in this darkest hour of the night?"

"I'm drowning. I know less than I did two weeks ago, before I went to Notre Dame."

"If I'm a sounding board, why don't you call me back in the morning?"

"I'm afraid." I clutched my gold locket.

A faint rustling sounded on the phone line, followed by the creaking of a door. Softly in the distance came the hum of crickets. I wondered if the lights of Detroit allowed him to see the constellations.

"I was awake because Rosa was dreaming. She kicked me in her sleep, but when I looked over at her, I couldn't fall back asleep. When she dreams, I see the same young woman I fell in love with over sixty years ago. I can't tell her that, though."

"She'd think you love her less now, because she aged. Even though it's not true." I thought again of Max, wondering if I'd ever be able to tell him just how different I was.

"If anything, knowing it wouldn't last forever has made me cherish her all the more." He cleared his throat. "I'm not letting you stay awake just to get philosophical. Tell me, why are you so afraid?"

After a moment's hesitation, the story spilled out of me. Tobias already knew about the unknown shift that had taken place six months before, when anything and any*one* who'd been helped along their way by backward alchemy began to have their life force reverse, from gold figures in museums turning to gold dust to living gargoyles returning to stone. And he knew about how, five months ago, Dorian had sought me out so I could help him decode *Not Untrue Alchemy*.

I smiled at the memory of my dear friend looking up at me from the wreckage he'd created in one of my shipping crates. I hadn't smiled at the time; I'd been terrified to find a living gargoyle, not to mention quite unhappy that he'd disturbed my carefully packed glass jars filled with alchemical ingredients. Dorian had apologized profusely and explained that he'd been hungry and was looking in the jars for food. When Tobias had visited, he'd been nearly as frightened to meet Dorian, and I hadn't known how to broach the subject of a living gargoyle who wasn't a homunculus to be feared. Since then, the two had bonded.

Now I told Tobias about what'd I'd recently learned of the formal origins of backward alchemy, in which a group of lazy men living in the 1500s, one of whom was Lucien Augustin, had found out how to shortcut true alchemy by using sacrificial apprentices, and had recorded their findings in a book that was meant only for themselves. Since alchemy connects as it transforms, the book took on the properties of backward alchemists, getting younger with age and not responding to fire as science would normally dictate.

In the flickering light of my half-finished alchemy lab, I grabbed the notebook on the table I used for recording plant transformations and began to scribble the ideas I was telling Tobias about.

"Why'd they create a book at all?" Tobias asked. "Sounds like they were selfish men who didn't want to share their twisted miracle."

"They're the laziest of men, Toby." I thought of Percy and snapped the pencil in my hand. "They didn't want to memorize even their most simple alchemical transformations. But they were so lazy they lost track of the book a couple hundred years ago."

"You don't know how it works yet?"

"Sometimes I feel like I'm so close to understanding, and sometimes I think I'm so far away I wouldn't understand it if I lived another three hundred years."

"Notre Dame didn't hold the key? I was so sure there was something it could tell you."

I hated to admit to Tobias how careless I'd been, but why had I contacted him if I wasn't going to be honest?

"Zoe?" he prompted.

"I was recognized. I had to leave before I was done."

Tobias swore.

"That's what started the mess I'm in. I thought at first the elderly woman who recognized me had sent a private investigator after me, but it was worse than that."

"Worse?"

"Two backward alchemists followed me home." I was glad he couldn't see my face as I explained how I'd learned a man I once knew in Paris had been murdered, seen a second stone gargoyle come alive for the briefest moment, and been tricked by Lucien about a nonexistent book that I hoped could lead me to a knowledgeable backward alchemist. I explained how I'd learned that Ambrose's son, Percy, was a clueless backward alchemist who'd killed his own father and that Lucien had died and shriveled inside an alchemy lab he'd set up in an abandoned cabin in Portland. It was all the more personal because Brixton had been a witness and now the police were suspicious of him and his mom, but I was so exhausted I was seeing alchemy everywhere I looked, even in Heather's paintings.

As I rambled, I picked up the shard of pencil and continued writing. Pouring my soul out to both Tobias and my notebook, I kept waiting for something to click. It didn't.

"I can see why you can't sleep," Tobias said.

"None of it makes any sense."

"On the contrary, it makes perfect sense."

"I remember you being a philosopher, not a comedian."

"I'm serious. *You're the one* everyone believes can figure it out. That's why they've all come to you."

"Misguided faith in an accidental alchemist."

"You really believe that?"

"Which part?"

"It wasn't an accident, Zoe."

"I never meant to find it—"

"You never meant to find the Elixir of Life for *yourself*. But you worked all hours to find it to save your brother's life. That's purpose. *Intent*. Not an accident."

"This isn't a problem with my ego. I know I'm great at many things. I can grow a thriving garden under the harshest of conditions, I can use spagyrics to create healing elixirs for an assortment of ailments, and I can fix the engine of just about any car produced before 1985. But I'm a terrible liar, I'm awful at turning lead into gold, and I never finished my alchemical training so I don't know how to decode formal alchemy."

"Do you realize the confusion you've told me about tonight sounds much more similar to listening to plants and putting a broken engine together than to speaking the secret language of some old white men?"

I swore. Why are we so blind to seeing what's right in front of us?

"I believe they're right that you can solve this," Tobias said. "As long as you get some sleep, kiddo."

"Kiddo? I'm almost two hundred years older than you."

"Then start acting like it. Stop thinking of what you don't know and focus on what you do. You know more than you think, my friend."

THIRTY-FIVE

I WOKE UP AT dawn, after approximately four hours of sleep, with a furious headache and a dry mouth that felt like it was filled with stinging nettles. Tobias was right—I shouldn't have stayed up. Was he also right that I knew more than I thought I did? With my brain in a fog, I wasn't much good to anyone at the moment.

Dorian saved the day. A breakfast feast was waiting for me. The spread took up half the dining table. Dorian had spent the predawn hours baking for me. He'd created variations on several of my favorite foods from my youth, from creamy almond milk porridge to cranberry nut bread. On the other half of the table, Dorian had arranged a set of notecards, written in his impressive cursive script. I helped myself to a serving of porridge and a slice of bread while Dorian explained the notecards.

"Each card is a piece of the puzzle," he said. "It is similar to the notes you wrote last night. By writing each separate point on its own notecard, we can move these items around in ways that are not simply chronological. My method is much more fruitful than yours."

"You snuck into my room and took my list?" I'd carried the note-book upstairs with me after talking with Tobias, hoping I'd have further revelations during the night. I didn't.

Dorian blinked at me innocently. "You left your door open. This was a sign you wanted my assistance."

It was a sign it had been a warm night, but no matter. "So you've rearranged my notes in a different order so they make more sense?"

"*Oui.*"

I stared at him. "You have?"

Dorian tapped one of his horns and raised a stone eyebrow. "I have cracked the case!" He grinned triumphantly. "Lucien was not an alchemist! Percival has misled you, Zoe."

"We know Lucien is the dead body. Brixton saw him."

Dorian waved away my concerns. "Brixton is an impressionable boy. Yet buried in your notes are dismissive descriptions of Heather, the very woman the police believe to be behaving suspiciously. It is *she* who is our most viable suspect."

I popped a bite of cranberry nut bread into my mouth and thought about how to refute the ridiculous idea. Dorian hadn't had an opportunity to interact with Heather. He could see in stone statue form, so he'd once stood still next to the fire place during a dinner party I'd given, and had observed Heather then. But most of what he knew of people was what Brixton and I told him.

"Heather wouldn't kill anyone." I saw Dorian open his mouth, so I quickly continued. "No, you're right. Anyone could kill someone, given the right circumstances. But for Heather, this doesn't make any sense. That's the more important point. Since you read my notes, you know I don't think those detectives are a good judge of character."

"*Non.*"

"No?"

"It is your own thoughts that betray you."

205

"My own thoughts?"

"You forget that you and Brixton have both said how strangely she has been behaving of late."

"It's true," I admitted. "But people have all sorts of things going on in their lives. Heather has a teenage kid and a husband who works out of town. That's not easy. But she doesn't have any connection to Lucien."

"How do you know there is no connection?" Dorian asked. "Her paintings at Blue Sky Teas—"

"We're reading too much into those paintings, Dorian. Brixton told her about the things I sell at my shop, and she's really creative."

"You are missing the point, Zoe. The motive could be any number of things we do not have enough information to understand. It is impossible to see into the hearts of men. No, my point is that your notes contain many points in history that are linked to one another in theory, such as the unfortunate coincidence of being recognized by a woman who knew you when she was a child. But there is only one true fact: science does not lie."

While science doesn't exactly lie, it's subject to the same human limitations as anything else. Accepted science in one era is later looked upon as laughable. Bloodletting to restore the balance in a sick body, mercury to treat syphilis, aether to explain light and gravity. Concerning forensics, DNA evidence was evolving as other tools had before it. And science didn't tell the whole story.

"Alchemy is science," I said, "but that doesn't do us any good because they don't understand it—"

"Yes, alchemy may be *foreign* science to these investigators, but they are seeking DNA evidence. You said they have the DNA of the killer, and yet Heather *refused* to submit to the test!"

"Do you remember the Phantom of Heilbronn?" I asked.

"The Phantom of the Opera? Have I told you about the time I snuck into a theater performing the musical and newspapers wrote that the phantom himself had appeared at the show?" He chuckled.

"No. Heilbronn. An example of when DNA science lied. A supposed female serial killer in Europe who killed dozens of people."

"Oh, yes. One of her crimes was committed in France."

"She didn't exist, Dorian. Laboratory results were contaminated with 'sterile' cotton swabs. It was the DNA of a factory worker."

"This is not bad science. It is human error."

"That's my point. It's perfectly reasonable to fear what will become of your DNA."

"Ah, so." He scratched his gray chin.

I looked at the set of carefully placed notecards and thought about how to turn the police onto Percy without revealing alchemy. Percy, whose wounds I'd washed. Aside from his head wound, he didn't have any scratches on his body.

But there was someone else who did. I felt as if the room was spinning around me.

"You are ill?" Dorian asked, his gray forehead creasing with concern. "Your face has gone as pale as a ghost from one of Father's magic posters."

"Yes. No. Where's my phone?"

I texted Brixton: ONCE YOU'RE AWAKE, WE NEED TO TALK.

———

An hour later, Brixton pulled up on his bike.

"I'm not going to get mad at you," I said, "so I need you to tell me the truth."

"About what?"

"I know you didn't want to worry me, which is why you didn't tell me. But you didn't only follow Lucien from afar, did you?"

Dorian gasped. "You cannot mean the boy killed him!"

Brixton and I both rolled our eyes.

"Of course not," I said. "But I think Brixton got closer to Lucien than he wanted to admit, when Lucien was spying on Ivan at his house. He didn't want to admit his mistake."

"Is this true?" Dorian asked Brixton.

Brixton fidgeted but didn't reply.

"Your wrist," I said. "I didn't think there was anything sharp on the table. It's not a scrape from when you hit my table, is it?"

Brixton shook his head but didn't look at me.

"Did Lucien grab you?" I asked. "Is that why you were extra careful to hang back when you saw him again?"

Brixton stared at us. "You mean it's *my* DNA they'll find under his fingernails?"

The air felt heavy and stifling. Brixton had a juvenile record. "Did they save your DNA in juvenile court?"

"I don't think so. That's why they had to ask my mom for DNA for that family match thing."

"At least your mom didn't give her DNA to the police. They won't have any way to match it to you."

"Actually," Brixton said slowly, "she decided to do it. It was killing her, not knowing for sure if it was her dad. When it seemed less likely it was him, that's when she realized how much she cared."

I stared at Brixton. "This is bad," I said. "Very bad."

"What happened?" Dorian asked.

"It wasn't a big deal," Brixton insisted. "He didn't think I was spying on him on purpose or anything. He just thought I was being nosy. I followed him around the side of the house, and he grabbed my arm and told me to get lost."

"It doesn't matter that the event itself wasn't a big deal," I said. "Nobody was there to see it, so nobody can back you up."

Brixton bit his lip and looked at me with fear in his eyes. I knew he was thinking the same thing: he already had a record. Even if a jury wouldn't be told, the police knew.

"They won't believe me, will they?" he said. "Even if I leave out the part that I was spying on Ivan because Dorian wanted to know if he was a trustworthy new alchemist."

"If they're looking at you as a suspect," I said, thinking it through as tendrils of worry spread over my body, "they'll be sure to notice you're lying about *something*. And even if you tell them the complete truth—*especially* if you tell them the complete truth—they'll think you're lying." I didn't add that they might even suspect he was crazy and lock him up somewhere worse than a juvenile detention facility.

"Why are you scaring the boy?"

"He's not a boy," I said.

Brixton was now nearly fifteen, older than my brother had been when he helped me escape from Salem Village. In the modern world, it was easy to dismiss a fourteen-year-old as a kid, and Brixton was indeed immature in many ways, but in important matters like this, I needed to treat him as an adult. He had to understand the full consequences of what was happening.

"What do I do?" Brixton whispered.

"You forget we had this conversation. Concentrate on supporting your mom, and leave it to me and Dorian to figure out what really happened to Lucien in that shed in the woods. Don't say a word about this to anyone, Brixton. Not to anyone."

THIRTY-SIX

DORIAN PACED THE LENGTH of the attic, past the shelves filled with antique books on herbal remedies, around the articulated skeleton of a pelican, steering clear of my set of Victorian swords once owned by a famous English physician. With his chin jutting out, left arm hanging limply at his side, and right arm tucked behind his back, he looked like a Victorian caricature. I sat on the old wooden trunk, my knees tucked up under my chin.

"We must assume that the police have not yet figured out Lucien's identity," Dorian said. "He must have left his identification papers elsewhere, since he was working undercover while he was sneaking around Ivan's home. Yet he was not staying in the shed as his lodgings, so his hotel will soon notice his absence. They will report this to the authorities."

"That's a good point," I said.

"I have many good points." He tapped his gray forehead beneath his horns. His *little grey cells*.

"We might not have much time until his identity is discovered," I said, "but we already knew that. Who knows how quickly the police labs will finish the DNA testing—that's the more important problem. Even if they learn who Lucien is, it doesn't necessarily connect him to Brixton. Lucien was a bookseller from Paris. If anything, that will connect him to me."

Dorian stopped pacing. He nodded his head only once, and the solemnity of his expression made me shiver.

"If it would help," I said, "I would take the blame." If it came down to it, I had no doubt in my mind that I would sacrifice my freedom for Brixton's. But the connection between me and Lucien was based on alchemy. Would anyone believe I was telling the truth, not simply trying to help a young man I cared about?

"I know you would," Dorian said. "Yet you could not do so even if you wished to."

"I might be able to convince them about alchemy. My old photographs. If I could prove my true identity, I'd do it to save Brixton, regardless of what it meant for us."

"I do not speak only of alchemy."

"Then what?"

"You do not know what it was that killed him. A 'head injury' is meaningless. And they are unlikely to tell you the specific method of death. Thus, the police would never believe your confession. No, we must figure out who killed Lucien."

"Maybe I was wrong about Percy. Could he be that good an actor? Maybe he doesn't actually believe the superstition that one alchemist can't kill another."

"Perhaps, though I doubt it. He does not appear to be a very intelligent man."

I steadied myself, pushing away the raw memory. "Who besides me would have a reason to harm Lucien?"

"You could return to Paris and examine his life. While you are there, you could also visit my brother again."

"I *can't* go back to France. The French authorities must have flagged my passport by now."

Dorian frowned. "Ask Brixton's young friend Veronique to hack into his personal life."

"Her name is Veronica. But she's fourteen. And she's a coder, not a hacker."

"It is the same, no?"

"No. Plus, hacking into someone's life isn't nearly as easy as it looks on television."

"Unless one can guess their passwords." Dorian drummed his claws against the side of a shelf containing Chinese puzzle boxes and apothecary jars. "A French alchemist would most likely select passwords in French or Latin, but this does not help us narrow things down."

"Ivan," I said.

"Ivan does not know how to hack into personal records."

"No. Lucien was spying on Ivan. I dismissed him as a suspect because he's too ill to hurt anyone. But unlike Percy, he doesn't believe the alchemy superstition that you can't kill another without killing yourself. Therefore Ivan could have *hired* someone."

"We suffer the same problem as we did with Brixton's mother. *Why* kill Lucien? Even supposing you are wrong about Ivan's quest for true alchemy, and he indeed turned to the dark side of backward alchemy, it makes no sense that he would kill the man who could teach it to him."

"We're missing something," I said. "I should talk with Ivan."

Dorian picked up a hefty glass paper weight from the shelf and handed it to me.

"What's this for?" I asked, turning over the heavy piece of practical art. The glass-blown piece was filled with flower petals, giving it the illusion of being lighter than it was.

"Protection. In case Ivan is a killer."

THIRTY-SEVEN

I BROUGHT IVAN A picnic basket filled with lunch sandwiches, potato salad, and multiple desserts; a thermos full of homemade ginger-turmeric tea; and a garlic tincture.

Yeah, I may have been overcompensating because I felt guilty for suspecting my friend. And also, assuming he was innocent, for ignoring his quest to discover the Philosopher's Stone and the Elixir of Life. But I'd taken the paper weight. It weighed down my purse.

"*Dobrý den,*" Ivan said in greeting as he let me in and ushered me through to the kitchen.

"Sorry I haven't been around much," I said, setting the food on the counter.

"Young love." He winked at me. "I completely understand." He shuffled around his library, tidying up.

I would have told him not to bother with tidying, but at the moment I didn't mind that he was turned away from me. His comment had made my cheeks flush. Was I blushing? Not very dignified for a 340-year-old.

"I'm glad you didn't forget about me for too long," Ivan said. "I have a question for you about how I've set up my laboratory."

We stepped into his garage.

Ivan had done his homework. He'd followed the descriptions in historical accounts of alchemists exquisitely. My little basement lab looked pathetic by comparison.

I hadn't had a true laboratory in more than a century. My goal for buying the dilapidated Craftsman house was to ease myself back into alchemy, one step at a time. Since life never seems to turn out quite as we expect it to, I hadn't had time to build my Portland laboratory, at least not properly. I'd been thrust into solving a much more urgent problem than purifying my own alchemical practice.

As I walked through Ivan's lab, I dismissed my concerns that he might be taking backward alchemy seriously. Since the last time I'd been at his house, Ivan had done a lot more to build his laboratory. He wasn't cutting corners.

I felt like I had stepped into a workshop on Golden Lane from Rudolph II's court in Prague. I wouldn't have been surprised if John Dee or Edward Kelley stopped by for tea. In addition to having alembics, matrix vases, and a pelican vessel, Ivan had a spirit holder. Glass jars were filled with ingredients. As much as I wanted to touch them, I knew I couldn't invade his space with my own touch.

One wall bore instructional posters—the torn pages from the books he'd destroyed. Only here, the destruction made sense. From their placement on the wall, the torn pages were close at hand, looking over him as he worked. A page on the steps of the Emerald Tablet, a map of the solar system with planetary metals, and an enlarged woodcut illustration of the *tria prima*: mercury, sulfur, and salt. The only thing missing was an athanor furnace, needed for cooking the philosophical egg.

"It's perfect, Ivan," I said.

The main thing that had led me to be suspicious of Ivan was that he was becoming obsessed, but was that so bad? Many a true alchemist had focused their obsession into a discovery.

"Not quite complete, I'm afraid. My furnace is being installed in the backyard next week."

"The athanor," I said.

"I won't tell you how difficult it was finding a vendor that had something similar to what's described in these alchemy books."

"A brick pizza kiln wouldn't do it?"

Ivan groaned. "You could have saved me time if you'd simply told me that. That's exactly what I settled on."

"Sorry. I didn't think you were at that stage. But truly, it looks like you don't need my help at all. I told you I never finished my training. At this point, I'd probably only hold you back or lead you astray."

"If I didn't know you to be a terrible liar, Zoe, I would think you were simply being polite."

"Shall we go back into the house?" I asked. "That way we can keep your laboratory strictly for you."

"In one moment," he said. He tapped on his cell phone before returning it to his pocket. "I've hung this Emerald Tablet poster on the wall here. It is my favorite so far, so I'm using it as my guiding model as I create my own."

Every alchemist must create their own fourteen steps of a personal Emerald Tablet to guide their work.

"Isaac Newton's?" I asked, looking over the yellowed page Ivan had taken from an antique book.

"I knew you were good, Zoe."

Working on Ivan's ideas in his library, I lost track of time. I pointed out that Ivan was trying to be too literal, as opposed to letting his intent guide him.

"I used to think these coded woodcuts were charming," Ivan said. "But now I wish to strangle the king and the queen here in these illustrations, and even their child. Look at the smug expressions on their faces. They hold more secrets than Mona Lisa."

I couldn't blame him for the sentiment. The king and queen, representing sulfur and mercury, come together in a marriage that results many months or years later in a philosophical child: salt. The two were sometimes shown as royalty, sometimes lovers, and sometimes as the sun and moon. Regardless of how they were represented in ink, they always hid their secrets.

Frustrated, Ivan declared he needed a break. Wincing as he rose from his seat, he led us to the kitchen. He'd cleaned up much of the mess of books I'd seen the last time I was there. The house was much more orderly, but the hard work had taken a toll on Ivan. He was thinner than he had been just days before.

"I could bring you some groceries," I offered.

"Brixton brought me a big bag of groceries yesterday."

"That was good of him."

"So many people grumble about 'kids these days,' but Brixton and my neighbor Sara are two of the most considerate people I know. Brixton's shopping choices contain more desserts than I'd have chosen for myself, but with all this work I have to do, a little sugar will do me good. Energy to complete the process." The flicker of obsession in his eyes had returned.

Only that's not what it was, I realized as Ivan collapsed into a chair. I rushed to his side, wondering if I had an appropriate tincture I could fix for him. I hadn't been making many lately, in proportion to how many I'd given out, so my supplies were low.

"It's nothing." He waved me off and glanced at the antique clock on the wall. "It's later than I thought. We've been working and talking for longer than my body can handle these days."

"Do you need any—"

"No." His hands shook as he spoke. "Leave me."

"Are you sure you—"

"Go."

THIRTY-EIGHT

HUMAN DIGNITY IS A complex thing. Ivan didn't want me to see his body's failings any more than Dorian wanted me to see his. I wished I could do more for Ivan, but my primary goal was helping Dorian— and now, Brixton.

After visiting Ivan, I was no closer to figuring out who killed Lucien. If I didn't make progress soon, the police would connect him with Brixton. And if I didn't get back to focusing on Dorian's life force reversal soon, his whole body would return to stone.

I could think of only one person who might have been able to help me. Why had I acted so impulsively and sent Percy away? I didn't even know his cell phone number! I'd reacted emotionally, but it was a stupid decision.

Berating myself, I shuffled up my stairs to the attic. The private and cozy space with a rooftop escape hatch was where Dorian and I had set up our research center. Dorian was using my laptop, since his clawed fingers didn't work well on the touch screen of a phone, leaving me to use my phone to go online.

Was Dorian right that I'd made unfounded assumptions? I wasn't so sure. All of the mysteries surrounding me were related to alchemy, so I couldn't help thinking they were connected. Occam's Razor: the simplest explanation was most likely the right one.

While I tried to put together the pieces of the puzzle, was Madame Leblanc working on a plan to get her nephew or a private investigator to find me and expose the fact that I was an alchemist? What would they find when they looked into the murder of my old acquaintance Jasper Dubois?

Because of more pressing matters, I hadn't spent enough time either worrying about Madame Leblanc's vendetta or researching Jasper's death. Dorian hadn't found anything, but I needed to try anyway. I again searched online library archives. As I narrowed my search, so many newspaper articles involved the police that I found myself distracted by thoughts of Max. If only I hadn't been encumbered by the secrets of alchemy, he and I could have had a normal life together.

Normal life ...

Damn. There was something else I'd been ignoring. I hadn't checked my business orders in days.

I only listed high-end alchemical artifacts on my website, so I didn't do a brisk pace of business. But when a customer bought an expensive matrix vase crafted in Prague or a set of apothecary jars once owned by a famous Bohemian painter in Paris, they expected good service.

I checked my orders through Elixir and found I'd made a sale two days before. I took a break to pack the item—a handwritten speech by Sylvester Graham. I added a small puzzle box as a gift to thank the customer for the delay in my acknowledging the purchase. Since the activities that had transpired earlier this spring, I hadn't been too keen on having puzzle boxes around me anyway.

There was one more parcel I wanted to send. It was Rosa's heart that ailed her, so I packaged a healing Hawthorn tincture for Tobias. Before sealing the padded brown paper envelope, I stepped outside and clipped a sprig of ivy growing wild along the side fence. Tobias would understand I meant it as a symbol of friendship.

After bringing the packages to the post office, I felt myself compelled to stay outdoors in nature. My sanctuary. I took a long walk. Too many ideas were flitting through my mind, and being outside with the early summer flowers of Portland would help me focus. Dozens of varieties of roses were beginning to bloom in the Rose City. Across time and cultures, roses have symbolized many things. Today, I let myself believe the fragrant new petals represented rebirth and life.

When I came home, I was much calmer. And hungry. I called upstairs to Dorian, but he didn't answer. Since he hated it when I interrupted his reading these days, I let him be.

I ate leftovers for dinner. A small hearty scoop of Dorian's secret garlic tomato sauce remained in the fridge in a glass mason jar, so I slathered it on crusty French bread and sprinkled arugula on top. A perfect combination of spicy and mellow flavors, and sharp and velvety textures, danced on my tongue. I had to remember to ask Dorian how he got the sauce so creamy.

There was enough food in the fridge to feed us ten times over, so I thought it would be nice to bring Ivan something else. I took out a nut loaf and a wild rice salad from the fridge and headed off. If I was honest with myself, it also served as another excuse to go for a walk outside.

Ivan wasn't home. At least I hoped that was the case, and not that he was too sick to come to the door. Our alchemical discussion that afternoon had taken a lot out of him. Had it been too much for him?

I peeked in the window of his library, much like Lucien must have done. I didn't see Ivan, but I saw something else I recognized.

Percy's leather jacket. My throat clenched and I staggered away from the window. The bag of food in my hand dropped to the ground.

Percy was staying with Ivan.

That's why Ivan had glanced at the clock. He wasn't feeling as ill as he pretended; he was expecting Percy to return.

This connection couldn't be good. Using tricks I'd learned from watching Dorian use his claws to pick locks, I tried to pick the lock to Ivan's back door, shielded from view. I failed miserably.

I checked all the windows and found one that wasn't locked. It was a high one, but I was glad to find that slipping into a narrow high window was a skill one didn't forget. Either that or I had enough adrenaline pumping through my veins that I could do anything at that moment.

On Ivan's desk I found a copy of a flight itinerary. Ivan was going to Paris. Was he going with Percy? Why?

I rushed home and up to the attic to share these latest developments with Dorian.

I found my gargoyle friend tied up. His wrists were bound behind his back, rope had been wound around his body to prevent him from flapping his wings, and a handkerchief stuffed in his mouth.

His precious *Non Degenera Alchemia* was nowhere in sight.

THIRTY-NINE

I SHOOK MYSELF AND pulled the handkerchief from Dorian's mouth.

"*J'en ai ras le bol*," Dorian spat. "I have had enough, Zoe! This is too much."

"Who did this to you?" I asked, even though I already knew.

"I knew Ivan was not to be trusted!" Dorian screamed, fidgeting as I worked to untie the rope. "Hurry! We must go after them."

"We're too late."

His shoulder's fell. "*Non*. I suppose you are correct. They were here hours ago. I heard you come home, yet you did not come up when I did not answer you."

"You've hated to be interrupted lately."

Dorian sniffed. "Is a small modicum of privacy a bad thing?"

"No. Not under normal circumstances. I'm sorry. With everything going on around us, I should have checked on you. Ivan tied you up and took your book?"

"*Oui*." Dorian shook out his wings and rotated his one working arm. "Ivan and Percival."

222

"They're taking it to Paris."

"You know?"

"I saw the flight itinerary at Ivan's house. The plane already left, we're too late. What happened?"

Dorian chuckled.

"It's *funny*?"

"At least when I spend eternity trapped in stone, I will always have the memory of Percival's terrified face when I came to life and refused to let go of *Non Degenera Alchemia*. He is a most annoying man, Zoe. You have the worst taste in men."

"It was his father I was in love with, not Percy. And what's the matter with Max?"

"He wishes to cook in my kitchen! He leaves things in the wrong place."

"Because he's nice enough to clean up—" I stopped myself and shook my head. "How did we get off track? You're *not* going to be trapped in stone for all eternity, Dorian. You're going to tell me what happened, and we're going to fix it."

"*D'accord.* The two men, Ivan and Percival, forced the lock to the attic. They must have had a key to the front door, because I did not hear them until they opened this one. By then it was too late for me to flee. I could only turn to stone and hold my book tightly. Yet with only one working arm ..."

"You couldn't hold on tightly enough."

"Nor put up a fight. If I was at full strength, they would not have been able to tie me up. That Percival wished to chip me into little stone pieces. He is a very bad man, Zoe."

"You're all right?" I looked him over, terrified I'd see pieces missing beyond his two toes that had chipped off earlier that year.

"Ivan stopped him from hurting me."

Dorian looked at me thoughtfully. "Ivan was less surprised than Percival when I began to move. It is as if nothing else in this world can surprise him."

"He's dying. He has nothing left to lose."

"Yet he did not wish to kill me. He is the weak link. It is Ivan who has not yet gone too far."

"I need to figure out why they're headed to Paris."

Dorian blinked at me. "You said you knew."

"I knew they'd booked tickets to Paris. But what are they going to do there?"

"*Merde.*"

"What is it?"

"I wish you already knew. Then I would not have to tell you."

My heart thudded. "It's bad?"

"They spoke of a backward alchemy lab in Paris. A powerful one used by all the backward alchemists throughout the ages. It is where they perform their sacrifices. Ivan and Percival plan to use the book to bring back backward alchemy."

"Percy didn't tell me there was an alchemy lab like that."

"Of course he would not. He left out many things when he brought you into his confidence. He has done the same thing with Ivan. Percival is leading Ivan to his doom."

"And you to yours," I said, "unless I stop them."

FORTY

I WAS TOO LATE. The next flight to Paris wasn't until the next day. But even if I could have purchased a ticket and boarded a flight, what would happen when I entered France on my own passport? Would there be a flag on my passport that I was a criminal? The man who'd helped me with IDs for decades was dead, so I needed to find someone to forge me a new passport.

It was shortly after seven p.m. and the teashop was closed, but Blue was still there cleaning up. She opened the door for me. Her gray curls gave the impression she'd been struck by lightning. With the smile on her face, it was a magical lightning bolt of happiness.

"Have you heard if Heather is all right?" she asked.

"I haven't heard anything."

"I'll put on some tea."

I shook my head. "I'm afraid this isn't a social visit. I need to ask you for help."

Blue gave me a crooked smile. "Trying to help me feel at home since Brix is at an age where he's too cool to ask for help?"

"I need a fake passport," I blurted out.

Blue choked. "Honey, we definitely need to put on a pot of tea. A relaxing blend." She locked the front door and led me to the area behind the counter.

"I wouldn't ask if it wasn't an emergency."

"I figured that part out."

"Do you still know the people who helped you change your identity?"

"Tea first, criminal activities later."

Blue brewed dandelion tea that was both calming and invigorating.

"I've always said you were an old soul, Zoe," Blue said as I sipped the tea out of a solid curved mug like the kind found in 1950s diners. "But you're taking it too far. You look like you haven't slept since I left. And if I'm eating and sleeping better in a jail cell than you are here at home, I know something's wrong."

The tea warmed my hands and belly, but with Brixton and Dorian in danger, the comforting sensation didn't reach my soul. I pushed the mug away. "When you faked your death and started a new life, you knew people who helped you set up that fake identity."

The blank look on Blue's face made me wonder if I'd misunderstood how she started over here in Portland. But then she smiled and took my hands in hers. They were calloused but full of vitality. "Whatever you're running from, doing what I did isn't the answer. Trust me, I know."

"Then you do know people. People who can work quickly."

"I'm not going to ask what's going on. It's up to you to decide whether you're ready to tell me. But I will say that however desperate you feel, it *can* get worse."

Not the reassuring words I wished to hear. "I thought you'd tell me it'll get better."

"Ha. That too. But it won't get better if you go this route."

"You don't understand what I have to do."

"I would if you'd tell me. No?" She let go of my hands and ran her fingers through her curly gray hair that was as untamable as a ferocious storm. "All right, Zoe. If you're sure."

"I'm sure. I know what I'm doing."

"I hope you're right, sugar. I do hope you're right."

———————

I stared at the number for Blue's contact, wondering if I should call. It was so late at night that it was difficult for me to think clearly. Dorian had gone on a nocturnal walk to work out his own tension, along with living up to his nightly responsibilities at Julian Lake's house and at Blue Sky Teas. I'd made too many mistakes. I needed to get some sleep to make the right decision.

When I woke up at sunrise, I saw that I'd missed several calls from Max from the middle of the night. Because I'd wasted precious energy staying awake longer than I should have, I'd slept through the phone calls.

I called Max back. It took several rings for him to answer. He must have been sleeping. Understandable, since his calls had come in only hours before.

"Is Brixton staying with you?" Max asked.

"No. Why would he be with me?"

Max swore. "He missed dinner with his parents last night. They thought he was out with his friends, but when Abel checked Brixton's room before going to bed at around midnight, he found some of Brix's clothes missing, along with the passport they just took out of their safety deposit box so he could go on a summer trip with his friends. Abel and Heather called Ethan and Veronica and woke them up, but Brixton isn't with them. Last I heard, he still wasn't home."

No, it couldn't be …

"I'd better check with his parents again," Max was saying. "He's run off for the night before. It's the missing clothes and passport that make this case different. Zoe, are you there?"

I couldn't speak. This was far worse than I had imagined. Brixton wasn't only implicated in a murder—he might become a murder victim himself.

Brixton knew about alchemy. He trusted Ivan, and he'd been bringing him food to help the dying man. Ivan likely didn't know that an alchemy apprentice would give his life when he performed backward alchemy's death rotation.

Brixton had gone to Paris with Ivan and Percy to be the latest unknowing victim of backward alchemy.

FORTY-ONE

IF ONLY I'D HEARD my phone during the night, I would have known Brixton had gone with Ivan and Percy. We could have alerted the authorities in Paris that they should meet the flight on the other end to find a kidnapped child. Max put me on hold while he looked into the flight.

We were too late. The flight had already landed. Brixton was gone. In Paris.

Max said he'd be right over to my house to talk in person, after he told the authorities what he knew. I hung up the phone and ran to the attic. The door was locked.

I pounded on the door. "Dorian, let me in. I know you need your own space, but this is an emergency. Brixton has been kidnapped."

The door flew open. "Kidnapped?"

"Yes. No. Sort of. Effectively, yes."

Dorian cocked his head and wriggled his horns. "You are delirious, *mon amie.* Come inside and sit down." He took my hand and led me to a steamer trunk we used as a bench.

I breathed deeply as Dorian hopped up onto the trunk to sit next to me. A drop of a dark red substance clung to his bottom lip.

"Oh, God," I said. "You're bleeding. I didn't think you could bleed."

"I'm bleeding?" Dorian whipped his head around and flapped his wings. One of them hit my shoulder and knocked me off the trunk. "*Pardon*." He scrambled off the seat and helped me up.

"Your lip," I said. "It's your lip." I held my breath. His health was worse than I thought, with a new symptom.

"Ah. Only tomato sauce."

It didn't look like tomato sauce. Was he lying to shield me from how close he was to death? But as awful as it was, Dorian's unnatural death wasn't this morning's priority. "Brixton left for Paris with Percy and Ivan."

"Along with *mon livre*. Perhaps he wishes to be a superhero and is attempting to retrieve my book."

I shook my head. "Brix doesn't know it was stolen. I've been trying to keep him out of this."

"Then why would he go with them? They are very bad men."

"He doesn't know that! He's friends with Ivan. Ivan now believes in alchemy, and if he's working with Percy, he believes what Percy has told him."

"Backward alchemy," Dorian whispered.

"Which requires a sacrifice."

"*Mais non!* Why would the boy agree to such a thing?"

"I'm sure Percy lied to Ivan and Brixton, like Lucien lied to Percy to trick him into the lazy route of becoming a backward alchemist. Ivan doesn't realize what Brix would be doing to help him."

The doorbell rang, and I moved toward the door. Dorian put his one good arm on his hip. "Max Liu?"

"I'll talk to him in the kitchen so you can hear us, okay?"

In the kitchen, I explained to Max that Ivan had grown delusional as his health deteriorated, and that I thought he'd stolen a valuable alchemy book of mine because he thought alchemy was real. I theorized that Ivan had convinced Brixton to go to Paris with him, because that's where a certain type of alchemy supposedly draws its power from.

"Why didn't you report the theft?" Max asked.

"I didn't want to get Ivan in trouble. I thought I could get it back once he came to his senses. I didn't realize he'd go so far."

Max checked with passport control and found that I was right. Brixton had arrived in Paris earlier that day. He'd used his passport to visit his stepdad before; a well-traveled teenager accompanied by two respectable-looking adults hadn't been questioned.

Max wanted to go through the proper channels, but I knew there wasn't time. Besides, it would be impossible to explain to the authorities where they should look for Brixton, especially since I wasn't sure myself.

There wasn't time for me to get a fake passport, either. If I wanted to save Dorian and Brixton, I had to get to France today.

FORTY-TWO

I HAD NO TROUBLE clearing customs in Paris with my own passport. Madame Leblanc's nephew must not have moved forward with the cold case.

With my adrenaline pumping, I set out to search Paris for the trio. I tied a white scarf over my hair and put on sunglasses, hoping to deter the eagle-eyed Madame Leblanc if she happened to cross my path.

I started with Notre Dame, the center of backward alchemy. I waited impatiently in the line of tourists that snaked across the courtyard. Many of the visitors carried umbrellas to shield themselves not from rain but from the spring sun. It made it difficult to identify individual people in the crowd. I listened for voices instead. Chinese, Spanish, Italian, and English with accents ranging from Australian to the American South. Nothing that sounded like Brixton, Ivan, or Percy.

Inside the cathedral's sanctuary walls, I showed a photograph of Brixton to every guide and worker in the cathedral. With the heavenly stained glass above casting a glowing light throughout the stone church above us, they all shook their heads.

Unlike many cathedrals, Notre Dame didn't contain a large crypt beneath its floors. The "official" crypt was a tourist attraction located across the courtyard from Notre Dame. Through miniature displays and audio recordings, it told the story of Paris. When construction of Notre Dame had begun in the 1200s, Paris wasn't yet known as Paris. The bishops had wished to build a monument to God in a spot where people from across Europe had gathered, and the cathedral quickly became a pilgrimage site.

As for the crypt that contained bones of bishops and other important Frenchmen, many were entombed on the street level inside the cathedral, leaving only a small crypt—and it was off limits. I gave a generous "donation" to the same security guard who had given me access to the crypt the previous week.

Brixton wasn't there.

Before leaving the Île de la Cité, I stopped inside the tourist crypt. Just for good measure. Again, nothing.

What was I missing?

I was run-down both physically and emotionally. I stopped in a café in the shadow of Notre Dame for a glass of Perrier for hydration, *pain au chocolate* for energy, and a cup of tea for my spirits.

A siren sounded, but I couldn't see where the sound was coming from.

A crowd of people rushed to the edge of the Seine, and I realized why I couldn't see the vehicle with a siren—it was in the water.

I tossed coins on the table and rushed through the crowd. From the edge of Pont Neuf bridge, I watched helplessly as the emergency boat came to a splashing halt in the river. The text on the side read SUCCURS AUX VICTIMES: SAPEURS-PUMERS DE PARIS.

Divers jumped from the boat and swam toward a still figure.

A shiver like shards of glass covered my body. I couldn't breathe. Was I too late? I imagined Brixton dumped unceremoniously into the Seine once he was no longer of use.

The first diver reached the body. And there was no question that it was a dead body, not a living person. The diver turned over the body. It was a young man, but it wasn't Brixton. I looked on in horror.

It was the police officer who had interviewed me the previous week. Madame Leblanc's grandnephew.

I was sure I was going to vomit over the side of the bridge. I felt claustrophobic in the crowd of people surging forward to catch a glimpse of the dead body. I held my head and pushed my way through the throng, also trying to push away the thought barreling through my mind: *Death follows you everywhere you go, Zoe Faust.*

Who had killed Madame Leblanc's police officer nephew?

I raced down the stone steps that led to the riverbed, but Gendarme Gilbert's body had already been pulled onto the boat. Its engine revved. From the edge of the river, I called out in my most authoritative French for them to stop.

To my surprise, it worked. Sort of. They didn't change course, but they paused for long enough for me to call out a few words to them.

I told them how sorry I was for the loss of one of their own, and asked what had happened.

"You are mistaken, mademoiselle," the officer answered, then motioned to his colleague to continue onward. The boat stirred up a froth of dark water and disappeared down the Seine.

I was mistaken? What did that mean? Did he differentiate between the branches of the police and not feel bad when a man from another division was killed? Or was I mistaken that Gilbert was dead? No, that wasn't right. I'd seen enough death to know what I was looking at. Was it possible it wasn't Gilbert? Could my mind be playing tricks on me?

I jumped as a hand pressed against my elbow. I was standing too close to the Seine. The strong hand pulled me back.

"*Je suis desolé, mademoiselle,*" he said. "I did not mean to frighten you. You seemed so distressed, I did not wish you to fall. Yet I have made things worse."

I studied the newcomer. His eyes were sharp and he spoke in polished French, but he wasn't dressed with the effortlessly put-together fashion sense one imagined such a man to have. In spite of the warmth of the day, he wore layers of ragged clothing and carried a dirty backpack over his shoulders. Two newspapers, *Le Monde Diplomatique* and *La Tribune Internationale*, poked out of his torn coat pocket, and a beaten-up book of Victor Hugo's poetry rested in the side pocket of the backpack.

"No harm was done," I said. "Thank you for your concern, monseiur."

"You knew poor Gilbert as well?"

I hadn't been imagining things. The body floating in the river was indeed the police officer who'd driven me from France.

"Please," he said, "There is a bench just here. You must sit."

"How did you know Gilbert?" I asked, letting him lead me to the bench.

"I am in between residences." He chuckled. "Being outdoors much of the time, I meet many people. Gilbert was one of the better ones. He often brought me a croissant when he took walks here."

"On his rounds as a police officer?"

The man cocked his head and laughed again. "Gilbert? He was not police."

"Not the National Police. A *gendarme*."

He shook his head. "Gilbert was an actor."

"An actor?"

FORTY-THREE

WITH THIS NEW PIECE of information, reality snapped into focus on a different plane. A slight shift in the lens I was using to examine all the facts gave everything a new perspective.

Gendarme Gilbert wasn't affiliated with the police.

Had Madame Leblanc hired an actor to impersonate a police officer to scare a confession out of me? I thought that through. It was a weak plan. If she truly believed I was an immortal Zoe Faust, surely she wouldn't think I'd so easily confess. There also hadn't been time for her to coach an actor with so many facts. He did consult a notebook, though. Even if I granted he was a good improvisational actor, why had he been killed?

"Are you all right, mademoiselle?" the homeless poetry connoisseur asked.

"His death is a shock. I'll be fine. I just need a moment."

I tugged at the ends of my hair and watched the ripples of the Seine. Gendarme Gilbert hadn't been the only person acting.

I hadn't stopped to think about how implausible it was for Madame Leblanc to have such vivid memories of her childhood. Finding a dead body would leave an impression and be hard to forget. But the rest? She could very well be acting.

That meant an unknown person had hired two actors—an old woman to impersonate someone who knew me in the 1940s, and a young man who could play a rookie police officer. Why? The only answer that made sense was to convince me that I should leave France.

So not Lucien. He'd wanted me to stay so he could steal Dorian's book, and it had inconvenienced him that he'd had to follow me to Portland. Who else was there? It had to be an alchemist.

That only left one person: Ambrose's son Percy.

But why kill the actor? Was he a loose end? Was the woman who played Madame Leblanc next? Was there any way I could find the actress to warn her?

"Monsieur, did you see where exactly the police found Gilbert's body?" I spoke before realizing how odd the question must have sounded. "I mean, I'd hate to think about the indignity of him floating in the river for a long time. I hope he was found quickly."

"A woman walking her terrier saw him floating in the river right here, under the shadow of Notre Dame. I cannot imagine he was in the river long. Between the tourists and the locals, it would be impossible to miss him. Rest assured, mademoiselle. I will not be so philosophical as to assert he is now in a better place, but his dignity is intact and he will be adequately mourned by his friends."

"*Under the shadow of Notre Dame,*" I whispered. "Beneath the city."

I now had an idea what I was looking for. The actor's body had washed up not only next to Notre Dame, the very place connected to alchemy and Dorian's book, but *beneath* it.

I looked around but didn't see any obvious entry points. But although I didn't know how to find it, I had an answer for how backward alchemists could have a space connected to Notre Dame without being observed as being part of it. The perfect place to hide a backward alchemy lab that needed to be close to Notre Dame. Not only a basement, but truly underground. A secret space where a backward alchemist could perform a transformation.

But where? Invisible to the city above were an assortment of catacomb passageways, bunkers that had been built during World War II, metro tunnels, shafts for water and sewage, and quarries that had been mined for limestone and gypsum for centuries, causing many a cave-in. Those cave-ins were much more common when I'd lived in Paris decades before, causing me to be wary of climbing beneath the surface of Paris.

"I hope, mademoiselle, that you are not looking to venture beneath the city to avenge Gilbert's death. People have died down there, after they've gotten lost and not been able to find their way out."

"I have a young friend," I said. "Just a boy. I think he might be with the same people who did this to Gilbert."

"Even if this is true, your death would not help him."

"There are people who know the city's underground well," I said, thinking of how it was now a trendy thing for artists to stage art shows or dance parties underground.

"You'll never find them."

"Who?"

"The Urban eXperimenters. That's who you're going to try to find, yes?"

"That's what they call themselves?"

"One of the groups. And I've tried. Believe me, I've tried. They don't like to reveal their identities. I once thought the underground might be a good place to stay during winter, but it is not what one would expect. I wish you good luck finding your young friend. But heed the words of an old man who has seen where such folly can lead. Following your heart is beautiful in the pages of a book, but in life, remember to think before you descend."

I thanked my new friend with a handshake while surreptitiously tucking a few Euros into his Victor Hugo book with the sleight-of-hand skills I'd learned from Dorian, then ran down the riverbank.

He was right: I couldn't find Brixton alone, but I now knew how to get the help I needed. I ducked into a quiet square filled with Honey Locust trees to make a phone call to my secret weapon: a fourteen-year-old.

"Hi, Ms. Faust," Brixton's friend Veronica said.

I'd never get used to the fact that people could see your name when you called them.

"I need your help finding Brix," I said.

"Mr. Liu and Brix's mom already asked me. I don't know where he went. My dad even searched my room. Like he'd be hiding in the closet! Can you believe that? I really don't know where he is."

"I think I do. But I need your help."

"You do?"

"I need to get a message to the Cataphiles of Paris."

"Paris? Brixton is in *Paris*? How did he get to Paris? I mean, I knew he had a passport cuz he went to visit his stepdad somewhere a couple of years ago."

"Veron—"

"But I always thought the two of us would go together, you know? Backpacking before college. He knows how much I wanted to go. The City of Lights. The—"

"Veronica. Please listen. He's not here on vacation."

"*Here?* You mean you're in Paris, too?"

"He's in trouble."

A pause. "Really? It's not just a crazy idea to get to Europe before Ethan?"

"I promise I'll explain everything as soon as I can. But first, I need your help."

"Okay. Um, what's a Cataphile?"

"People who like to explore underground. Sort of like what you, Brixton, and Ethan did when you explored Portland's Shanghai Tunnels."

"That was different. There aren't *graveyards* underneath Portland, Ms. Faust. That's who you mean, right? The explorers who sneak into creepy old tombs underneath Paris to walk through old bones and things? I saw the creepiest photos online from an art show and pop-up kitchen set to candlelight in Paris."

"That's them—"

"Oh, you should totally do something like that in the Shanghai Tunnels, where it's cool without being weird with all the skulls and things, you know? Is that what Brixton is in Paris for?"

"Sort of. But because what these groups do is illegal, they don't like to be found by people who aren't part of their group."

"You want me to post a message to this online group?"

"I know it's a lot to ask," I said, "but I think it'll help me find Brixton. I don't know how else to find them, but I thought if you tried you might—"

"Sure."

"What?"

"While we've been talking, I found them. Um, I've only had one year of French, though. Can you tell me whatever your message is *en français*?"

FORTY-FOUR

An hour later, I sat at a crooked wooden table scarred with key carvings in the back room of a Left Bank café with Constantine and Emma, who insisted they would only use their first names. That was fine with me, since I wasn't going to reveal more than my first name to them. Yet we huddled together like old friends, speaking in low voices as we constructed our plan.

Veronica had posted a message that a boy had been kidnapped and taken to the tunnels, and that the police hadn't followed up on the tip. Anyone who wanted to help me could meet outside a café near the entrance to the catacombs. I knew the tourist attraction wouldn't be where we descended, but with urban explorers hiding their discoveries almost as well as alchemists, I couldn't think of a better place for a group of people to meet.

The eight others who'd shown up had departed as soon as they realized this wasn't a piece of performance art. They had wanted to be part of a murder mystery-themed game like a similar one staged in a newly discovered section of the catacombs the previous month. Constantine and Emma were different. They were hardcore Cataphiles who'd taken Veronica's note seriously and come prepared. They arrived in thigh-high rubber boots and carried small backpacks filled with maps, lights, and other items they didn't reveal to me. I guessed they were brother and sister, for they both had tiny bodies, ginger hair, and a familiarity that I remembered from long ago.

The first words out of Constantine's mouth, after listening to my plea and extinguishing his cigarette, were, "You were right to contact us."

"Below ground," Emma added, "we will be of far greater help than the police."

I'm not a perfect judge of character—as my misjudgment of Percy and Ivan reminded me—but in spite of their youthful arrogance, the thing that told me I could trust Emma and Constantine in this situation was their healthy skepticism of the authorities. They hadn't once asked me why I didn't try again to convince the police. Instead, they followed me to a private corner and quizzed me for details of Brixton's disappearance so we could construct the best plan of attack.

"This is our best way in," Constantine said, using his index finger to circle a hand-drawn mark on a wrinkled photocopy of official blueprints.

Emma clicked her tongue. "*Non.* That passageway is always muddy."

"But it gets us close to Notre Dame," I said. "That's what matters."

Emma's pale cheeks turned scarlet.

"Emma brings up a good point," Constantine said, his eyes not leaving the map.

"I'll pay your laundry bill," I said, not caring about the naked desperation in my voice. "I'll pay whatever you want. You know the life of a child is at stake here. *Please.*"

"You misunderstand," he said.

"The *reason* for the mud in that tunnel is the problem. I forgot there's a blockage there, after another section collapsed. We might not get through."

"Can't we climb down in a big tunnel you know isn't blocked, and go from there?" I asked. This was taking too long. What had become of Brixton?

"This attitude is why people have died down there," Emma said derisively. "It is not as easy as looking at a map. There are not only side tunnels, but different levels and many underground landslides we don't know about. There's a whole world beneath Paris."

"She exaggerates," Constantine said, "but not by much. Here." He jabbed his finger onto another spot, not far from the first. At least I thought it was close by. I wouldn't have been able to read the map without them.

"*Oui*," Emma said. "That will work."

Constantine gave a single curt nod. "*Bon.*"

"Are you ready?" Emma asked me. Without waiting for a reply, she stood and tucked the tightly folded map underneath her shirt.

I tossed coins onto the table and chased after them.

———

When we reached the rusty metal grate that was to be our entrance, Emma handed me a hat with built-in flashlight and an extra set of gloves. I looked down at my own green ankle boots, gray cotton slacks, and black cardigan. Even with my guides, I was far from prepared for this. All that mattered was that I reach Brixton in time.

Willing myself to forget about the people who'd died during tunnel cave-ins of previous centuries, I took a deep breath or five and climbed into the darkness below.

We walked for what felt like an eternity, passing through limestone and gypsum corridors that had been mined in the Middle Ages, and passing near the more modern Metro, sewer, and water tunnels. In many of the tunnels, empty plastic water bottles and other trash was strewn about. I stepped on more than one long-dead glow stick from the parties that must have taken place here. The trash gave me hope, though. It meant we were traversing where others had recently come. We weren't going to end up as a statistic, another stupid explorer who starved to death underneath Paris.

At a crossroads, they stopped and consulted a map. After only a few seconds, they pointed to the left path.

"Why that way?" I asked. "It's going away from Notre Dame. It looked like we were almost there."

"You will not find them there," Emma said.

"But that's where I think he's been taken. That's why we're here."

Constantine exchanged a look with Emma before speaking. "Nobody goes there."

"Why not?"

"Perhaps it would be best to call the police now," Emma said softly.

I put my hand on her grimy shoulder. "They can't help," I said. "I need to go."

"You don't," Emma said, gripping my hand. "If this is where your young friend has been taken, you won't find him."

"Why?"

Emma didn't answer.

"Death," Constantine said. "Only death awaits down that corridor."

A mixture of panic and hope welled inside me. That had to be the right way.

"I'll pay you for a map and headlamp," I said, hoping they could hear the desperation in my voice. I didn't care if they asked me for all the money I possessed. "I need to find him."

The two communicated wordlessly for a few moments. I think I held my breath for every second.

"No money," Emma said finally. "But you must be safe. Take these breadcrumbs." She pressed a map and what looked like a bag of plastic sticks into my hands. No breadcrumbs in sight.

"Glow sticks," Constantine explained. "At every turn you take, break one and leave it there. You'll be able to find your way back."

Breadcrumbs to find my way out of the dark forest.

————

My solitary route took me through catacombs and crypts of bones as I continued the search for Brixton. It was a disheartening image that reminded me too much of the very real possibility that I could be too late to save his life.

I remembered to leave a glow stick at each turn, though in these tunnels the curves were deceptive rather than clear cut. I hoped I'd used enough.

The sound of a man's voice speaking made me stop in my tracks. A moment later, I breathed in a familiar scent that blended metallic and sweet. I ran forward, slowing only as a sliver of light cast its glow in front of me. I forced myself to slow down and approach with caution.

I found myself in an alchemy lab like no other I'd ever seen before. Instead of the complicated assortment of dozens of glass vessels, hundreds of ingredients, and countless books, a cozy armchair took up more space than the single table of alchemical apparatuses and ingredients. Candles illuminated the 50-square-meter space that looked more like a child's playroom than a serious alchemy lab.

And a child *was* there. Brixton's body was sprawled on the cold stone floor.

He wasn't moving.

A lone man stood next to Brixton. He clutched Dorian's book in muscular hands. The man turned, and I saw his face. Ivan.

FORTY-FIVE

Only ... Was I mistaken? The hands that gripped *Not Untrue Alchemy* were too strong to be Ivan's. His face and his body looked different as well.

"You don't have to do this, Ivan," I said.

"Zoe? How—"

"Why don't you come over here?"

"What? Oh, Brixton isn't hurt. He's sleeping."

"He's not sleeping, Ivan." A ferocious anger welled up inside me. "He's dying."

Ivan looked hesitantly at Brixton, then shook his head furiously. The motion startled me. Ivan normally moved slowly. Not any longer. That's why he looked different. A vigorous middle-aged man stood before me. There was no way I could take on this new Ivan physically. If it had only been me, I would have risked fighting him. But with Brixton unconscious beneath him, I had to be smart. I had to reason with Ivan.

"The apprentice sacrifices their life," I said. "I know Percy kept the truth from you. That's how backward alchemy works. That's how it begins."

"No. That's not how it works. You're lying."

"It's Lucien and Percy who lied to you."

"Lucien? Did he find you? Where is he?"

"You don't know?"

"I now know of backward alchemy's true potential. You lied to me, Zoe. You said it was dangerous, you said *he* was dangerous. That's why I didn't embrace backward alchemy sooner. If only—"

"Lucien is *dead*, Ivan. He's the man who was found in the shed in the woods last week."

"You're trying to confuse me. That man was Heather's father."

"No, it wasn't. Backward alchemy changes how quickly a body deteriorates. It misled the police. It was Lucien. And if Brixton survives—" I swallowed hard and looked at his unmoving form on the cold floor. *Don't look, Zoe.* I couldn't let myself break down. "If Brixton survives, he's going to be implicated as a murderer unless we find out who killed Lucien."

"This is madness. The boy is simply exhausted from the Death Rotation. And there's no reason for the police to suspect him."

"Lucien caught Brixton following him and grabbed him. Brixton's skin cells ended up under Lucien's fingernails."

"You're trying to distract and confuse me. Nothing you're saying makes any sense. Can't you see backward alchemy's potential? Look at what I've become. When Brixton wakes up, he'll be stronger too."

"You don't understand—"

"You weren't honest with me, Zoe. How can I believe you now?"

"You're right. I'm sorry. It's hard for me to open up. But I'm ready to talk now. To share everything I know. Why don't you come over here and we can talk about it?"

A pained expression crossed Ivan's face. "I see what you're doing. You think I wish to hurt Brixton. How little you know of me. I would never do that."

"I don't think you would do so intentionally." I spoke as calmly as I could manage. "It won't hurt to get him medical attention, will it? Now that you're done with the transformation, we could—"

"We're not done. Not yet."

I said a silent prayer. There was hope for Brixton. "This isn't you, Ivan. I know you're a good man. You don't know what you're doing. You've been lied to."

"Only by you. You twisted the facts so I didn't believe what Lucien had to tell me."

"You spoke with him?"

"He wanted my help. He saw that I had a vast library of books on alchemy and wanted to know if I had *Non Degenera Alchemia*—the book that you've so desperately wanted to understand. You've been lying to me since we met. You never wanted to understand that book for the sake of knowledge. Percival told me the truth. It was to save that creature who lives in your attic." His eyes were pleading. "You could have trusted me, Zoe."

"Because you're showing yourself to be so trustworthy," I snapped before I could stop myself.

"This is your fault," Ivan boomed. "Not mine. If only you'd been honest with me, I could have had the Elixir of Life so much sooner."

I looked at Ivan from head to toe. Was he as strong as he now looked? "How do you feel, Ivan?" I asked quietly.

He frowned and smoothed his wild hair. "Percy said I would feel decades younger immediately, but—" He shrugged. "It must be because there's more to the process."

I thought back on my own true alchemy transformation. I had discovered the Elixir of Life while searching for a cure for my brother, who was dying of the plague. I was so grief-stricken that I didn't realize what I had become until I saw that I wasn't aging.

But true alchemy was different from backward alchemy. The shift in true alchemy was more subtle, because it wasn't a quick fix. From what I'd seen of backward alchemy, the effects were visible and immediate. Ivan did look much healthier than I'd ever seen him, but the full power of backward alchemy was being diminished by the shift that had taken place six months ago. No matter what Percy claimed, Ivan wouldn't be able to experience the full effects of backward alchemy until that fissure was fixed.

"There's indeed more," I said, "but not in the way Percy told you. Did he tell you that a shift occurred six months ago and that everyone who'd been granted an extended life through backward alchemy began to die?"

"It was because you were hoarding that book! That's why he and the others had to make and smoke Alchemical Ashes, to fight for their lives. He had run out of his supply."

"It's not the book, Ivan. The book contains the secrets of backward alchemy and is tied to Notre Dame, but it has nothing to do with why the power is fading."

"You're still lying. I should have believed Lucien when I had the chance."

"What happened when he came to you?"

"Seeing that I was a scholar of alchemy, he confessed to me that he was a backward alchemist who had been alive for centuries. He suspected you had stolen a book that was his. But I trusted you. I foolishly trusted you, Zoe. He wanted me to steal the book from you, as he said you had done from him. He became angry when I refused. I shoved him out the door."

"You shoved him?"

Ivan snorted. "You have always thought me a weak old man, but Lucien was weaker. It was not difficult to push him out of my house. He fell down the front steps."

I gasped.

"It doesn't take much strength to hurt a frail man," Ivan continued, "as I know all too well."

"It was you. It was you who killed him."

"No, he was not dead. I told you—"

"Did he hit his head when he fell?"

Ivan narrowed his eyes that were no longer tired and blood-shot. "He might have, but he got up and left."

"To go back to his makeshift alchemy lab to try to make more Alchemical Ashes. He died before he succeeded."

On the floor, Brixton groaned. Ivan jerked back, startled.

"Brix?" I said, rushing to his side. "Can you hear me?"

His eyes were still closed, but he moaned again. Sweat coated his body.

"Ivan, please," I pleaded. "We've got to get Brixton help."

"He's not supposed to be hurt," Ivan whispered. "He must be faking it. Yes, that's what's happening. He's an attention-seeking kid."

"He's not faking it. And he's going to be arrested for murder."

"I would never let that happen," Ivan said. "You think so little of me? If it comes to that, I'll tell the police what happened."

I recoiled when Ivan's shoulder touched mine as he knelt over Brixton.

Ivan cried out. "This isn't right." He shook Brixton's still shoulders.

"He's not pretending."

"He's cold," Ivan murmured. "Too cold. We must help him."

"Let me call an ambulance."

"No."

I squeezed my eyes shut. I'd been so sure I'd gotten through to Ivan.

"We can't call an ambulance," Ivan said. "They'll be back soon. We have to get Brixton out of here ourselves."

I opened my eyes and saw the good man I'd thought of as my friend.

Ivan handed *Not Untrue Alchemy* to me. With his newfound strength, he lifted Brixton into his arms and carried him out of the backward alchemy lab beneath Notre Dame.

In the darkness of the tunnel, Ivan swore. "I don't know if I can find my way out without them."

"That," I said, "I can help with." I turned him towards a faintly glowing light. The glow sticks Constantine and Emma had brought were the perfect breadcrumbs to make our way out.

As I watched Ivan carry Brixton's limp form from the subterranean gloom out into the summer sunlight, I was filled with two of the most conflicting emotions I'd ever experienced together. The all-encompassing relief of having found Brixton in time was weighed down with the realization that the only remaining hope I had of saving Dorian's life was the backward alchemy transformation I'd been denying: a sacrifice.

I now knew, with all certainty, that I would have to sacrifice my own life to save Dorian's. And I knew that I would do it.

FORTY-SIX

THE HOSPITAL CALLED BRIXTON'S family, explaining that he'd been found unconscious and dehydrated, but was stable.

I hated hospitals, with their overbearing astringent scents that assaulted my senses and my memories of the horrors of medicine of past centuries, but I didn't want to be far from Brixton. Ivan stayed with me. We hadn't yet talked about what had transpired, but he'd been the one who carried Brixton's body from subterranean Paris, and he spoke to the hospital staff so I could keep my name out of it.

There was another reason it was difficult for me to talk with the staff. I was so thankful Brixton hadn't died like the actor who played the policeman that it was difficult for me to speak. My eyes kept welling with tears of relief.

Ivan and I sat together in an outdoor courtyard waiting room. People had recently been smoking here, but the scent was far better than the sterilizing chemicals and strong medicines inside. Neither of us could sit still. I paced the length of the courtyard, and Ivan prodded the newly regenerated muscles of his arms. How long would it last? I couldn't let myself begin to feel sorry for Ivan. His blind selfishness had nearly killed Brixton.

"Would you sit with me for a minute?" Ivan asked. "I see your hesitation to be near this monster, but I wish to apologize. And to understand."

I joined him on a wooden bench, not wanting to hear his apologies, but wanting even less for the other visitors to hear what he had to say.

"If I'd performed the Death Rotation experiment properly," Ivan began, then faltered. "If I—" He cleared his throat and looked up at the wispy clouds above. "If I'd done it right, the boy would be dead?"

"If you'd finished the transformation," I said. "Brixton only survived for as long as he did because of his own strength."

Brixton had survived for the same reason that my own backward alchemy transformation *hadn't* worked well the last time I'd tried it to make Dorian's Tea of Ashes. He'd lived for the flipside of the reason I'd been sickened.

"Brix was tending to my garden," I explained. "He has a green thumb, and the garden flourished. His energy gave strength to the plants he tended, and that energy flowed back into him, giving him strength and protecting him."

"Alchemy doesn't create something out of nothing," Ivan said. "You tried to teach me that, but I wouldn't listen."

"Alchemy transforms, and the power of the transformations is tied to the practitioner and their materials."

"You can tell them the truth," he said. "Max and the beast. I can see on your face that you want to call them."

"He's not a beast," I said. The man sitting next to me was much more of a beast than Dorian would ever be. "And what could I possibly tell Max?"

"The truth. I was blinded by my desire to live, so I believed a hoax. I put Brixton's life in danger with a desperate plan."

"You're owning up to this?"

"Of course. I'm mortified by my actions, and thankful alchemy isn't real so I didn't harm Brixton."

I nodded. He understood we couldn't explain alchemy to the world. I stepped to the quietest corner of the courtyard and called Max. I kept an eye on Ivan, who wasn't interested in me. He flexed his fingers and stood on his tiptoes. It must have been a strange sensation to have one's body transform within hours.

My call to Max went to voicemail, which I was thankful for since it would be easier to stick to the somewhat truthful lies if I kept to the script I'd rehearsed in my mind. Next I called Dorian. Even with the coded timing of rings he insisted we use, he didn't answer. Where was he? With me gone, he knew he shouldn't be baking at Blue Sky Teas.

Frustrated, I hung up the phone and looked up at the sky for a few seconds. When I turned my attention back to the courtyard, Ivan was gone.

In his place on the bench was a torn piece of paper. Caught in the gentle breeze, it fluttered to the ground. I ran to it and snatched it in a tense hand. The handwritten scrawl read *I'm sorry*.

I crumpled the note in my hand and rushed inside but caught no sight of him. I asked everyone I saw, down every hall I could find, but nobody had seen him. The hospital appeared to be more labyrinthine than the catacombs.

I wasn't giving up. I looked from room to room. As I finished searching a hall of patient rooms, a news story on the television in the waiting room caused me to stop my search. On the screen was a face I recognized, one that still bore the marks of bee stings. Professor Chevalier, the scholar studying the gargoyle statue, was being interviewed by a reporter. I turned up the volume.

Professor Chevalier was explaining the mystery of the curiously posed gargoyle statue thought to be stolen from Notre Dame in the

1860s. There had been a break-in at the university, and thieves had ransacked the whole Architecture Department. The reporter asked the professor how he first noticed the theft.

"No," Professor Chevalier protested. "It was not thieves who stole the chimera. The stone creature came to life."

The reporter abruptly ended the interview and the camera switched back to a reporter sitting at a desk with a plastic smile frozen on her face. But she wasn't able to hide the flush filling her cheeks.

Was it possible? The Death Rotation Ivan and Brixton performed must have also enlivened the gargoyle. Perhaps because I'd left the Alchemical Ashes in his mouth, the nearby alchemy had woken him enough that he could swallow the ashes and escape.

If I were a gargoyle who once stood atop Europe's most famous cathedral, where would I go? I left the hospital and headed for Notre Dame.

————

People see what they expect to see. They believe what already makes sense to their understanding of the world. Therefore it didn't surprise me when the tourists I spoke to said they'd seen a disfigured man. They assumed him to be homeless because he wore only a sheet and carried a bottle of liquor. They pointed in the direction they had seen him go.

I thought I was going to lose my mind as I waited in line to climb to the top of Notre Dame, but it was the only way to gain access to the stairs. I used the time to look up a few things on my cell phone. Now that Brixton was safe, I felt guilty that I hadn't found the actress who played Madame Leblanc, to warn her that her colleague was dead and she might be next. I found the *gendarme* actor's website. He didn't have any affiliation with an actress who looked like Madame Leblanc.

A tap on my shoulder alerted me to the fact that the line was moving. It was time to climb the winding steps of Notre Dame once more. I hadn't heard any screams from above, so I wasn't entirely certain my theory was correct. But I had to try.

The first place I looked—near the famous Gallery of Gargoyles—was a bust. But while the guard was dealing with two people blocking the way with banned selfie sticks, I slipped into an off-limits area near the bell tower.

A scuffling sound startled me.

"*Allo?*" I said softly, hoping it wasn't a cathedral worker.

A burp broke the silence. I stepped forward and saw a lumpy sheet in the corner. The sheet moved.

"Do you remember me?" I said. "I tried to help you last week."

"*Va t'en!*"

"I'm not leaving. I can help you."

The gargoyle poked his head out from underneath the sheet and glared at me. "*T'es conne.*"

Great. That was all I needed. A drunk gargoyle telling me to get lost and calling me dumb.

"Are you drunk?

"'It is the hour to be drunken! On wine, on poetry, or on virtue, as you wish.'"

"You've only been *awake* for an hour ... But if you've already found liquor, I suppose you don't need this." I held up a bottle of absinthe, the same brand that had been found in his frozen hand in Prague.

He lunged for it. I put the bottle behind my back, hoping he wouldn't tackle me. This gargoyle was more than a foot taller than Dorian, almost five feet tall.

"Only if you talk to me," I continued. "What's your name?"

He chuckled. "Leopold. *Je m'appelle* Leopold."

Now that he was standing before me, I got a better look at him. Leopold did look like he could be an older brother to Dorian. Since he'd once stood with the other stone creatures on the Gallery of Gargoyles, he was larger than Dorian in both height and girth. His body was a similar gray color, but his eyes were gray, not black like Dorian's. His horns were larger than Dorian's, yet he had no wings.

"I'm a friend," I said. "An alchemist."

Leopold blinked at me. "Your name is Alchemist?"

"No. My name is Zoe. I'm an alchemist."

He shrugged. "*D'accord*." Did he not realize alchemy had brought him to life? This was too big a conversation to have a few meters away from the tourists atop Notre Dame.

"Myself," he continued, "I am a *poète*."

A gargoyle poet? I supposed it was no stranger than a gargoyle chef.

"You have another friend, too," I said. "Another gargoyle, like you."

He drew his horns together. "You mock me, mademoiselle."

"Let me call him, so you can see." I dialed Dorian for a video call. "I think you'll feel more comfortable talking to him."

A moment later, Dorian's beaming face appeared on the screen. An amazed Leopold grabbed my phone.

The two gargoyles spoke rapid Latin to each other, so I wasn't able to follow most of what they said. But when they switched back to French, they told me they'd agreed Leopold would accompany me back to Portland. I hadn't thought that far ahead, but who was I to stop two living gargoyles on a mission? We quickly constructed a plan where Leopold would turn to stone in a completely different shape than he'd been found in on the Prague bridge, so nobody would suspect he was the gargoyle "stolen" from the university.

"Now we need to get you out of here," I said.

Using his sheet to disguise himself and his drunken state as an excuse to keep his head down and lean on me, Leopold and I wound down the Notre Dame stairs and away from the cathedral as quickly and quietly as possible.

Leopold spent the evening in our small rented room alternately drinking the bottle of absinthe I'd offered him and reciting poetry to it.

———————

I flew back to Portland the next day with two special deliveries. Heather had authorized me to accompany Brixton home after I went to the hospital first thing in the morning. The doctors had determined he was suffering from dehydration and severe jet lag but was otherwise healthy, so they wanted to discharge him as soon as possible.

Brixton and I traveled with a special piece of luggage: a storage crate containing a statue I claimed to have found at a flea market. Also in the crate was a case of absinthe. It was meant to last our new friend a month, or at the very least a week. When we arrived at PDX, the bottles were empty.

FORTY-SEVEN

BACK AT HOME IN Portland, Brixton was safe; that was the most important thing. But I couldn't rest easy. Brixton was still recovering and not yet back to his usual self. Ivan and Percy's whereabouts were unknown. And I hadn't figured out how to cure the deterioration of backward alchemy with anything short of the ultimate sacrifice: giving my own life.

Further down the line, I worried what would happen with the police investigation into Lucien's murder. They hadn't yet discovered his identity, but it was only a matter of time before they connected him to Brixton via the boy's DNA under his fingernails.

In spite of his partial backward alchemy transformation, Ivan hadn't lost his humanity. At least not yet. It was a small silver lining, but I was willing to take it. Even though he hadn't yet come forward to confess that he was responsible for Lucien's death, he'd helped Brixton escape the tunnels in Paris and had accepted that he'd been misled by Percy. I hoped he'd come through before the police got their DNA results back.

In the meantime, I had my hands full dealing with two gargoyle roommates.

I came home from visiting a subdued Brixton to find a smoky scent permeating the house.

"It is his fault," Dorian said as soon as I came through the door. "He distracted me and the bread burned in the oven."

"It's all right, Dorian. So … where's Leopold?"

Dorian frowned. "Taking a nap in the attic. I do not understand, Zoe. He does not need to sleep."

"Maybe he's just lazy."

Dorian and I climbed the stairs to the attic and found Leopold curled up on a stack of pillows on the steamer trunk. The pillows looked suspiciously like the ones from my bed.

"He's not asleep," I said, sniffing the air. "He's drunk."

Dorian gaped at Leopold. Our gargoyle guest stretched luxuriantly and sat up.

"Where is the art in this mansion?" Leopold asked. "Your walls are quite barren. Monsieur Robert-Houdin informed me this is a new abode for you. Have you not yet finished unpacking?"

"I collect books and other alchemical items, not art."

Leopold's gray eyes grew wide. "*C'est vrai?*"

"It is true," Dorian answered. "I have already explained to you that Zoe is an alchemist. This is how she understands how you and I were brought to life. We have not yet discussed the intricacies—"

"No art?" Leopold said, again completely ignoring the reference to alchemy. "*Quelle horreur!* I may as well return to stone."

I wouldn't have believed a gargoyle could be more dramatic than Dorian if I hadn't seen it with my own eyes.

"Without art, what do you do for amusement?" Leopold asked Dorian.

"Before you stated your strong desire to take a siesta," Dorian said, "I was showing you my kitchen—"

"Cooking? This is your idea of fun? I believed you to be joking. This is women's work, no?"

Dorian puffed up his chest. "I am a chef of great distinction."

Leopold giggled. Then burped. "*Pardon.*"

"Perhaps," Dorian said in his most diplomatic voice, "if you have now recovered from your journey, you will tell us of your life."

The gargoyle rolled off the steamer trunk and clasped his talons together. "'How little remains of the man I once was,'" he said softly, "'save the memory of him! But remembering is only a new form of suffering.'"

"Baudelaire," I said. "You're quoting Baudelaire. You quoted his poetry when I first met you too. You said you were a poet. So you enjoy Baudelaire's poetry?"

"*Enjoy?* Is this the right word to describe the influence of the great man? To handle language so skillfully is to practice evocative sorcery!"

"You knew him," I said. Dorian remained speechless.

"*Oui.* Monsieur Charles Baudelaire brought me from the shadows."

"*Bon!*" Dorian chimed in. "I, too, had a great man teach me. Jean Eugène Robert-Houdin. Surely you have heard of—"

"The stage magician? *Pfft.* A common entertainer."

Dorian sputtered several words, none of them intelligible.

"You have more wine?" Leopold asked. "Or hashish?"

———

Dinner that night was a tense affair. We learned that Leopold had been taken in by a group of Bohemian artists and writers who were loosely affiliated with Victor Hugo's romantic army. Critic and poet Charles Baudelaire was the man Leopold was closest to, and upon his death, Leopold mourned him tremendously. Much poetry was written during those dark days. Leopold claimed that some of Baudelaire's last works were ghostwritten by Leopold himself. I was disinclined to believe him. Then again, Baudelaire had been drunk when he wrote many of his famous poems.

Dorian cooked a classical French feast in honor of his newfound brother, sending me to buy expensive wine in addition to a short shopping list to supplement what we already had at the house. The menu consisted of marinated olives, spinach and walnut terrine, and lentil pate for appetizers; Breton onion soup for a starter; cider casserole for a main dish; and apricot tarts for dessert.

Leopold drank nearly all of the wine himself but barely touched his food. "A man can go without food for two days," he declared, "but not without poetry."

———

After dinner, Leopold didn't offer to help with the dishes. I began to help Dorian, but he said it would be easiest in the small kitchen for him to take care of the dishes himself, even with only one good arm. I didn't argue. It was difficult for me to talk with him alone, knowing the sacrifice I was getting ready to make. He would never agree to it, so I had to keep it to myself until the preparations were ready.

Once it was late enough, Dorian left for Julian Lake's house to prepare food for the following day, after which he'd go to the tea-shop kitchen to bake pastries before dawn. It felt strange to follow such a simple daily routine after the crazy events of the past few days and weeks, but there was really nothing else to be done.

I made my rounds through the house, making sure it was tightly secured. As I passed back through the first floor, I found Leopold passed out. In the middle of the dining room table.

FORTY-EIGHT

THE NEXT DAY THE Portland police declared Brixton well enough to talk with them about what had happened with Ivan. He told the police that Ivan had gone crazy and started to believe all the historical alchemy books he was studying. Brixton also said that Ivan had convinced him he needed his help to save his life. Of course he'd wanted to help. But Brixton swore he didn't know what Ivan had in mind. Max knew him well enough that he might have picked up on the fact that Brixton wasn't telling the whole story, but with the detectives on the case, Brix played the role of an innocent, gullible, and slightly selfish kid to perfection.

The police thankfully hadn't yet gotten the results of the full DNA testing, so they hadn't connected Brixton to Lucien's dead body. As soon as I was sure Brixton was truly safe, then I'd be ready to make my sacrifice for Dorian.

I visited Brixton after he returned home from the police station. His mom was sitting on one side of his bed.

"I'm never letting this one out of my sight again," she said. She pulled him close and planted a kiss on the top of his head. "He's grounded for the rest of the summer."

Brixton rolled his eyes. "Very funny, Mom."

Heather's breezy smile turned almost as grim as the day I'd seen her at the morgue. "I'm dead serious, Brix."

"But I—but you—I mean, I nearly *died*."

"Exactly," Heather said. "You're too old to get away with acting so stupidly. Running off to a foreign country with a delusional neighbor? I liked Ivan, too, but you can't do things like that, honey."

Brixton leaned back on the assortment of pillows his mom had propped up. I had a feeling his summer of being "grounded" would consist of a fair amount of TLC from his parents and probably visits from his friends Ethan and Veronica.

"At least I haven't been keeping a secret," Brixton said, making a face at his mom. "You want to know why Mom has been disappearing lately, Zoe?"

"Brix!" Heather said, "I'm not telling people yet!"

"You said it wasn't a secret anymore."

"Not a secret to *you*, silly."

"Zoe is family, Mom."

I felt a lump form in my throat.

"You're right," she said. "I'm sorry for the secrecy. I didn't want to tell anyone, especially Brixton, before I knew if I'd succeed."

"You'll succeed," a deep voice said. Abel leaned against the bedroom door. "She's studying for her GED."

"That's wonderful," I said.

"You know I dropped out when I had Brix," Heather said. "In a year, he'll have more education then I do. That's not a great example."

"You're a great mom," Abel said. He strode across the room and gave them both a hug. "Stay for dinner?" he asked me.

"I wish I could," I said.

Heather pulled Abel to the bedroom door. "We'll let you two visit a few more minutes while Abel starts dinner."

I'd never been inside Brixton's room before, yet it felt to me like something was missing. "Your mom took away your guitar?" I asked.

He shook his head. "I sorta ... sacrificed it."

"Why would you—"

"Ivan said I had to make a sacrifice for the alchemy to work. That's what we thought the sacrifice was. Giving up something I loved."

"Oh, Brix. I'm so sorry. Your heart was in the right place. Where did you toss it? The Willamette?"

"Pawn shop. I used the money for my ticket to Paris. Ivan talked about *intent* being important in alchemy. My sacrifice used my intent and got me to Paris. Wicked city, by the way." He smiled mischievously for a few seconds before growing serious again. "I'd do it again, you know. To help him not die. I mean, as long as it didn't mean dying myself. Which is totally messed up."

A happy tear slid down my cheek as I walked back to my truck. I'd leave my truck and trailer to Tobias, I thought to myself. Since Rosa was dying, he'd soon need a change. He liked my truck when he visited a few months ago. Maybe he'd like the Airstream too.

————

At home, Leopold was still passed out, although now his hefty gray body was sprawled on my green velvet couch. I poked the bottom of his foot. He twitched but didn't open his eyes. I poked his foot again.

"'I have felt the wind of the wing of madness,'" he mumbled, then rolled over.

I felt myself roll my eyes like my young friend would have done. Leopold wouldn't be disturbing me anytime soon. I unlocked the door to my basement alchemy lab and began the preparations for my sacrifice.

I lit a kerosene lamp and walked to my main work table. A prickle made its way up my spine. Someone had been inside my lab. *Recently*. My gold leaf was gone, as were all of my salts.

But Percy was the one who'd searched my lab before, and he was long gone. Wasn't he?

Where *was* Percy?

FORTY-NINE

"This is one of my favorites," Leopold said. "*Un moment.*" He rubbed his jaw and opened his mouth terrifyingly wide, revealing rows of pointy teeth. Squaring his shoulders, he took a stance that made it look like he was howling at the moon.

"Or this one," he added. He moved out of the werewolf position, shaking his body as if stretching after a workout. Next he crossed his arms, held his head high, and looked down his nose at us.

"That pose does not look scary," Dorian said. He tried to make a frightening pose himself, spreading his wings wide, but he nearly lost his balance. The speed of his deterioration was quickening.

"You miss the point, *mon amie.* In this simple posture, I inch closer ... and closer .... It instills fear in the hearts of men!" He guffawed.

"Er, yes," Dorian said.

"Or how about this one?" Leopold thrust out his chin, baring his bottom row of teeth, and hunched his shoulders.

Dorian circled him. "Too humorous."

"*Oui*, I suspect you are right." Leopold shook out the pose.

At least the two gargoyles were getting along better.

For the last half hour, Leopold had been showing Dorian the various ways he'd stayed hidden since being brought to life. His family of drunken artists and writers had known of his existence (though I suspected half of them thought he was a figment of their collective imaginations), but nobody else did.

Like Dorian, Leopold had learned how to live in the shadows. As we were coming to realize, though, he pushed the boundaries. He went where he wanted then simply turned to stone on the spot if he was in danger of being seen. Often in a bizarre pose, to keep people off balance.

"And nobody ever saw you?" I asked. "Truly?"

Leopold shrugged. "In the music halls and museums, the people think with their hearts, not with their minds."

We all gave a start when my phone buzzed. It was Brixton texting me that he was at the front door.

"You really need a doorbell," he said after I let him inside and we were walking up the stairs. "I've been knocking for five minutes. You're always in the attic."

"Leopold Baudelaire, meet Brixton Taylor."

"Wicked," Brixton whispered, staring at the gargoyle.

"Your servant?" Leopold asked me.

"Our friend," Dorian corrected.

Leopold rubbed his chin and nodded. Dorian prodded him to shake Brixton's hand.

"I thought you were spending time with your family," I said. "And grounded."

"Yeah, Mom is studying for her GED in the open now, but then she and Abel … " He cleared this throat. "I think they wanted to do things no mom should do. Ever."

"'From love there will be born poetry,'" Leopold recited, "'which will spring up toward God like a rare flower.'"

"My life is too weird," Brixton mumbled. "Anyway, I snuck out."

"Now that we have made introductions," Leopold said, "we have important matters to discuss. A council of war, if you will."

Finally. He'd put me off every time I tried to address the problem of backward alchemy turning the gargoyles back into stone.

"It has been brought to my attention," Leopold continued, "that you are cavorting with *un flic*. This will not do. The police are not to be trusted."

I groaned. "My love life isn't your concern. I thought we were going to talk about—"

"If you think this is unimportant, you are *assez stupide*!"

"Not cool," Brixton said. "That's so not cool."

"Why don't you play some music for us, Brixton," Dorian said diplomatically. "I see you have brought your banjo."

Skeptically eyeing Leopold, Brixton picked up the banjo he carried slung over his back. He strummed a 1960s folk song.

"This is not music," Leopold said. "This is—"

He broke off when two phones began to ring at once. Grateful to head off that argument, I picked up mine and smiled.

"Max," I said into the phone. "It's wonderful to hear your voice, but this isn't really a good time."

"I won't take long. This isn't a social call—but I hope it's a good one. Is Brixton there with you?"

"Yeah, he is." How could this be good? Brixton had answered his own phone and stood in the corner, his back to us.

"Good," Max said. "Ivan gave a confession."

"Ivan," I whispered, closing my eyes as I let out a sigh of relief.

"Not what I expected either," he said, misinterpreting my surprise. "He emailed a confession, and we know he's not lying to protect anyone, because he gave us details that led to blood evidence. The man was apparently an aggressive salesman who came to the house while Brixton was there. Grabbed Brixton's arm, which is why Ivan threw him out. I'm betting it'll be Brixton's DNA the lab finds under his fingernails when they conclude their analysis. It was an accident, so I wish Brixton had just told us what happened, but I understand that he's scared. This has been such a strange case—but now life can go back to normal."

Normal. I bit back my true reaction. Everything would be all right without me now. It was time to make my sacrifice.

FIFTY

BRIXTON USED THE INTERRUPTION of the phone calls as an opportunity to escape the rude gargoyle. I walked him downstairs.

"I can let myself out," he said.

"I need a break from those two too," I said. "You hungry? Before you go, you can grab something from the kitchen."

He turned to me, and I saw in his face the caring man he was growing into. "You're different today, Zoe. I don't know what it is. I don't think it's your frustration with Leo—even though you're gonna have to watch that dude."

I gave him a hug. I hadn't meant to, but I was overcome with emotion realizing that I wasn't going to live to see Brixton grow up. "I'm so proud of you," I said, blinking back tears.

Once I was sure I wasn't going to cry, I pulled back from the hug. Brixton was rolling his eyes. "Okay, Zoe. Whatever."

I watched Brixton ride his bike down the driveway with his banjo slung over his back. When he reached the street, he briefly glanced both ways. Catching a glimpse of his profile, I was struck by the handsome man he would soon be.

Instead of going back upstairs, I grabbed my silver raincoat. I scribbled a note to Dorian so he wouldn't worry, then set off on foot.

For the next three hours, I walked around my Hawthorne neighborhood of Portland, stopping to speak to the locals walking their dogs, browse the wares of the quirky stores, pick up a cup of tea at Blue Sky Teas, and literally stop and smell the roses.

Without realizing the route I was taking, I found myself in front of Max's house. The sun hung low in the sky. The day was coming to a close. As was my life.

I was here to say goodbye.

I stood in front of the red door with a gold dragon knocker but paused before I raised my hand to lift it.

The door swung open and a very wet Max grinned at me. In jeans and a white t-shirt, his feet were bare and he held a towel to sopping wet hair. "I thought I saw someone out here. Sorry, I didn't hear the door."

Inside, I walked through the uncluttered living room, filled with a white couch, pewter coffee table, and paintings of forests that were taller than either of us. I came to a stop in front of the sliding glass door that led to the backyard garden. Max laced his fingers through mine as I looked out at the wooden bench where we'd spent so many happy hours together.

When I'd been in a reckless mood, I'd allowed myself to fantasize about spending years with Max, sitting on that bench watching the night-blooming jasmine unfurl and the morning-blooming California poppies awaken with the day.

"You want to go outside?" Max whispered. "Let me grab my—"

I stopped his words with my lips. He didn't object. And it was a good thing he didn't have many things in the house to bump into. Only that plastic skeleton in the hallway.

An hour later, Max fixed us a pot of lemon balm tea using his grandmother's iron tea kettle.

"Sorry about that skeleton," I said. "I can put it back together. I'm good with my hands."

"I know." He kissed my shoulder. "But don't worry about it. It's time I got rid of it. Time I moved on." He added a sprig of fresh mint to the tea, then handed me a white porcelain cup with deep blue Chinese characters. The minty steam made it the perfect choice.

It hit me that it had been selfish of me to come here. While I was here to say goodbye, Max was ready to take the next step with me.

"I'm not entirely convinced the stories about the skeleton are true anyway," Max said.

"You didn't tell me the story. Only that Chadna wanted to draw it out so you'd learn more about it each year as you grew old together."

"Supposedly this skeleton originally contained some *real* human bones."

"That's how med schools used to train their students, you know."

"Apparently some of them still do. My guess was that it was a secret society type of thing. Creepy, huh?"

"Oh my God," I whispered.

"It's not *that* great a story."

"Max, I'm so sorry, but I have to go. I lost track of time."

"You're not staying?"

I kissed him hard and fast. "No, but I'll be back."

Maybe this wasn't goodbye after all.

I ran home, my silver raincoat flapping behind me and hope surging within me. I might not have to sacrifice myself. I now knew what had changed. As a true alchemist, I was looking at it the wrong way around. I was in control of my own life force, but backward alchemists weren't. They relied on the remains of other willing sacrifices.

In spite of the late hour, I was energized with hope. Too energized. I failed to notice the front door of the house wasn't as securely locked as it should have been.

Only as I bounded up the attic stairs, calling for Dorian and Leopold, did I notice something was off. The house was quiet. Yet it was too early in the night for the gargoyles to be on the prowl.

I thought to myself that I'd have to lecture Dorian about not following Leopold's lead of trying be cool. Did gargoyles even care about being cool? Never mind. I'd have years to find out. Since I now knew a better way to save the gargoyles. A way that didn't involve sacrificing my life. I knew that—

I stepped into the attic and froze. I saw not two gargoyles, but two *people*: Percy and Madame Leblanc.

Only Madame Leblanc wasn't quite herself. This woman was decades younger. Her daughter? Granddaughter?

No, it couldn't be …

The woman in my attic looked almost identical to the woman with movie-star good looks in the black-and-white photograph Percy carried in his wallet.

Madame Leblanc wasn't an innocent actor like the man who played the part of her nephew. She was the backward alchemist who'd killed him. This whole time, she was the mysterious mastermind.

FIFTY-ONE

ALL THE PIECES FELL into place. Madame Leblanc—or whatever her real name was—was the true charismatic leader of the backward alchemists. Not Lucien. Not Percy.

I should have seen it sooner. In Paris, Madame Leblanc played her role with me so lyrically it was almost theatrical, and she'd believed in my immortality all too readily. She knew I worked with Jasper Dubois, who was an aspiring alchemist, so she was able to create a believable lie. The actor who played her grandnephew policeman had looked young from afar but up close he looked tired—because he was a backward alchemy apprentice. Back in Portland, Percy had said "only three of us left" while telling me about backward alchemy. The woman in the photo in Percy's wallet had looked familiar. And when Ivan had said "*they'll* be returning soon" to the alchemy lab, as opposed to "*Percy* will be returning soon," it was Madame Leblanc he was referring to.

"Cat got your tongue, Zoe?" she said. The accent was English. "Don't look so surprised. I'm sure you've figured everything out."

"I was so gullible," I hissed, barely able to control my anger at having been so close to the truth but also so far off.

"Don't be too hard on yourself, dear. I really am an actress. Made quite a splash in the West End for a while. That's where Percy found me." I could believe it. Though her skin was pinched, her large eyes and lips were stunning. Her hair was a rich, lush black, and it flowed past her shoulders.

"You killed the actor playing your nephew," I said. "He was your apprentice. That's how you look so young again."

"Oh, do catch up, my dear. And hand over the book. *My* book."

I smiled. Now *I* had the upper hand. If she didn't already have Dorian's book, that meant Dorian and Leopold had gotten away through the hole in the roof. It also meant Madame Leblanc hadn't figured out the book was, as Dorian would have put it, a McGuffin. Everyone was searching for the damn book, but it *wasn't* the key. It was only the clue that pointed to Notre Dame.

"Why are you smiling? Percy, restrain her."

So strong was Madame Leblanc's presence that Percy had faded into the background. He now stepped forward, though the movement was half-hearted. His eyes darted between the two of us. His hair was flecked with gray, and his jowls sagged. While Madame Leblanc had grown younger, he'd grown older.

"Don't touch me, Percival," I said.

He stopped.

Madame Leblanc sighed. Theatrically. "Do I have to do everything myself?"

"You have me at a loss," I said. "I don't even know your real name."

She smiled wickedly. "I wondered if I'd gone too far there. Blanche Leblanc: White White. The embodiment of a Ms. Goody Two-Shoes."

Mentally kicking myself, I edged my way toward the attic door.

"I see you moving, Zoe. Stop right there. Don't you want to know my true name?" The look in her black eyes told me I wasn't sure I wanted to. "The name I've used since my transformation is Raven. And you don't want to mess with the Raven."

The skin on her forearm had firmed enough for me to realize that what I'd mistaken for faded numbers from a concentration camp was actually a tattoo of a raven. My subconscious had noticed it and turned it into a dream.

"You will give me that book," she said. She didn't yell. Her words were so soft that I barely heard them. Yet there was a cold forceful-ness to the directive that made me shiver. "I will be restored to my former beauty for eternity."

"I don't have it," I said, matching her strong, stoic intonation.

"Wrong answer." She drew a sword from behind her back.

FIFTY-TWO

It was one of *my* swords from my collection of antiques that Raven held in her hand.

"Percy," I said, "you don't have to go along with—"

"Enough!" Raven thrust the sword into the creaking floorboards, showing its might.

"I swear I don't have the book here," I said. I knew I was convincing, because it wasn't a lie.

"I know. We've searched the house. But I have very persuasive ways of making people talk."

I nodded. Not too quickly. I couldn't let her think I was eager. I couldn't let her know I now knew more than she did. "I'll tell you where it is," I said, "if you let me understand what's happened. I need to know."

"Why?"

"I have a friend who's dying, like you."

"The gargoyle," Percy said, raising his hand in earnest like a syco-phantic schoolboy. "The gargoyle I told you about."

Raven and I both ignored him.

"I don't care what happens to me," I said, "but I want you to help Dorian."

I knew she wouldn't, but there was still a chance I could, if I could think of a way out of this.

"All right," Raven said cautiously. She motioned for Percy to close the attic door. He rushed to oblige.

"I thought you would find our secret alchemy lab," Raven continued once the door was bolted. "That would have ruined our plans to sacrifice the actor. I couldn't kill you without hurting myself, so I devised a plan to get you to leave Paris of your own accord."

"Because an alchemist can't kill a person without hurting themselves."

She smirked. "Nice try. Percy convinced me it was true, long ago. But now, thanks to you, I know the truth. It's only a superstition."

Me and my big mouth…

"I never suspected that you had Lucien and Olav's backward alchemy book," she continued, "or that you could help us. It was Lucien who realized you had the book and could help solve what the rest of us could not. You aroused his suspicions, and when he asked Percy about a woman called Zoe Faust, Percy told us who you were. That's why Lucien followed you to Portland."

"I made it so easy for him. I even gave him my address."

"Most backward alchemists aren't 'friends,' so we don't keep each other's confidences. Stupid Lucien didn't tell us his suspicions that you could help us. And I didn't tell Lucien of my plan to get rid of you."

"That's why Lucien was truly shocked when I said I was leaving Paris. He was upset that you'd messed up his plans, so he followed me to steal *Non Degenera Alchemia*—which he originally planned on doing more easily in Paris, before you ruined his scheme."

"Lucien was almost out of Alchemical Ashes. He was smoking them frequently to stay young until we could permanently stop our life forces reversing. Lucien was arrogant, and thought he could get the book without much effort."

"That's why he lost his temper so quickly at my friend Ivan's house," I said, using the word *friend* automatically before I could think better of it. "Lucien was upset that Ivan refused to help him."

"I've never trusted Lucien, so I sent Percy to follow him. Can you believe Lucien once said theater was for the mindless masses? Yet it was my acting skills that fooled you. I'm the one who has outlived them all—"

Percy cleared his throat.

"Oh, yes, my love," Raven said. "Of course I meant *we* are the ones who have outlived them all. And now we are going to retrieve our long-lost book and live on forever as the beautiful specimens we once were."

Raven had to come to Portland to do her own dirty work. And she still mistakenly believed Dorian's book contained the secret to the "change" that had reversed the transformations of backward alchemy.

"You're forgetting the most important part of the story," I said. "*What was the shift that occurred six months ago?*"

She blinked at me. "What do you mean?"

"What happened six months ago?"

"We began to age and die."

"Percy already told me that much," I said. "I need to know what *triggered* the change."

"You're trying to confuse me. Percy warned me that you were overly intellectual. Half of your antiques are books. What good are books? Scripts for the theater are different, of course. The only book I need is the one Olav and Lucien created."

Was my theory right? "Who was the first to die?" I asked.

"Why does it matter?"

"Humor me."

"Olav," she said, a look of suspicion creeping onto her face.

"Percy said he wasn't very intelligent. Is that right?"

"He was a stupid, stupid, man," she agreed.

"How did he die?"

"The same as the rest of us. He began aging rapidly."

"You saw his transformation take place?"

She hesitated. "We weren't friends. Who wants to associate with a man less interesting than a rock?"

"How did you know he died, then?"

"I found him," Percy spoke up. "Inside the underground tunnels not far from the alchemy lab. The smell . . . I went to investigate."

"What was he doing in there?"

Percy shrugged. "It's trendy for people to go down into the catacombs and tunnels these days, so I assumed he was making sure our laboratory entrance remained hidden, as I was."

"People get lost down there," I said. "Especially people—"

"The idiot!" Raven shrieked. She grasped the hilt of the sword and paced back and forth on the creaky attic floor, her silky black hair snarling around her face. "You mean he got lost in the tunnels and starved or froze to death, like other stupid explorers have done. We're not immortal, we just don't age."

"Exactly," I said.

"Hang on," Percy said, "I don't get it."

"Olav didn't die because of a shift," I said. "His death *was* the shift. Because backward alchemy is a shortcut *tied to another person*, Olav's death broke the link. That's why you're all dying."

"The sacrifices," Raven said, comprehension sinking in. "The sacrifices aren't enough?"

"What happened to Olav's bones, Percy?" I asked. "What happened after you found him?"

"When I touched him," Percy said, "he turned to ash."

I nodded. "And the ashes?"

"I sprinkled them in the Seine."

"So it's over," I said softly. "The link is broken."

Bones and ash are our core essence. That's why relics have significance. And that's why Max's skeleton helped me see the possibility that a person's physical body was tied to the shift.

Raven's eyes locked on mine. "No. There's got to be another answer in that book."

I shook my head sadly. I didn't think there was.

I understood the truth about *Non Degenera Alchemia*. Backward alchemy was a quick fix for lazy people who were willing to sacrifice the life of another for their own unnatural immortality. To get around the core tenet of alchemy—using guided intent to transform the impure into the pure—backward alchemists had to sacrifice an innocent.

An alchemist's lab is their sanctuary and thus inexorably linked to their work. The pure intent of Notre Dame Cathedral balanced the impure intent of the two men who recorded their backward alchemy steps in *Not Untrue Alchemy*, allowing for some sort of stability. Because Dorian and Leopold were *innocents* from the cathedral, the book itself was able to bring them to life without an external sacrifice. Yet when the original intent was broken, everyone given life through backward alchemy faced the consequences.

Steps sounded beneath us. Had Dorian gone to Max to get help?

The attic door opened. Ivan stepped inside and relief washed over me. He'd had a change of heart after all.

Ivan wasn't quite as young and vigorous as he'd been when I saw him at the alchemy laboratory in Paris, but he was strong enough to help.

"The book?" Raven asked him.

Ivan shook his head. "I searched again. It's not here."

My relief turned to cold terror. Ivan was still working with the backward alchemists?

But it didn't matter. The quick deterioration of Ivan's body showed me that backward alchemy was over. And Dorian's life along with it.

FIFTY-THREE

"It's over, Ivan," I said. "We've figured out that backward alchemy is done for."

"She's lying," Raven said. "She's trying to trick us into thinking there's no solution. But her beastly friend is hiding the book that will save us."

"I'm telling you the truth," I said, wondering where my decidedly non-beastly gargoyle friend had gone. "She and Percy misled you—"

"It's because of *us* that you're healthy again, Ivan," Raven said. "Zoe would have had you die."

"And *you* would have had him kill Brixton," I said.

Ivan winced.

"I forgive you, Ivan," I said. "I know you didn't know—"

"Enough with the sentimentality," Raven said. "Do you want to survive or not, Ivan?"

He nodded silently, his jaw clenched. He refused to look me in the eye.

"How many more sacrifices will you make?" I asked. "With the link broken, it will never stop."

"Men will always willingly give me this gift," Raven said. "Jasper jumped at the chance."

I gasped. "It *wasn't* a lie that Jasper Dubois was murdered. Only it was *you* who did it."

"I'll let you in on a secret, my dear: if you want to tell a convincing lie, stick to the truth as closely as possible."

I glared at her. That was *my* secret. And she'd killed *my* shopkeeper assistant. Not that I'd been all that fond of the misogynistic Jasper, but still, he didn't deserve to be murdered.

"Didn't you wonder how I knew you wouldn't be able to trace Jasper's movements?" she continued.

"Because you knew he was already dead." I should have thought of it, but she'd thrown me off balance by appearing in my attic today.

"I can practically feel my face sagging," Raven said, feeling her neck with the hand that wasn't clutching the sword. "Percy, Ivan, stop standing there like useless lumps."

Now I was *really* angry. Not only had she manipulated me, but she'd turned Ambrose's son Percy and my friend Ivan against me. I lunged for the second sword that was part of the pair. I'd been so calm until now that she didn't anticipate the movement.

"Stay out of my way, Percy. Ivan." My voice didn't sound like my own, but I was fairly certain it was me speaking. "This is between me and Raven."

Decades ago, I'd taken some fencing lessons with a lovely German man named Anton. I hoped I'd remember what he taught me.

The men stepped back as Raven and I lunged at each other. In our rage, we weren't going for proper form. We were trying to kill each other.

Raven was already aging, so she wasn't as strong as she thought she was. She was the first to draw blood, a shallow wound to my hip. While she regained her balance, I slashed a long cut across her shoulder. She cried out, more in shock than pain, I expect. Her sword dropped from her hand and she gripped her arm.

I immediately thought of Tobias, who carried cayenne pepper with him in his role as an EMT, as an unconventional herbal remedy to stop blood loss. I kept a glass jar of cayenne on an antique spice rack there in the attic and wondered if it would help staunch the flow of blood from the wound I'd inflicted.

I knew then that I couldn't kill Raven. It wasn't in my nature.

But there was something else I could do. I grabbed the jar of cayenne, tore the lid off, and threw the spice into her eyes.

Raven screamed in pain, blinded and writhing on the floor. Since she was no longer a threat, I pressed a towel to her bleeding shoulder and looked for something with which I could tie her arms.

A piece of rope secured a curtain in the corner of the attic that Dorian kept for his private reading room. I yanked off the rope and turned back to Raven. But she was no longer sprawled on the floor. She stood in front of me, red-faced and wielding her sword.

Then the look on her face morphed into surprise. A spot of deep red formed in the middle of her chest. The tip of a sword burst through her chest. A metallic scent filled the air. She looked down at her chest for a brief moment before her eyelids closed and she crumpled to the floor.

Behind her stood Ivan, a blood-drenched sword clutched in his hands.

FIFTY-FOUR

"ON MY GOD!" PERCY screamed. He repeated the words again and again until I slapped him.

Unlike Percy, Ivan stood as still as a nonliving gargoyle statue.

"Ivan?" I said quietly.

"She was going to kill you," he whispered. "I couldn't let her. I couldn't."

As we stood there, the three of us in shock, Raven's body shriveled from a woman into a skeleton, then before our eyes changed from bone to ash.

A siren sounded in the distance.

I swore. "Dorian and Leopold must have sent for help."

"Nobody will believe what has happened," Ivan said.

"Oh my God!" Percy started repeating again. Goodness, that man was tiresome. And he hadn't lifted a finger to help me.

"Percy," I said, shaking him by the shoulder. "You're not doing anyone any good. You're going to give me your cell phone number and then get out of here. All right?"

He nodded, wide-eyed.

"Ivan," I said. "Pick up Raven's ashes and then leave. The cut on my leg will explain the mess. I'll tell the police there was an intruder." The sirens grew louder. "Hurry."

I scooped Raven's ashes into a set of glass apothecary jars. After a quicker cleanup of Raven's remains than I thought was possible, I collapsed onto the attic floor. I hadn't attended to the cut on my hip. There wasn't enough blood loss for me to pass out, but it was the middle of the night. I didn't have the natural energy from the sun to draw upon.

I closed my eyes and felt the cool hardwood floor on my cheek. I'd rest for a few moments . . .

"Zoe?" a distant voice called. "Zoe?"

"Mmm?"

"You're awake," a familiar voice said, followed by a sigh of relief.

"No, I'm not," I mumbled.

Max's lips found mine. "I hope you're awake now."

I opened my eyes. I was still sitting on the attic floor, but now Max had wrapped an arm around my shoulder. His other hand pressed a cloth to the wound on my leg.

"EMTs are on their way up," he said. "Hang on."

"I could hang on better if you put both of your arms around me."

He laughed. "You scared me, Zoe. You said you'd come back, but you didn't. Instead I got a call from that French friend of yours—the guy I've never met. He said you were in danger. He wouldn't give me details, but insisted I rescue you. He's a strange guy. I don't know how he knew, if he wasn't involved—"

"He didn't do this to me."

"I know. We saw Ivan Danko leaving your house."

"You have him?" What would Ivan tell them?

"No, he got away. I can see that you rescued yourself, so I'll have to play hero another day, but what exactly happened here, Zoe?"

"That question can wait, Detective Liu," a woman said. She and a man rushed over to me and examined my hip. "We're having a hell of a time getting a stretcher up here. These old houses aren't up to code. Let me check out this wound and get you downstairs."

My wound was deemed superficial, so I was treated by the paramedics but I wasn't forced to go to the hospital. Max, however, wasn't happy about my decision to stay home.

"If you won't go to the hospital," he said, "you could at least stay with me. Or I'd be happy to …"

I swept an errant lock of hair from his forehead. "I appreciate the offer, but I won't get any rest if you stay. I need to sleep."

He took my hand and kissed it. "I promise I'll let you get some sleep."

With how much my insides melted with that gentle brush of his lips against my hand, I gave him a truthful answer. "I don't trust myself to make you keep that promise."

That seemed to appease him. I sent him home and awaited Dorian's return, which was the more important reason I couldn't have Max stay.

I wasn't sure what I was going to tell Dorian, now that all hope was lost. There was no cure for the backward alchemists and those who'd been brought to life by backward alchemy's power. I could continue making the Tea of Ashes frequently enough to keep Dorian alive temporarily, but I'd be killing myself while he'd continue to slowly die. I should have accepted the truth earlier, but I hadn't been open to the possibility that I wouldn't be able to save Dorian.

I wished Dorian would return home. Everyone had left over an hour ago. A detective had taken my statement. I told him that Ivan Danko had returned to seek revenge on me after I thwarted his crazy attempt to kill Brixton. I hated that it was the lie closest to the truth. I really had wanted to save Ivan.

I fixed myself a chocolate elixir in the blender in an attempt to stay awake, but I fell asleep on the couch waiting for a gargoyle who never came.

———————

At dawn, I awoke to the sound of singing and the scents of cinnamon and smoke.

Dorian stood at the kitchen counter, whisking batter in a stainless steel bowl. Turning at the sound of the swinging kitchen door, he hopped down from the stool and grinned at me. "*Bon*, you are awake, *mon amie*. I have only just returned from Monsieur Lake's home."

"I have so much to tell you, Dorian."

"And I you. Why do you look so sad?"

"Why didn't you come home sooner?"

"I was confident you could defeat the insane woman who was after my book, as you have. I also knew you would not be alone. I was certain Max would come to your aid. He is a good man, and he cares very much for you. I decided it was best to remain hidden and attend to pressing matters."

I sat morosely. "I have news. It's bad. I don't know how to tell you this, so I'm going to come right out and say it."

Dorian rocked back and forth on the linoleum floor and looked at me expectantly.

"There's no cure, Dorian. There's no cure for a backward alchemy transformation."

"Ah. Is that all?"

"Is that *all*?"

"I will share my news." He gave a little hop and clapped his hands. *Hopping and clapping …*

"You're moving your left arm. And your ankle. It bends again."

"*Oui*. And all the rest of me. He wriggled his horns and flapped his wings gracefully. "You see, my friend, I have discovered true alchemy. I have found the Elixir of Life!"

"But how?"

"Through cooking."

FIFTY-FIVE

"LIKE ALCHEMY," DORIAN SAID, "cooking, at its core, is about transformation."

"You truly found the Elixir?" I asked. "You're not joking? Trying to make me feel better about failing?" I'd had so much false hope that I was scared to hope again.

"*Il est trop vrai.* It is as true as true can be. This is why I returned to Julian Lake's house last night instead of coming to check on you. I knew you were safe, so I wanted to complete the transformation."

"At his house rather than your own? I'm sorry if I haven't made you feel like you belong—"

"Not *inside* his house. His backyard, you may recall, has an outdoor brick kiln. It is meant for pizza, but it is the same heat—"

"As an athanor." The fire to cook the philosophical egg.

Dorian grinned. "I cooked many foods in that oven, each of which represented a step to create the Philosopher's Stone."

"You're the one who was moving things around in my laboratory! I worried that was Lucien or Percy. I had the locks changed for nothing."

"*Oui*. I apologize for the deception. But it was necessary."

"And you weren't even bleeding the other day, were you? I knew it wasn't tomato sauce."

He shook his head. "Cinnabar."

"I *knew* someone had taken my dragon's blood."

"I am sorry, my friend. But as you know, alchemy is a personal process. That is why I roped off my own meditative space in the attic."

"Your reading space."

"Yes, only it was not a reading space. I was meditating on alchemy. Did you not wonder why I had not asked you to obtain more library books lately?" He smiled sheepishly.

"What was your philosophical egg?"

"Can you not guess?"

I smiled. "A food?"

"An avocado." He beamed at me. "It was the perfect ingredient for the first step to my Emerald Tablet: Gourmet Food Version."

I burst out laughing.

"It is perfect, no? The avocado is the shape of an egg, and it represents life and fertility. The tree lives hundreds of years. It is even green, like an emerald."

"And your last step must have been salt."

"But of course. Salt purifies and protects foods from being corrupted, as alchemy's transformations purify the impure. Salt is the truest, most natural, and most essential of all foods."

"The product of mercury and sulfur. The child of the spirit and the soul."

"You alchemists are more clever than I gave you credit for. I knew there was a reason I sought you out, Alchemist. We are a perfect balance, you and I. You claim you are not prepared to train others in the art of alchemy, yet it was your guidance that enabled me to find the Elixir."

"But I didn't—"

"You are too humble, Zoe. You are the one who showed me that a meal need not be complicated to reach perfection. You are the one who taught me that salt is the child of the alchemical king and queen. And you are the one who sacrificed yourself for me by creating the Tea of Ashes, showing me that backward alchemy was not the way I wished to live."

I hugged my friend, and he wrapped his wings around me. His wings were no longer the stiff-yet-malleable stone they once were. Now they felt like I imagined the wings of an angel would feel.

I squeezed Dorian's strong, feather-like wings, then pulled back to look at his transformation. He looked much the same as when I'd met him six months before, but his gray skin held a radiance that hadn't previously been there.

"Where's Leopold?" I asked.

Dorian blinked. "Is he not in the attic?"

"I don't think so."

Dorian ran up the stairs. I tried to keep up, but now that he was healthy again, it was all I could do to keep him in sight.

"*Merde*," Dorian said from the attic doorway. "He promised he was coming back here. I had to leave him so I could finish my transformation alone."

"It's not your fault. I'm sure he'll turn up."

"Zoe, you do not understand. He has *my book*."

"You don't need it anymore. And what could he do with it on his own?"

Dorian rubbed his chin. "I wonder."

We tromped down the stairs, me pestering Dorian about the fourteen food steps he used to create the Elixir of Life.

"To the kitchen," he said. But as soon as he opened the pantry door, he flapped his wings in earnest. He turned around, clutching a mangled note in his clawed hand. "From Leopold," he sputtered.

"He has taken the last of my wine from the pantry. And look, that is the least of the affront."

I eased the wrinkled note from his hand.

It is by universal misunderstanding that we agree with each other, it read. *You have convinced me, my friend, that I must come to understand this foul alchemy that has given us this malady of life. This is why I must borrow your book, say farewell, and accompany my new friend Ivan to the land of alchemists.*

Adieu.

L.B.

Leopold and Ivan together, with Dorian's book? That couldn't be good.

I quickly looked up the local Portland news on my phone to make sure there hadn't been any gargoyle sightings. Thank goodness for small favors.

"Zoe," Dorian interrupted. "I hate to alarm you, but your leg is bleeding."

I put my phone down and looked at my healthy friend once more. "I wasn't kidding when I said I had a lot to tell you about what happened last night."

"Let me cook us breakfast. We have much time to talk, and much grand food to eat."

THE END

RECIPES

Each of these recipes is an easy dish that Dorian was able to make with only one good arm. Using simple ingredients doesn't mean sacrificing flavor.

CREAMY GARLIC TOMATO SAUCE (VEGAN)

Total cooking time: 1 hour
Makes 4 servings

Ingredients:
- 2 tbsp plus ¼ cup olive oil, divided
- 10 medium-size cloves garlic
- 24 oz. jar tomato puree or strained tomatoes
- 1 tsp salt (or to taste)
- ¼ tsp red chili pepper flakes (or to taste)

Directions:
Smash the garlic cloves, and let them rest for 10 minutes. Heat a medium saucepan on low heat while peeling and mincing the smashed

garlic. Add 2 tbsp olive oil and garlic. Cook garlic and oil slowly on low heat for 20 minutes. Add tomato puree and simmer for another 20 minutes, minimum.

Remove from heat and cool for a few minutes, then stir in ¼ cup olive oil. Use an immersion blender or transfer to a blender. Watch the color of the red sauce transform to a lighter shade of pink before your eyes, as if you'd added cream.

Once blended, stir in salt and red chili pepper flakes.

Add to 4 servings of a grain (e.g., pasta or freekeh) or use as a dipping sauce for bread.

Note:

You can skip the step of letting the garlic rest for 10 minutes, but the most health benefits will be released by letting it rest for at least 10 minutes once smashed or chopped before heating.

Note:

The trick of transforming these simple ingredients into more than the sum of their parts is *time*. For the best results, don't skip the step of letting the garlic and sauce simmer.

CHOCOLATE MOUSSE (VEGAN, RAW)

Total cooking time: 10 minutes
Makes 2 servings

Ingredients:

- 1 large ripe avocado
- ¼ cup cacao powder
- ¼ cup maple syrup (or ⅓ cup for a sweeter mousse)
- ¼ cup cashew milk (or other nut milk of choice)
- ½ tsp vanilla
- dash sea salt

Directions:

Add all ingredients to a food processor. Puree for at least 1–2 minutes, until smooth and creamy. If lumps persist, stop the food processor and stir the mixture before resuming blending.

Divide into two dessert serving bowls. Optional: garnish with fresh berries on top.

Note:

Skeptical that avocado is the main ingredient? Tasters were surprised to learn the mousse even contained avocado.

FROZEN LEMON CHEESECAKE DROPS (VEGAN, RAW)

Total cooking time: 15 minutes hands on (plus overnight soaking time, and time to set in freezer)
Makes 6 servings (approx. 24 drops)

Ingredients for the topping:
- ¼ cup dates (or up to ½ cup, if you prefer a sweeter crust)
- ½ cup walnuts (or substitute almonds)

Ingredients for the cheesecake:
- 1½ cup raw cashews
- ⅓ cup maple syrup
- ⅓ cup coconut oil
- 3 tbsp lemon juice (add an additional tbsp lemon juice for a tarter tart)
- dash of salt
- dash of turmeric (optional)

Directions:

Soak the cashews in water overnight. Or, if in a rush, boil water and soak in hot water for 4 hours.

To make the topping, chop the dates and walnuts in a food processor. Set aside in a small bowl.

To make the cheesecake drops, drain and rinse the cashews. Melt the coconut oil. Puree all cheesecake ingredients in a blender or food processor until smooth, around 1 or 2 minutes. Line a baking pan with parchment paper. Scoop heaping tablespoons of batter onto the parchment. Sprinkle with the date and nut topping. Let set in the freezer for at least 2 hours.

AUTHOR'S NOTE

As with the other books in the Accidental Alchemist mystery series, *The Elusive Elixir* is a work of fiction, but the historical backdrop is real.

The façade of Notre Dame Cathedral in Paris includes several alchemical carvings, including a person carrying a shield with a salamander in flames. My addition of Dorian's alchemy book to the carving is fictional, and there aren't currently any alchemists using Notre Dame as described in the book—as far as I know.

Dorian Robert-Houdin is based on the famous *Le Penseur* gargoyle that sits high on Notre Dame. If you're ever in Paris, he's worth the long line and stairs to visit.

Nicolas Flamel's house still stands in Paris at 51 *rue de* Montmorency, and is now a restaurant. *Rue Nicolas Flamel*, a street in the 4th Arrondissement in Paris, is also named after the famous alchemist. Le Cabaret de L'Enfer was a real Hell-themed café that opened in the 1800s in Paris's Pigalle neighborhood, the red-light district famous for the Moulin Rouge.

The Death Rotation is a real concept in alchemy, but backward alchemy as portrayed in this book is fictional. I enjoyed developing this idea because alchemy is so shrouded in secrecy that it's easy to imagine what some of the codes and concepts might have meant. Alchemy is an example of a subject where the Internet doesn't reveal all. In my research I came across many old books that have not been digitized, filled with fascinating historical facts about alchemy and old alchemical drawings.

Alchemy, in reality, is both a figurative concept and a precursor to modern chemistry. As Zoe explains, alchemy is about transformation. Alchemists of previous centuries wanted to transform their bodies (seeking the Elixir of Life for immortality) or the elements (transmuting lead or other metals into gold). Their experiments resulted in many discoveries that led to chemistry as we know it today. Zoe is a spagyric alchemist, someone who uses alchemical processes to extract healing properties from plants. Spiritual alchemy is the practice of inner transformation.

I'm not an alchemist (nor am I a French gargoyle chef), but my life transformed five years ago when I was diagnosed with breast cancer in my thirties. I began writing this series steeped in alchemy and cooking transformations while I was undergoing chemotherapy. I took cooking classes and learned how to cook healing vegan foods that nourished both my body and soul. As I write this, I'm four years cancer-free and working on the next Accidental Alchemist mystery.

ACKNOWLEDGMENTS

What would I do without my critique readers? Huge thanks go to the ever-insightful and supportive Emberly Nesbitt, Nancy Adams, Brian Selfon, Stephen Buehler, Juliet Blackwell, Susan Parman, my agent Jill Marsal, and my editorial team at Midnight Ink: Terri Bischoff, Amy Glaser, and Nicole Nugent.

I'd go crazy without the support from the writers in my life. Local pals Emberly Nesbitt, Mysti Berry, Juliet Blackwell, Lisa Hughey, and Michelle Gonzales make sure I make it to the café and keep writing. Sisters in Crime, especially the Guppies, provide endless online support. And Diane Vallere, my kindred spirit on this path, is always there to bounce around ideas.

My parents always told me I could be anything I wanted to be. Without their early encouragement, there's no way I would have conceived of this series. And my amazing husband James encourages my dreams in every way.

© *Michael B. Woolsey*

ABOUT THE AUTHOR

Gigi Pandian is the *USA Today* bestselling author of the Accidental Alchemist mystery series and the Jaya Jones Treasure Hunt mystery series. A breast cancer diagnosis in her thirties taught her two important life lessons: healing foods can taste amazing, and life's too short to waste a single moment. Gigi spent her childhood being dragged around the world by her cultural anthropologist parents, and she now lives in the San Francisco Bay Area with an overgrown organic vegetable garden in the backyard. Find her online at www.gigipandian.com.